J. A. BOULET

1833 BROTHERS & SISTERS

Also by J. A. Boulet

Whichever Way The Road Leads

1956 Love & Revolution

The Origins

The Wars Between Us

The Strong Within Us

The Strong Amongst Us

J. A. BOULET

1833 BROTHERS & SISTERS

Published by J. A. Boulet

Book cover design: J. A. Boulet

ISBN: 978-1-0697950-0-7

This book is dedicated to my family. May they always stay true to the values they grew up with.

Note to Reader

This book is a work of historical fiction. I have attempted to be accurate with many of the historical events, although some details have been intentionally skewed to fit within the story. This is a fictional saga of family, marriage and integrity. Many of the background historical events were researched extensively, although, this book should still be read as fiction.

J. A. Boulet September 22, 2025

Cast of Characters

EASTMAN FAMILY

Ellen Eastman, widow of Bob Eastman

Jesse Eastman, son of Ellen and Bob

Zee (Zelda Collard) Eastman, Jesse's wife and eldest Collard sibling

Xavier Eastman, Zee's illegitimate son, Jesse's adopted son

Janey Eastman, Jesse and Zee's firstborn daughter

Scott and James Eastman, twin sons of Jesse and Zee

Johnny Eastman, Jesse and Zee's youngest son

Rosie and Eva, twin daughters of Janey Eastman

Billy Eastman, estranged brother of Jesse

Katie, Bridget, and Joshua, Jesse's other siblings (in order of birth)

Georgina, illegitimate child of Bob Eastman, Jesse's half-sister

COLLARD FAMILY

Charlotte Collard, younger sister of Zee

Betty, Hanna, and Elise Collard , younger sisters of Charlotte

Jacob Collard, youngest brother of Zee

Jack, Jacob's son and youngest nephew of Zee

Alice, Julia, Clara, and Joey, Charlotte's children

Sam Collard, Jacob's twin brother, died young in 1825

George Collard, Zee's father, died in 1825 after the death of Sam

OTHERS

Samuel, Jesse's best friend and security advisor for the Eastman Empire

Bartholomew Mato, hostile businessman from Texas

Thomas, Bartholomew's associate

Jeremiah Williams, runaway black slave

Bemidii, native Ojibwe trail guide

Sarah Freeman, freed black slave

Laura, Bartholomew's girlfriend

PART I

HOSTILE TAKEOVER

Chapter 1

"You will treat her as one of the family!" Jesse shouted, his face reddening.

Billy Eastman sneered and squinted his eyes at his brother. "She is still a black slave to me. Nothing more."

"Georgina is your half-sister!" Jesse yelled, pushing his chair back as he stood angrily in confrontation. Jesse removed his suit jacket roughly, throwing it on the chair behind him. "You will treat her as such!"

"We only have her word, no proof," Billy countered, softening slightly. The murderous rage showing on Jesse's face subdued him for the time being. "Her slave mother is dead, and our dear father is also dead. Nobody is alive to prove Georgina's claim."

"Father never would have admitted to siring a child from a slave," Jesse spat back, a twitch starting on his left eyebrow. The War of 1812 had left him with many permanent changes in his behavior, and his temper with his brother was one of them. Most days, he feared that he would lose his control with Billy and the result would be a family tragedy. The brothers were like oil and water; two completely different people from very different backgrounds. Jesse sometimes wondered how they were related.

But the festering sibling rivalry is exactly how they had all ended up in the mess the family was facing today. An unscrupulous businessman named Bartholomew was threatening to take over the Eastman Empire. BMato Investments, Bartholomew's acquisition company, had made an offer to buy the entire Philadelphia shipping empire for less than half of what it was worth. Jesse immediately refused with a veiled threat for them to stay away and even physically shoved the company's representative out the door. It seems that Jesse's temper had raised the ire of Bartholomew.

The worst complication was that his younger brother, Billy, had verbally agreed to the sale without Jesse's approval! It had ignited a festering resentment between the brothers that had started back in 1815, when Jesse had introduced his family to his wife, Zelda. Her family, the Collards, were originally Loyalists back in the Revolutionary War. Billy's side of the family were fierce Patriots. The two sides did not mix.

"Georgina will never be my sister," Billy sneered back, standing up to his full 6-foot-4 inches tall. "I'm done arguing with you. You never do anything positive for the family. You brought Loyalists into our family and supported our slave girl with a wage!" Billy yelled, throwing up his arms in exasperation.

Jesse stood his ground. "I have done more for this family than you ever could!" he shouted, his eyes glowering murderously. His blood started pumping behind his ears, and his fists naturally curled into balls.

Billy cursed, turned on his heel, and swung open the large oak office door, fearing for his personal safety. The murderous rage on his brother's face was no joke. Billy was taller and stronger than Jesse, but he had never been to war, and Jesse's rage was something that frightened him to the bone. He turned his head briefly, glared at his brother, and left without another word.

Jesse watched the large oak door creak closed. He slammed his palm down on his massive teak desk and willed himself to calm down. He rolled up his white sleeves methodically, getting ready for a physical confrontation if Billy came back.

A slight knock sounded on the door.

"What is it?" Jesse hollered angrily.

The door gently creaked open, and Zelda's beautiful face peered in. "What happened?' she asked, removing a stray lock of dark blonde hair from her eyes. "What was all the shouting about?"

Jesse released his balled-up fists to his sides and felt the stress of the day slowly dissipate. His wife Zelda was still just as beautiful as when he had met her twenty years ago. Everyone called her Zee, and Jesse thought she had grown even more beautiful over time. After five children, Zee's hips had widened, her breasts had grown larger, and her thighs were pleasantly thicker. She was a tall woman, just a few inches under his own height, and the changes of growing older had been kind to them both. Jesse was forty years old and had a few grey hairs starting in his brown beard and peppered throughout his thinning, dark hair. Zee was the same age, but the physical similarities ended there. She had fair skin and long blonde hair, with very little grey hair visible. Along with her different colored eyes, one blue and one green, she was a striking woman. Many people assumed she was much younger, which infuriated Jesse at times. He was grateful to have such a beautiful wife, but disliked the stares from younger men.

Jesse smiled and stepped around the desk. "Nothing unusual. Just my brother, Billy," he answered, his voice softening.

"What's he causing trouble about now?" Zee asked, walking into the office with her dress flowing behind her.

"The usual," he replied. "Georgina."

Zee reached Jesse and wrapped her arms around his broad shoulders, hugging him. "After all these years, he has never accepted Georgina into the family, and it seems, he never will," she stated.

Jesse bent his head and kissed her briefly. "You speak the truth, my darling. Billy never once accepted that slaves should no longer be an acceptable solution to households in the Upper States. Most of the blacks are fleeing to Canada because of people like Billy. Even in the Northern States, I am still surprised by the refusal of some people to let go of past ideals and accept that blacks are people too." Jesse shook his head at the absurdity of it all. "Georgina was always a sister to me, all the years that I grew up with her. When she told me that we had the same father, I believed her without a doubt. I was delighted, actually! We had such a strong bond as youngsters, and it explained so much. We were brother and sister all that time." Jesse frowned at the differences between his family members. He loved Georgina, his half-sister, and hated Billy, his closest full brother.

Jesse sighed heavily, then smiled. Just seeing Zee melted his coldness and anger. He was always astonished at the effect his wife had on him. "I am so glad that you are my wife." He chuckled softly as a memory from the past lifted in his mind. He watched his wife smooth her dress and sit down in the intricately carved leather guest chair.

"What are you chuckling about?" she smiled, stroking her hand along the lion head carvings at the end of the armchair. Zee had never gotten accustomed to the rich, lavish lifestyle of the Eastmans. It seemed every piece of furniture she sat in was made from leather or had been forged from silver.

Jesse's eyes softened. "I just remembered how much you used to hate dresses," he responded, a slight grin curving the corners of his lips. He caressed her shoulders lightly with his large hands. "When I met you, you were wearing homemade britches."

Zee's nose wrinkled up. "I still hate dresses," she laughed. "I just wear them more now. I'm certain your associates would be appalled if you were married to a woman in men's britches."

"You do it for me, then?" he asked, genuinely concerned.

"No," she replied, her voice softening. "Honestly, after four pregnancies, I appreciate many things about dresses now."

"Well, you look amazing in this dress," Jesse complimented.

Zee smiled and covered his hand with hers. "Thank you, my dear."

Jesse leaned down and kissed her full lips. His body instantly responded, and he wondered how long it had been since they had been intimate. It seemed like over a month ago. His emotions became instantly appalled at his obvious neglect. Jesse's hand shifted higher up towards her blouse. He would make it right with her, right now if he had to.

A knock on the door quickly interrupted them.

"Who is it?" Jesse growled.

"Samuel," the voice mumbled through the thick door.

Jesse straightened and let his hand fall from her breast. "Come in," he shouted.

Zee's hand slid wordlessly from his hand as Jesse approached the door. She stifled a small cry and struggled to keep the disappointment from showing on her face.

Samuel entered the room along with several other men. He held a long, straight staff in his hands.

"What in the blazing is that?" Jesse asked, grinning at the staff his long-time friend held.

"I found it on the grounds back near the tree line to the ocean," Samuel replied, examining the staff's pointed end. "What do you think it is?"

"It looks like an old Army flagstaff," another man answered.

"You may be right," Jesse agreed. "So many battles happened around here in Philadelphia during the Revolution. We are bound to keep finding relics like this."

"I found an old powder horn once!" Another man stated.

"I found an old sword!"

"My grandfather was killed in one of those battles," Jesse interjected. He slapped an arm playfully around Samuel's shoulders in an effort to find the real reason for the sudden visit. "But what were you doing that far back in the tree line?"

"Trying to clean up the yard from that windstorm!"

"Let the yard personnel do that," Jesse replied.

"What yard personnel?" Samuel countered. "Ever since the last few black workers left for Canada, we haven't had anybody. Just me and Bemidii are left."

"We have no yard personnel?"

"That's right," Samuel stated. "The only man who stayed was our trusted trail guide, Bemidii."

Zee stood calmly and laid her hand lightly on Jesse's arm. "I will leave you all to your business. I will see you later at dinner." She moved towards the door, her dress swishing from the sway in her hips. Several men watched her leave.

Jesse glared at the men angrily, and they all immediately looked down. "Okay, sweetheart. I will see you at dinner," he replied back.

Zee closed the door gently behind her as the men resumed addressing the many issues afflicting the Eastman Empire. She slipped quietly away to the library and tried valiantly to keep her emotions from escaping down her cheeks in tears.

♎

The sun streaked into the room as the afternoon turned to evening. Zee sighed and closed the book she was reading. The leather chair she was sitting on had similar intricate carvings on the legs, just like in Jesse's office. She exhaled heavily and looked up to the ceiling. It had been two months since her husband had shown her any affection. She had been counting the days. Her eyes drifted over the carved tiles and detailed artistry on the ceiling. She chuckled sadly to herself. People always thought being rich and influential solved all problems. It did not.

Zee tried to keep her composure but was helpless to stop the tears from welling up in her eyes. She felt almost selfish about her need for intimacy. It almost seemed like a petty reason to feel so disenchanted. Zee was still attracted to her husband after twenty years of marriage. But lately, she wasn't quite certain that he felt the same. Jesse Eastman had changed a lot since 1813, but she loved him all the same. He rarely wore anything but suits and expensive shoes now. He told her it was the image that came with the job of running one of the most profitable companies in America. Jesse always had his hair slicked back, and his appearance was always so polished. In Zee's mind, she always saw him as the twenty-year-old American sergeant with blood on his hands and mud caked on his boots. She didn't care about the suits or how everybody thought her husband should dress. Zee Collard knew her husband was made of more substance than just a wealthy background. Jesse was the perfect man for her; he always was. Her body craved her husband's attention so badly that, some days, the aching made her stomach upset.

Zee knew that Jesse was embroiled with the hostile take-over. She heard that Bartholomew had sent his associate to initiate the deal on the spot. Nobody had met Bartholomew personally, so he remained a mysterious face to the Eastmans. But every businessman knew Bartholomew's reputation. He was a wealthy thug who was traveling up from Texas, acquiring many businesses along the way. A few rumors spread that he had even murdered several property owners and taken over with no money exchanged.

Zee was afraid for her husband and family. She was closest to her twin teenage sons, Scott and James. They were always overly protective of her. She didn't know why, although maybe it was because delivering twins had been very difficult for her. She hypothesized that they both somehow held childbirth sympathies because of the extreme chaos it had put her body through. After the birth, doctors had struggled to stop the flow of blood. For several stressful days, she had thought she was going to die. Jesse had stayed by her side and prayed. After a week, they were relieved that the bleeding had ceased and her body had begun the process of repair.

It was a perilous delivery and had definitely scared both Jesse and herself. Even though years later, she still managed to have another son, Johnny. Nothing was wrong about that pregnancy or delivery except a painful, slow recovery that lasted almost a full two years. After that period, Zee had conceived multiple times, all ending in miscarriages. It was a sad and heartbreaking day when the doctor informed her that she was unable to conceive again. Jesse adored Johnny and treated him especially well. He was the miracle baby of the family after all.

Zee rubbed her shoulder and felt the muscles all knotted up with stress. She didn't like living in the grand Eastman estate. Every room was as uninviting as the rest. She yearned to be back at the Collard farm or the cottage they still held near Lake Huron in Upper Canada.

But she wanted her husband more. So, she stayed at the estate.

Zee could still have sex, of course, and her body craved it on a daily basis. Although Jesse had become a lot gentler since all the miscarriages, she now feared that he had lost his desire for her. A slew of negative thoughts filled her mind, and she began to weep. Zee couldn't even begin to categorize her emotions, but her mind briefly wondered if she should talk to Jesse about it. Zee felt slightly ashamed that she wanted sex. She wasn't sure if it was normal or not, because so few people talked about their desires. None of the ladies of the Eastman empire ever spoke of such things. Her mother, Clara Collard, had died when Zee was twenty, and all her sisters stayed in Upper Canada. She had no female confidantes in the US.

Zee exhaled heavily and stood, wiping the tears from her eyes. She smoothed her dress and wondered if she should try to look more attractive. Maybe that would entice her husband to spend more time with her.

She witnessed Jesse's mother, Ellen, applying lotions and a homemade face powder many times. One of Jesse's sisters also rubbed ashes on her eyebrows and stained her lips with berries. It was the only way women could safely add beauty to their looks. No one wanted to be labelled a painted lady.

Zee closed the door to the library and passed a hallway mirror. She looked younger than her age, but her complexion was not the same anymore. Maybe she would ask Ellen if she could borrow some face powder and then rummage through the kitchen to find some red berries.

Chapter 2

The most attractive man at the table had an air of importance to him. Everyone at the Tremont Restorator knew this. The serving staff were very diligent with keeping up to the man's every culinary whim. The man was a tall gentleman with short and thick dark hair, slicked back from his forehead. The tall gentleman lit up the room with a charismatic smile. His lips were oddly full, his skin slightly tanned, and his arms heavily muscled. All the ladies seemed to be instantly taken in by his smooth charms, Latino looks, and devilishly handsome face.

"Bartholomew," his assistant spoke calmly. "We need to close this deal as soon as possible with the Eastmans. The younger brother, Billy Eastman, agreed to the sale. Whatever Jesse Eastman says should be null and void."

"Did you get Billy's signature?" Bartholomew asked, waving at a server.

"No, not yet."

The waiter approached the table, and Bartholomew scowled at his assistant, Thomas. "Please bring me another serving of oysters for my men," he stated charmingly. "And if you can conjure up a loaf of bread, you will be greatly compensated."

The server nodded and whisked away back into the kitchen.

Bartholomew turned his gaze to Thomas, his dark eyes almost turning a shade of black. "Why didn't you get his signature?"

"I did not have the agreement prepared in writing at the time," Thomas responded coolly. He was not afraid of his unscrupulous boss. Thomas was Bartholomew's right hand after all. "I had it drawn up later when I set up the meeting with Jesse. Billy assured me it was a deal. I will get our men to find Billy, and we will obtain his signature."

Bartholomew nodded and accepted this as fact. But Jesse Eastman continued to bother him. The man had vehemently said no, threatened him, and almost physically thrown Thomas out. This man, Jesse, was quick to anger, it seemed. "I would like to know more about this Jesse Eastman," he stated. "Find out as much about him as you can. I like to know my enemies."

"I will do that," Thomas responded, nodding at another man to his right. He turned back to Bartholomew and spoke again. "All I know personally about Mr. Jesse Eastman is that he was extremely confrontational during our meeting. Apparently, Billy and Jesse don't see eye to eye." Thomas plucked three chunks of juicy shellfish from the closest platter of oysters set on the table. Several of the eight men at the table did the same, devouring the five platters of fried oysters. Thomas licked his long fingers. "Jesse told me that he had controlling interest of the estate and nothing would be sold at this time. Troubling information, yes, but we will find a way around that with Billy."

"I have a feeling Jesse Eastman might be more trouble than we think."

Thomas frowned. He knew Bartholomew. He had been working for BMato Investments for fifteen years. The only thing that scared him about Bartholomew was when he started conjuring up plans to eliminate stubborn owners with physical means. It was a dirty, malevolent side of Bartholomew's ego. He could never lose a fight.

"Don't look at me that way," Bartholomew laughed. "You look like you just saw your mother's ghost."

Thomas forced a smile onto his face. "Not at all," he answered quietly. He finished chewing and then swallowed another delicious oyster. "Just another day at BMato."

"That's right," Bartholomew chuckled as a young lady walked by, swaying her hips. All the men at the table watched her. She wasn't a painted lady because her face was relatively plain, but something about the way she moved raised Bartholomew's interest. He watched as she sat politely at a table and resumed her dinner. Bartholomew quickly waved for a server and whispered into his ear. "Send that beautiful woman at the far table a bottle of wine." The waiter nodded and did as he was told.

Bartholomew watched the young woman for several minutes. He hadn't been with a woman since his wife died suddenly two months ago. His wife, Lorena, was beautiful but never knew her place in the marriage. Bartholomew missed her but also thought that Lorena could easily be replaced if he chose to get married again.

The woman turned her head suddenly and smiled, waving at Bartholomew with the bottle of wine at her table. Her dimples pinched on both sides of her luscious smile as she flirted with him from across the room. Bartholomew waved back and then spoke to his entourage. "She will be mine tonight, men. Hands off."

♎

Georgina placed the warm bread from the rack onto the wooden serving board. She sliced it expertly as Zee opened the door to the cold cellar. "Zee, what are you searching for?" Georgina asked.

"Strawberries, red currants or raspberries," Zee replied, walking into the chilly cellar.

"We have plenty of strawberries," Georgina responded. "To the left, on top of the shelf."

Zee rummaged around until she finally found the sweet red berries. She placed three on a plate and was satisfied that it was enough.

"Dinner will be ready soon, Mrs. Eastman," Georgina offered. "Don't eat too many strawberries before dinner." Georgina noticed that Zelda Eastman had some white powder on her face, and her brows were somehow darkened. She wondered what the beautiful wife of her half-brother was up to.

"No, I won't eat many," Zee grinned shyly, then whispered. "I'm using them to add color to my lips."

"Oh," Georgina whispered back. She placed the wooden board of bread down, wiped her hands on her apron, then grasped one of Zee's hands. "Come with me, I will help you." She led Zee out of the kitchen and down the hall to a servant's washroom. They closed the door and giggled. Both women were close to the same age. Georgina was only slightly younger by a year. "Stand still," Georgina giggled, grasping the strawberries from Zee's hand. She rubbed the juicy fruit with her finger until her skin turned slightly reddish, then rubbed it onto Zee's lips.

Zee Eastman took the strawberry and rubbed it directly onto her lips, squashing the fruit recklessly against her full lips.

Georgina yelped. "Hold on, Mrs. Eastman!"

"Address me as Zee!" Zee argued. "I told you this a hundred times."

"Zee," Georgina screeched. "Don't rub too much! You are very fair, and your lips will come out looking painted!"

Zee smiled and looked in the mirror. It was a bit too red. Georgina was right. "My lips look perfect."

Georgina exhaled in exasperation. "If it is what you want, Mrs. Zee. You are beautiful without it. Jesse loves you the way you are."

Zee's eyes fell, and her heart thumped in her chest. "I'm doing this for Jesse."

"Whatever for?"

Zee sighed and let her arms fall at her sides. She was dressed in a lovely pink dress with embroidered pearls framing her ample bosom. Zee heaved with choked-up tears and turned away immediately to hide the moisture welling in her eyes.

"Mrs. Zee," Georgina asked softly. "What is going on between my brother and you?"

Zee inhaled sharply, holding back the tears. "Nothing. It's just that he's been working too much."

"Jesse works all the time. It's got to be something else, Mrs. Zee."

Zee straightened and leaned against the wall. "You won't tell?"

"I won't."

"We haven't been intimate in a while," Zee whispered, her green and blue eyes searching Georgina's.

"There must be a reason, Zee," Georgina stated. "He loves you like a thunderstorm."

Zee smiled meekly. She wished that it were true. After twenty years, could any man still love their wife so strongly? Zee smoothed her dress and kept her eyes on the tiled floors. "I think it may be from the repeated miscarriages. I think maybe he doesn't want to hurt me."

Georgina was silent for several seconds, musing over it. Then her eyes widened. "You must talk to him about it then!"

Zee analyzed her thoughts and faced Georgina strongly. "I will try this first. He's my husband after all. I should know him the best." She grasped the doorknob and stepped out into the hallway, just as Jesse's voice filtered loudly from the dining room.

Georgina walked out with her and patted Zee on the arm as they entered the dining room. It was a large room with a fifteen-foot ceiling, over 1000 sq ft of space, with a huge dining room table in the middle, with enough seats for 24 people. On two opposing walls hung several large gun racks and deer heads. A massive china cabinet with a long chest of drawers was placed strategically under one of the gun racks. Most of the relatives knew that it contained enough arsenal to start a small war or finish one.

Jesse stood, pulling his suit lapels around his muscular shoulders, and smiled warmly. "My darling, you look ravishing!" he exclaimed, grinning at Zee and then glanced curiously at Georgina. "What have you girls been up to?"

Georgina chuckled. "Nothing, Mr. Jesse. She was just helping with the strawberries for dessert." She turned and exited, calling behind her. "I will get the fresh bread."

Jesse immediately pulled out a chair and held Zee's hand, kissing her on the lips. "Sit, my dear, you look so vibrant and lovely today. Something's changed. What did you do?"

"Oh, nothing," Zee lied, seating herself. "Just a little freshening up."

Jesse turned his head when the large oak dining room door creaked open. Two loud, boisterous voices boomed in unison. "Father! Momma!" Scott and James entered the dining area and sat beside Zee. Scott hugged Zee and pecked her on the cheek. "Momma, what's for dinner?"

"I'm not certain," she replied. "Georgina was baking some bread. That's all I know."

"At least you don't have to do it anymore," James chuckled, chiding his mom.

Zee frowned and wrinkled her nose at her sons. "I got a lot better at baking bread!" she stated indignantly.

Scott punched his twin brother's arm. "Stop teasing Momma. She's the best mom ever, and you know that."

James snickered. "Just having fun," he said, pulling his chair in. "He's right, Momma, you're the best mother a son could ever have."

The door flung open again, and several people were ushered in. Xavier walked in, followed by the youngest son, Johnny, and everyone's grandmother, Ellen. They all seated themselves as more relatives filtered through the doorway. Jesse's two sisters, Kate and Bridget, walked in with their husbands and teenage children, along with Jesse's youngest brother, Joshua.

Jesse scanned the group of relatives. "Where's Billy?" he asked.

Joshua replied, "He said he had some business to attend to."

"Business?" Jesse scoffed, lifting his arm from Zee's hand and gesturing in the air. "That rotten brother of ours is trying to sell the Eastman Empire for half its worth and leave us all in ruins!"

Ellen interrupted, "Now, Jesse!"

"It's true, Mother!" Jesse responded, sitting in his chair roughly.

"Jesse, you never really got along with Billy," Joshua interceded. "But honestly, I never got along with him either. Billy is greedy and always will be. He only cares for himself. He was father's favorite."

"It is the truth, Momma," Jesse agreed, waving his hand toward Joshua in confirmation.

Ellen Eastman scowled and pursed her lips. Her mouth opened to protest just as Georgina walked in with three large platters of sliced bread.

Georgina frowned questioningly at Jesse and placed the bread on the massive rectangular table.

Ellen found her voice and cleared her throat. "Let's enjoy dinner, my sons," Ellen conceded. "It's not every day that we are together for Independence Day."

"Look who's here!" Zee shouted enthusiastically, standing up and rushing to the door.

A dark-haired beauty with green eyes stood at the door with her husband and two babies. "Momma!"

"Janey!" Zee screeched, wrapping her arms around her only daughter. "It's been so long! I haven't seen you in years."

"That's a lie!" Janey teased, hugging and kissing her mother on the cheek. "I was here for Christmas."

"Christmas!" Zee exclaimed, laughing. "That was last year!" She held her arms out and cradled one of the babies. "Eva looks just like me." Zee smiled proudly as the blonde-haired baby girl cooed in her grasp.

Jesse stood firmly beside Zee and gently clutched the other twin baby. "And my darling Rosie has Janey's dark looks. Just like me!" He chuckled and raised the baby girl up over his head as two musicians entered the long dining hall.

Georgina showed the musicians in, gesturing to the guitarist and drummer to set up in the corner of the dining hall.

Johnny leaned over and started chatting to his cousins. Joshua's, Bridget's, and Kate's sons and daughters were the only relatives close to his age, other than his older twin brothers, Scott and James.

The group of teenagers, ranging from thirteen to seventeen, chatted amicably as the guitarist started strumming a country song. Scott and James joined the group of teens as the drummer set up his equipment.

The musician placed a polished military-looking drum between his knees and sat on a tall chair. The instrument was made with cowhide stretched and tied over a hollowed tree trunk. The drummer's palms began to lightly tap on the stretched cow skin, and the sound of a rhythmic beat filtered into the room, adding to the harmony.

A cluster of servants entered the dining hall with several plates of food to start off supper. Boiled oysters in the shell, green turtle soup, salmon with anchovy sauce, and a selection of breads adorned the table. Jesse, Zee, and the remaining relatives all sat down at the smell of the delicious food. As they settled at the table, Jesse laid his hand on Zee's and smiled. She felt a sensation run through her spine at the gesture of affection. The makeup and dress had worked! Zee smiled back at her husband, wondering if this was the start of a new beginning for their marriage.

Everyone started consuming the soup and fish at once. Several more plates started arriving. The hot entrees steamed with a delicious aroma. Tenderloin of beef with mushrooms, mutton leg, and saddle of venison were also placed on the long table.

"Eat!" Jesse announced. "And enjoy! Thanks to every-one for celebrating Independence Day with us!" Jesse raised a glass of wine and toasted his relatives near the end of the table. Everyone followed suit. Jesse watched Georgina place another plate of food on the table. He grasped her wrist. "Sit with us, Georgina," he instructed. "Let the other servants bring the rest. You've worked all day on this. Sit down and eat."

Georgina nodded. "I will just bring another plate of mutton out, and then I will sit down with you all."

Ellen glared at Jesse, then placed a forkful of beef delicately into her mouth. She didn't have much say about Georgina any-more. Ellen was a 58-year-old widow with a full head of greying hair, and Jesse took good care of her at the estate.

Georgina had been accepted into the family, but obviously wasn't Ellen's biological daughter. Everyone knew that her late husband, Bob Eastman, had sexual liaisons with Georgina's slave mother back in the late 1790s. It was a dark stain on the Eastman's history. Bob Eastman had died in 1812. After his death, Jesse had come back home to help Ellen settle the estate. That's when Georgina had told everyone.

Ellen drank her wine daintily as Georgina sat near Jesse and Zee.

Jesse had always been close to Georgina. As children, they had often played secretly together. Jesse grew up with Georgina, never knowing that she was his half-sister until he had turned nineteen years old. It had all made perfect sense, and so many mysteries were solved when Georgina had told them the truth. Jesse did not doubt her. He had known her his entire life.

In 1812, Jesse had freed her as a slave and given her the choice to stay in the Eastman estate as a paid cook. She accepted and has been grateful to Jesse ever since.

Georgina accepted a glass of water and toasted the others after seating herself. She never drank alcohol because she believed it brought out the evils of humanity. She had joined the local Baptist church a decade ago and had since become a devout Christian. The church was nothing more than a small shack with wooden chairs inside, but it kept her connected with her faith.

Georgina placed a forkful of venison in her mouth. She hummed appreciatively. "The venison turned out perfectly!"

"As always, you are the best cook," Jesse responded.

"I didn't do that much with the venison. I just seasoned it. I made the bread mostly."

"Well, that is tasty too!" Jesse replied. "I'm glad you are here."

"Thank you," Georgina said, smiling. She tasted more of the venison and then tried some of the beef tenderloin with mushrooms. She broke a piece of bread off and placed it on her plate. The food was exquisite at the Eastmans. She had no desire to leave. Even at the age of 39, she was unmarried but quite content and happy. "I will always be here," she stated confidently.

"I hope so!" Zee added.

Samuel seated himself as one of the late arrivals and immediately started filling his mouth with the mutton and oysters.

"You finally made it," Jesse laughed.

Samuel looked up and finished chewing before speaking. "I had to get cleaned up. I was covered in grass and mud."

"Why?"

Samuel eyed Jesse. "I told you before," he replied. "You don't have enough yard maintenance staff. I'm doing security and the yard work now, too."

"Can you find someone to take over the yard work?" Jesse replied. "I trust your decisions."

"There is no one other than me and Bemidii," Samuel replied, his brows knotting together in frustration. "I have tried to recruit others. Only the blacks have an interest in this type of work, and they have mostly all left to Upper Canada."

Jesse frowned. "Since Canada invoked the Act to Limit Slavery in 1793, I know that many blacks have fled to Canada. I lost many workers. We completely stopped having slaves after Georgina and I thought we still had some yard personnel left. I didn't realize it was becoming a real problem for the estate now. Are you sure that you can't find anyone?"

Samuel chewed another morsel of mutton. He swallowed and continued. "All this talk of the Slavery Abolition Act in Britain has made many blacks hopeful that Canada will soon be a free territory." Samuel motioned with his hand. "There are so few men available in this area to take on these difficult yard-work jobs now."

"How do we manage then?" Jesse asked, concern evident in his voice. "It's a massive property. Two men cannot do it alone."

Georgina coughed politely and interrupted. "Jesse, I met a man just recently at my Baptist church. I think his name is Jeremiah Williams. He seemed to be a very strong, large man."

Jesse nodded. "What is his character like?"

"He seemed very kind to me," Georgina replied, looking up at the ceiling, trying to remember the man. "Oh yes, he had helped me when I tripped on the stairs leading out of the church. I didn't talk to him for long, but he seemed like a very strong gentleman." Georgina chuckled at the memory. "He lifted me almost straight in the air, preventing my fall."

"Could you ask him if he's interested in a paid grounds-keeper position the next time you see him?"

"I can definitely do that," Georgina answered. "I will be going to church this Sunday. I will ask him after the service, if he's there."

"Thank you," Jesse replied. "Keep me updated." He nodded at Georgina, then turned his attention to Zee. He grabbed her hand under the table, squeezing it lightly.

Zee smiled demurely and squeezed his hand back. It was always his sign that he wanted affection. Her heart burst open with butterflies, and she was truly delighted to have her husband back.

♎

After dinner, Zee realized she couldn't have been more wrong. Jesse was consumed with alcohol, his sons, friends, and family. The Independence Day celebrations lasted until early into the morning hours. Zee had finally gone to bed alone at 2 am, wishing that there was something more she could do to resurrect their marriage.

She curled the blankets over her shoulders and hugged herself. Zee smelled the pillow, and it only smelled of herself. She hadn't smelled her husband on her sheets for so terribly long that it made her stomach ache. They both slept in their own bedrooms, of course, as everyone did. But Jesse used to visit her bedroom in the deep of night regularly. When they first met in 1813, they slept together quite often, but lately it was becoming more and more of a rarity.

Zee crumpled the blankets in front of her nose and sighed. When they made love, afterwards, Jesse would wrap his arms around her waist, then slip his hand between her breasts, hugging her tightly from behind until she fell asleep. Often, he would fall asleep himself and then sneak out back to his bedroom sometime in the early morning.

Zee closed her eyes, imagined his touch, and how it used to feel. She groaned quietly and rolled over to her other side. Her breasts ached, and her inner thighs clenched oddly without her mind's consent. Her hands slid along her thighs and then up to her breasts, until her emotions abruptly grabbed a hold of her thoughts.

She missed her husband so much it felt physically painful. This must be why her breasts ached, she concluded. Zee hugged the sheets tighter, trying to hold onto someone who wasn't there. She allowed that familiar feeling of despair to creep back into her heart as her mind drifted off to sleep.

CHAPTER 3

The Baptist Church was full this Sunday, Georgina mused, looking around. Every chair was occupied, and she barely had time to secure one herself before the singing had started. Georgina sang loudly with the congregation, feeling her heart swell with joy.

She started attending the Baptist church eleven years ago, when she had turned twenty-eight. Like so many of the other former black slaves, she had the urge to leave to Canada. By law, she was completely free when she had turned twenty-eight, even though Jesse had never treated her as a slave. Her quest for freedom and clarity of life led her to the church for answers. When she first attended, she was welcomed wholeheartedly and had immediately joined the choir. Georgina made many friends, and it helped her to sort through her conflicting emotions. On one side, she was happy living at the Eastmans, but on the other hand, she still felt an emptiness in her heart. Georgina had never had children nor any men in her life and felt secluded from her peers.

Georgina was different from the other slaves. She even looked different. She was half-white, and her skin was light brown, almost whitish on her cheeks. Her eyes were brown like everyone else's, and her hair was black with curls, tightly held back in a bun. But that's where the similarities ended. Georgina was born in Philadelphia and grew up within the Eastman family. Her mannerisms were well defined, and even her speech was strikingly different. She spoke with clear American English and sounded more like the Eastmans than her colored peers.

She yearned to enjoy a life of her own, but could not envision a life outside of the Eastman household. Georgina had nowhere to go in Canada and knew no one there, other than Zee's side of the family. Georgina was raised as an Eastman and finally just accepted her path in life at the estate. Regardless of how she was born into this world, this was her life now.

It had taken many years for her to come to this conclusion, and the Baptist community had helped immensely. She no longer sang within the choir but joined the congregation with every song, clapping happily.

Georgina glanced around, trying to spot Jeremiah, the tall, dark man whom she had met only a few times. Unfortunately, she was much shorter than most people around her, and they were all standing by this point. She was only 5-foot-6 inches tall and quite shorter than most of her female peers. Georgina was slim and strong but still shorter than she would have liked.

She glanced behind her and could only see a wall of people. Finally, she gave up and joined the chorus, singing loudly with the closing songs.

When the service had ended, she weaved her way through the crowd and stepped outside, waiting for the mysterious Mr. Williams to emerge. Several worshippers shook her hand and hugged her warmly as she waited patiently, scanning the crowd.

"My dear," one tall woman approached, waving. "You must think about rejoining the choir. Your voice sounds like a dozen angels!"

Georgina smiled. "Thank you! I have too many commitments with my work now that I am head cook."

"Oh, yes," the woman replied. "I completely understand. But the choir is not the same without you!"

Georgina poked her head up over the crowd of people, and she thought she saw him, but the woman was distracting her search. Georgina's eyes darted to the other side of the steps and towards the center of the doorway.

"Are you looking for someone, dear?" the woman asked.

"No," Georgina answered. "Well, yes and no." She laughed.

At that moment, a large hand landed on her shoulder, and she could feel his presence before she could see him. Her heart fluttered strangely.

"Georgina," a large man cooed in a smooth African accent. "I have to agree with Frederica that your voice is soothingly angelic."

Georgina swung around and came face-to-face with Jeremiah. He was quite tall and towered over her, almost a full foot higher than her. She had to look up to meet his eyes. His skin was dark brown, almost completely black, and his white teeth gleamed when he smiled. He was smiling at her now with a funny, odd expression on his face.

"Jeremiah!" Georgina greeted enthusiastically. "I was looking for you the entire time. You must have been hiding. I didn't see you anywhere."

"I was in the back row, keeping to myself," he stated, his voice a smooth baritone that harmonized throughout his words. "Remember, I am new here. I only arrived with my sister a few weeks ago."

"Yes," Georgina replied. "You had mentioned that before. The congregation is wonderful here." She smiled appreciatively at him. "Did you manage to secure work here? Is that why you moved?"

"No," he replied haltingly. "I moved here with family." He stopped talking abruptly, almost like he was going to say something, and then stopped. He oddly didn't offer any more explanation.

"Oh," Georgina stated, unsure what he was about to say. She tried to change the direction of the conversation. "You met Frederica?"

"Yes, we met last week and she had humbly invited me over for dinner." He flashed his white smile.

Georgina felt oddly jealous. "Oh, I didn't know. That's wonderful of you to feed a newcomer, Frederica."

"It was my pleasure!" Frederica announced. "After my husband died, I am most grateful to cater to good company." Frederica batted her lashes and smiled at Jeremiah, clearly flirting.

Georgina felt uncomfortably out of place. "Well, I must be going, I don't want to intrude on the two of you," she stated and turned to leave. She glanced behind her, addressing Jeremiah. "There is something I have been asked to talk to you about, Jeremiah, if you have a moment one day. Maybe next week." Georgina waved and walked quickly away, feeling a plethora of emotions hijacking her senses. She had promised Jesse that she would talk to Jeremiah today, but now all she wanted to do was escape. She swung her slim hips towards the road leading back to the estate. It was an hour walk, but well worth it most Sundays. Georgina normally stayed and socialized, but for some reason today, she felt excluded.

Her shoes clopped against the dirt road as her dress swayed beneath her. She would talk to him next Sunday, she mused.

As the crowd dispersed behind her, a voice called her name.

"Georgina!" the soothing male African accent called. "Wait! I will walk you home."

She swung around and saw Jeremiah running to catch up to her. With his long legs, he managed to reach her in no time.

"Oh! You don't need to walk me home," she replied, a blush forming on her light-colored cheeks. "I walk this way every Sunday."

He stopped in front of her and took her hand. "Don't be silly," he said. "We can discuss what you wanted to speak to me about, and I can be assured that you arrive home safely."

Georgina let him lead her down the path, his strong hand in hers. It felt strangely calming, almost as if he was someone she had known for a long time. Georgina had never experienced any such reassuring sensations around men before. Normally, men invoked apprehension and sometimes fear within her. Why did this man calm her? Was it his voice? Then she realized blatantly what it was. She felt safe around him.

Georgina looked sideways at him, curiously.

He smiled at her, flashing his bright white teeth. "What is it, my dear?"

She chuckled at herself. "No, it's nothing."

"Oh, come on, you said you needed to talk to me about something," he replied. "So, talk to me."

"Yes," she replied, happy to talk business. "My half-brother had asked me to help him find a new groundskeeper for the Eastman estate. I mentioned you, but I wasn't sure if you were already employed. But it seems that you are with Frederica." She stumbled over her words, not completely understanding why she had mentioned Frederica. "I'm sure you have your hands full. She has seven children!"

"Frederica?" he replied, genuinely confounded. "I only had dinner at her house once. Me and my sister went. I'm not taking care of her seven children!" He laughed, with a deep baritone chuckle rising from his chest.

"Oh, I see." Georgina looked down at her shoes, slightly embarrassed.

"I would be delighted to work for the Eastmans as a groundskeeper," he declared keenly. "I have been looking for work and have only managed to find work cleaning stables since I arrived." He squeezed her hand gently and smiled. "I might be a perfect fit. I worked at an orchard before and have plenty of grounds experience."

"Oh really?" she replied, intrigued. "The Eastmans actually have a small orchard and garden on the grounds, mostly to supply the kitchen, not anything more. But the majority of the grounds are massive and secured by staff. They have recently lost much of the workforce, and there are lots of flowers, countless trees, and shrubs to maintain."

"That sounds like a fabulous job."

"You are interested then?" Georgina replied, genuinely surprised by this gentleman.

"Yes, most definitely!"

"I will introduce you to Jesse when we arrive, then."

"That sounds perfect," he replied, squeezing her hand gently again. "Do you mind my hand in yours? I have an odd feeling to be slightly protective over you, that's all."

She smiled broadly, and a warm feeling spread throughout her body from limb to limb. "I don't mind at all. It's nice." She felt her cheeks blush again, and she looked down to try to hide it.

"Well, then," he added, another smile creasing the corners of his lips. "I look forward to meeting your brother."

♎

Zee woke up to another sunny, beautiful summer day. She clutched her nightgown hem and padded silently down to the stairway. She descended down the stairs as several servants rushed towards her, asking if she needed anything.

"No, I'm fine," Zee replied. "I was just going to find some books for reading."

"You spend a lot of time in the library, Mrs. Eastman," a small woman servant stated. "You should take your books to the sunroom. It is a beautiful day."

"I might just do that."

Zee entered the massive library and picked up the book she had been reading the other day. Sunlight streaked in, competing with the dark leather furnishings. The bright rays seemed to be beckoning her to leave to sunnier rooms.

She accepted the challenge, grabbed her book, exited quietly across the room, and gently closed the library door. Zee stepped across the expansive foyer and rounded the circular sweeping staircase, continuing towards the back of the mansion. The sunlight shone brightly towards the south side of the mansion, long rays of yellow warmth filtering through the windows. Zee grasped the eloquently carved door handles and opened the double sunroom doors with both hands. A rush of warm, fresh air blew in her face. She looked at the windows and was surprised to discover that the servants had aired out the sunroom for her. A plush chaise lounge chair was prepared for her with a blanket and two rolled pillows. The lounge chair was made of fabric, gold in color, with a sleigh-type design. The legs were carved with rounded balls, one on top of the other, each one smaller than the other, until finally the leg met the foot, a triangular spike that touched the floor eloquently.

Zee folded her flowing white nightgown underneath her buttocks and lay down on the chaise lounge gently. An audible sigh of relief escaped her lips as the sunshine swathed her entire body. She stretched her head back and enjoyed the feeling of warmth all over her body. The book fell onto her lap as her mind wandered.

She wondered what else she could do to revive her marriage and found no answers. She felt that talking to Jesse about it at a time when he was dealing with so many dangerous situations was simply selfish and inconsiderate. But he had dealt with many other threats throughout the years, and it never stopped him from being intimate with her. The more she thought about it, the more certain she was that the lack of intimacy was because of the miscarriages. Jesse still loved her, she told herself, but her heart seemed to rationalize things differently.

Zee felt neglected and lonely. Her connection with Jesse used to be so strong in the past, right from the first day they had met, and through every childbirth. They were together and inseparable, it seemed. She racked her brain to examine what had changed since then.

The biggest life-changing event for Zee had been in 1825, when her youngest brother, Sam Collard, had died in a farming accident. He was only seventeen years old at the time, and his twin brother, Jacob, had tried to disentangle his body from the horse rake, but it was too late. Zee had received the news of Sam's death by courier and raced immediately back home to the Collard farm in the Niagara region of Upper Canada.

And that was the last time she had seen her father alive.

George Collard died a month later, when his heart could take no further pain. Zee's father had been through so much in his lifetime. He had been shot in the chest during the 1812 war and then returned home to discover that his wife, Clara, had died.

Zee looked up, trying to prevent the tears from forming in her eyes. The memory of keeping her mother alive during 1812 was still fresh in her mind. Zee was the eldest sibling and had been the strongest, doing whatever was necessary to keep the Collard farm operating until her father returned from war.

It was a very tough few years, and George finally came home severely injured. All Zee's siblings cared for him and helped him to heal, even after the devastating news of Clara's death.

Zee had eloped with Jesse into the Canadian wilderness, and the guilt of not being there with her family still pressed on her emotions. But she was pregnant and in love with Jesse, an American.

It was the only choice they could have made back then. Any Americans found in Canada were considered the enemy during the war.

Her heart thumped with the memories of the past. Zee inhaled deeply and stared out the large, picturesque windows, gazing across the expansive grounds of the Eastman Empire.

She missed her father greatly. He was her mentor, her foundation, and the person who had instilled strength within her. Pappa had taught her to be the last soldier standing, not just with his words but with his actions. When George Collard was a young man, he had walked for weeks from Philadelphia after the Revolutionary War to Upper Canada. George was given land by the British, and he built everything the family ever had, marrying Clara and having seven children, including Zee. George had even survived the bloody Lundy's Lane battle, when so many others had perished. He was the pillar of strength to Zee throughout her entire life.

Then her pappa's heart just stopped working.

At first, she didn't believe it. Zee had travelled back with her children and attended the funeral. A large contingent of military personnel was there, along with all the extended family and neighborhood friends. George Collard was a well-liked man of integrity. Zee felt like she was in a nightmarish dream and was waiting to awaken one day.

Eventually, the reality sank in that her father was gone, and her world began to somehow lose color. The autumn leaves of New York State and Pennsylvania were just leaves, not the vibrant colors of red, brown, and purple. The meaning of life became elusive to her as she searched for something deeper and more meaningful.

Jesse was there for her during the loss of her family members, but she still turned inward and secluded herself more often. She gazed out the window, wondering if she was at fault for the lost connection with Jesse. Maybe her emotional numbness had driven a stake between them.

Zee mused on this notion as she watched the new grounds-keeper trimming the bushes on the other side of the expansive Eastman property. He looked like a very productive man. She was glad that Georgina had found Jeremiah. It was a relief of stress for Jesse that at least the grounds were now in capable hands.

Zee pondered what the connection was between Georgina and Jeremiah. Jesse's half-sister was unexpectedly cheerful and jubilant. Normally a quiet, reserved woman, Georgina had turned into a smiling, laughing, bubble full of energy. Zee speculated that the two were having a secret love affair. She didn't tell anyone about her assumptions, but it did make her feel mournful about her own marriage. Jesse and Zelda once had a similar joyful, deep connection with each other.

Several tears unexpectedly slipped from Zee's eyes.

She could sit here and cry for days with no solution, she thought. Jesse was too busy preventing the takeover of the empire.

Then what was she to do?

Zee rubbed the back of her hand against her eyes, drying her tears.

What things could she do to bring back the color in her life without putting more pressure on Jesse?

Zee thought back to what made her so happy back in their younger years, living at the cabin on Lake Huron in the Canadian wilderness. Her babies were young, life was simpler, and the marriage was new.

She couldn't change the marriage to be new again, but she could certainly change her circumstances now.

The cabin was lovely. They slept together in the same bed for ten years before moving to the Eastman Empire. They hunted together and raised their family together.

A smile crept to her lips.

Maybe that was it, she thought.

The smile faded from her face quickly. The Lake Huron cabin was currently rented to a neighbor, who had lived there for almost eight years now. It was their rented home. She could not just take it away and live there herself.

Maybe there was another way, she thought. Zee ran her hands through her long blonde hair and twisted the ends in her fingers, deep in thought. Her passions and where she felt comfortable were with animals, hunting, and farming. That had been her purpose in life for so long. She had even become the unofficial animal doctor in the small town where the Collard home was located.

When Jesse had taken over the Collard home as a military hospital, she had fallen in love with him at first sight, and she knew the feeling was mutual. Jesse had loved her determination, medical expertise, and strength. But yet, it seemed she had lost all of those things when they had moved to the Eastman Estate.

Zee frowned and allowed her hands to fall helplessly in her lap. She had somehow lost her identity, everything Jesse had always been so attracted to. Even worse, when she had fallen into a state of mourning, Zee gave up tending to the animals at the Eastman property.

It was frowned upon by the servants to find Mrs. Eastman in the stable. It was unacceptable to be cooking anything herself or even to sleep in the same bedroom as her husband. High society had its rules, and Zee was finally realizing the toll it had taken on her soul.

She yearned to return to her roots, start farming and tending to the animals again. Maybe even shoot a deer or two for dinner with her twin sons.

But that wasn't allowed within the Eastman family. She was married to one of the richest men in the country. Zee Collard was an Eastman now. Her passions in life were secondary.

With the thought of the rest of her life stagnating, a torrent of tears spilled down her cheeks. Everything would simply stay the same as it was today, and she couldn't bear it for one more week.

Zee stood and smoothed down her nightdress. She never even used to wear dresses! She inhaled deeply and straightened her spine. Zee Collard could never truly be a rich, Eastman girl. She loved Jesse, but she realized now that she must love herself too.

She would have to find a way to return to her roots.

Ω

When Zee stepped back into the mansion, several angry shouts from the office raised the hairs on her neck. She padded quickly up the stairs and turned to look down the stairs behind her. Billy stormed out of the main floor office, flanked by Jesse, Xavier, and Samuel.

Jesse was waving a large document in his hand. His dress shoes clacked on the marble floors as he chased Billy from the house. "This is not a legal document!" Jesse shouted, his voice reverberating against the tiled ceiling. "You don't even have signing authority for the Empire!"

Billy brazenly turned and shouted back. "I am an Eastman! I can sign a bill of sale for my family business." His voice thundered across the entire mansion.

Jesse's face turned red, and his breathing expanded and contracted in his chest as he tried to control his urge to punch his brother in the face. "Get out," Jesse calmly stated.

"What?" Billy shouted.

"You heard me," Jesse replied quietly. Xavier and Samuel positioned themselves to quickly intervene if the two brothers began physically fighting.

"You're telling me to leave?" Billy's finger flew in the air and pointed accusingly at Jesse.

"Yes, Billy," Jesse glowered, the anger still evident in his voice. "You attempted to sell the company illegally for a fraction of what it is worth to a bunch of thugs from Texas." Jesse ground his teeth and clenched his hands into balls of anger. "You are officially extradited from the Eastman family. Father did it to me, and I am now doing it to you." Jesse took two large strides towards his brother.

Billy jumped to the side to avoid a direct hit, but that wasn't what Jesse was doing.

Jesse grasped the large oak front door. "You are no longer an Eastman," Jesse stated angrily. "Get out."

"I live here too," Billy stated incredulously.

"Not any longer," Jesse replied.

"I have my belongings here."

"I will have the servants collect your belongings and deliver them to you by carriage."

"You can't do this!" Billy yelled, indignantly.

"I sure can!" Jesse shouted back, systematically rolling up his sleeves. "I noticed that you signed this agreement today, probably at Bartholomew's office, and you came here right after. Big mistake, Billy. You are officially estranged from the Eastman Empire as of today. Get out and don't come back. Your signature officially means nothing as of today." Jesse straightened his shoulders and braced himself for the physical fight. "We have witnesses to attest to this." Jesse waved his arms around the room.

Billy's eyes darted toward the stairs where Zee was watching the entire event unfold, and to the hallway where several servants gathered from the kitchen. Almost ten people stared at Billy, waiting for his next move.

"You always were the one that Father hated," Billy sneered, hoping that his brother would do something stupid.

Jesse leapt at Billy. The younger brother took a few steps back and narrowly escaped the range of Jesse's arms.

Jesse came closer and growled in Billy's face angrily. "If you don't leave now, I will pick you up myself and throw you out."

Billy didn't doubt his brother's strength. When Jesse was boiling with anger, he could move an entire army.

Billy stepped through the doorway and turned his head back. "I will send word of my whereabouts."

"Good," Jesse responded. "I will let the servants know where to send your belongings." With that, he slammed the large oak door heavily in Billy's face. The force of the door reverberated throughout the front wall of the mansion, sending a chill through everyone's body. The servants, Zee, Xavier, and Samuel all stared at Jesse in astonishment.

"It's all over," Jesse stated calmly. "The threat has been dealt with. You can all go back to work or whatever it was that you were doing." He unclenched his fists and stomped toward the back of the house. He yelled over his shoulder. "I'm going for a horse ride." Jesse exited the house with his heart thumping loudly in his chest.

♎

Jesse gently closed the back door and took several large strides toward the barn. He could feel the eyes of everyone still on his back. Jesse had thrown his suit jacket off earlier in his office. He now only wore a blue vest, a white collared shirt, and dress pants. He frowned. Jesse truly hated these clothes. The summer morning air was warm, humid, and not suitable for dress clothes. Sweat was already collecting on his neck, sticking his shirt to his upper back. In stark contrast with the intense yelling in the house, the birds chirped happily outside, and the bugs hummed noisily.

Jesse stomped angrily towards the horse stable, crossing the manicured lawn. He hated everything about his appearance today. His suit and his shoes weren't meant for riding, and his hair was too short. He ran his fingers over his head and made a mental note to start growing his hair. Maybe he'd start wearing a wide-brimmed hat to hide the thinning on top.

Jesse wasn't the same man that he knew himself to be, and it was gnawing at his nerves. Ten years ago, he wore riding pants, rough working shirts, wide-brimmed hats, and leather boots. He had probably not even put his leather boots on his feet for ten years! Jesse Eastman scowled. He was a different man now, and he didn't like it.

He neared the stable with a deep frown on his face.

Jeremiah poked his head out of the stable as Georgina trailed Jesse from the house to the barn. "Is there anything I can do for you, Mr. Jesse?" Jeremiah asked politely.

"Saddle a horse for me," Jesse instructed. "I need to get away from this household for a while."

Jeremiah ran into the stable as Georgina caught up to Jesse. "Are you okay?" she asked, her breathing coming out heavy and fast.

Jesse stopped and turned around to face Georgina. His face was still red, and his jaw was squared. "I never wanted to live at the Eastman Empire," he confessed. "I never wanted to take the place of my father." His dark brown eyes searched for Zee in the large windows of the second floor, but he couldn't see her. He unbuttoned his blue vest and tore it off, throwing it onto the fence. "I never wanted this suit or these clothes, or this status. I never wanted any of this. My life was happier without all the money and influence. I was happy with the man I was. My life was simple."

At that moment, Ellen Eastman walked quickly from the back door onto the manicured lawn.

Georgina glanced behind her and watched Ellen advance. She turned back to Jesse. "Why did you come back to the estate then?" Georgina asked softly.

"My mother," he stated, watching Ellen walk briskly towards him. "I love my momma. She couldn't deal with Billy anymore. Momma couldn't handle the stress of running the Empire herself. She needed me."

Ellen quickened her steps as Jeremiah began to lead the saddled horse from the stable towards Jesse.

Georgina's eyes softened, and a glimmer of sympathy grew in her heart. "I know you were happy living in Upper Canada. It was a sacrifice for you to move back."

"It sure was," Jesse replied, removing his shoes. He shouted back at Jeremiah. "Do you have my leather boots in there? I think I left my old pair in the stable."

Jeremiah yelled back. "I will look!"

Ellen finally reached Jesse and stretched her arms around him in a warm motherly hug. She whispered into his neck. "I've wanted to throw Billy out for decades. I could never gather up the strength to do it."

Jesse stood there still as a statue, looking for Zee in the large second-floor windows. He thought maybe he saw her blonde head through one of the windows, but then she disappeared. He missed the way his marriage used to be. His arms finally softened, and he hugged his mother back. "Billy won't be coming back, Momma. It's for the best. Something evil has taken over that man. Sometimes I wonder if he's even my brother anymore."

Ellen hugged Jesse tighter. "Thank you for being the man the Eastman Empire needs."

Jesse felt his soul fall at his feet with her words. "I never wanted to be that man," Jesse spoke softly, almost whispering.

Ellen straightened and looked him in the eyes, holding his bearded chin in her small, wrinkled hands. "But you see, Jesse, the reluctance of riches that you possess is exactly what makes you the best man for the job."

Jesse felt the rage drain from his body. She was right. Momma knew him all too well. "I know, Momma. I know."

Jeremiah walked the black horse from the stable towards Jesse as the group watched. A calm descended upon everyone as the large horse trotted towards them. As Jeremiah neared, he handed Jesse the old leather boots. "Are these the ones?"

"Yes, they are," Jesse replied. "Those are my old boots. Much appreciated." Jesse pulled on the boots, then mounted the horse. "Don't wait up for me," he said to everyone gathered around, then turned the horse and galloped away.

♎

Thomas looked up sharply as a series of short, loud knocks banged on the office door. BMato Investments had bought a small commercial building and had just moved in, hopeful of the future in Philadelphia. Thomas stood up and walked to the door, momentarily confused. Not too many people knew of this office yet.

He yanked open the door and was taken aback by the murderous scowl on the man's face. "Billy," Thomas stated simply.

"You must provide me with a place to live," Billy demanded.

"Sure, we can do that."

"I left the Eastman Estate," Billy lied. "I no longer wish to live there."

Thomas narrowed his eyes, sensing a whole lot more had happened than Billy was willing to admit. Thomas turned his back and waved him into the office. "Bartholomew will be stopping by shortly. We can discuss it with him. It shouldn't be difficult to find a small private property for all of us."

Billy smiled. "I knew I could count on you."

CHAPTER 4

Georgina's face creased into a huge smile as she watched Jeremiah eating breakfast in the servants' quarters. He lived at the estate now, and she couldn't be happier. Over the past few weeks, she had become quite fond of Jeremiah. He was a very strong man physically. She had no doubt that he could lift her entire body over his head effortlessly. Although, what astonished her the most was his gentle nature around women. He wasn't overly chivalrous, but oddly thoughtful about Georgina's specific needs and requests.

At first, she assumed it was only because she had secured him an excellent job at the Eastman Estate. But after many weeks of being around him and enjoying each other's company, Georgina wondered if he was physically attracted to her. He hadn't held her hand again after their first chat. But lately, Jeremiah had started placing his palm on her hand. Like he was doing today.

"Your cooking is so delicious, Georgina," Jeremiah mumbled between bites. He reached across the table and laid his palm lightly on top of her hand in thanks. "I am grateful for everything you've done for me."

Georgina felt a shiver run through her hand from his touch. His dark brown eyes glimmered while he glanced at her briefly. "Jesse and Samuel are grateful for having you here," she responded sincerely. "I told you this many times before. They were having great difficulty finding someone skilled and strong enough to maintain the grounds and gardens." She inhaled sharply. "Especially after this Underground Railroad started luring so many skilled laborers to Upper Canada."

Jeremiah grew silent momentarily. He almost seemed unsure of how to respond. He pulled his hand away and concentrated on finishing his eggs and bread.

Georgina frowned worriedly. It seemed every time she mentioned the Underground Railroad, he froze up. "I hope I didn't say something wrong."

"No, not at all," he replied. "Just finishing up this delicious breakfast you cooked."

She tilted her head to the side suspiciously. She knew of the Underground Railroad movement from the church. It was inevitable that a system of volunteers would begin helping slaves escape. She never spoke of it to Jesse, actually, she rarely spoke of it, period. She felt comfortable enough around Jeremiah to speak openly, but it was obvious that he did not feel the same.

Jeremiah was often vague and mysterious about his past. It reminded Georgina that she really didn't know much about this man. He was strong and very accommodating with her, but she wasn't completely aware of his background. Every time she inquired, he would change the direction of the conversation or offer vague recollections of living in the South. She had given up trying to extract familial information about him. It seemed to be a sore point with him. Maybe he had a feuding family like Billy and Jesse, she thought.

"Would you like some more coffee?" she asked, standing up.

"Yes, I would appreciate that," he replied, holding his cup.

She poured the coffee into his cup and smiled. Every moment she spent with him felt pleasant. She looked forward to speaking with him, and if she was completely honest, she sought opportunities to spend more time in the areas he would be working in. Georgina couldn't help herself. When he was around, she felt so indescribably splendid and almost glowing inside. So naturally, she wanted more of those feelings.

It wasn't something she was accustomed to.

Georgina had devoted her entire life to the Eastman family. Even after being accepted as the half-sister, she worked hard to maintain a high level of trust with every member of the family, including Ellen. Twenty years of working hard to be accepted had paid off. She was now one of the highest paid servants in the household. She could afford her own property but chose not to. The prospect of living alone scared her. Georgina had always been surrounded by family and servants her entire life. To be going home every night to an empty house was like a nightmare to her.

"Why don't you come out in the garden this afternoon?" Jeremiah asked. "I'd like to show you the overgrown summer flowers that need to be divided. I will wait until fall, of course, but Jesse has given me permission to redesign what I see fit." He smiled and patted her hand once again. "I'd love to have your opinion on the placements of the flowers."

"I'd love that!" Georgina smiled and felt her cheeks grow warm.

"Okay," Jeremiah replied, standing up to his full height and unconsciously dwarfing Georgina. "I have to get back to work, but thank you so much for the food." He snatched her hand and kissed her knuckles quickly before she had a chance to protest. She froze, and he dropped her hand and then exited through the door. "See you later on!"

Georgina watched him leave and tried to will herself to speak. "Yes!" she finally shouted before the door closed behind him. She lifted her hand to her cheek and chuckled gaily. He had kissed her hand!

She twirled around and rushed to her room to change into better clothes. Maybe she would rub some strawberries on her lips like Mrs. Zee did!

♎

Bartholomew was tired of dealing with Billy Eastman. The man had no common sense and little knowledge of legal matters. It annoyed him every time he had to deal with Billy, and now the swine was living with them.

He stepped into the newly acquired property with a gorgeous dark-haired beauty on his arm. She was the latest in a recent string of women he had become obsessed with. They were all young and beautiful, but something was always missing. The lust and physical attraction always faded much too quickly. It wasn't the memory of his wife, he knew. Bartholomew was glad she was dead. Lorena had quickly become a thorn in his side, and he wondered now if he would ever remarry again.

But the lovely young women weren't giving him everything he needed. He yearned for a woman closer to his age, someone whom he could relate to on a generational level. He absolved that this was to be his next mission once he was done with the takeover of the Eastmans.

"Bartholomew," Billy nodded from the front sitting room. He stood and offered his hand in greeting. "And the lovely lady." He kissed her knuckles briefly and waved them in. "We just finished moving everything in last week. It's a good house. Close enough to the Eastmans but far enough away from the hectic harbor."

The young woman giggled. Bartholomew grasped her hand and led her up the stairs. "I suppose my bedroom is this way?" Bartholomew asked.

Billy swallowed and urged himself to speak. "Yes," he croaked. "Yours is the third room on the left."

The young woman's eyes widened, and the smile instantly fell from her face as she was herded up the stairs by Bartholomew. "Come on, sweetheart," he sneered. "I don't have much time."

Billy watched them disappear up the stairs, and the door clicked closed. Several minutes later, he heard the thumping of the bed against the wall. The woman let out a stream of high-pitched yelps that reverberated through the house. Billy pursed his lips in disgust and stood to leave when the front door opened.

"Oh, Billy," Thomas stated. "I was looking for Bartholomew. I need his signature on several documents. Did you see him? I thought I saw him come this way."

Another stream of high-pitched, passionate yelps filtered down the stairs. The thumping of the bed frame against the wall increased in intensity. "Umm," Billy stated. "He's busy right now."

Thomas laughed. "He's still recovering from losing his wife?"

"It seems, yes."

"I will wait," Thomas stated, sitting on the sofa in the front room. The thumping increased until a whoop sounded and then several deep-throated groans.

Billy chuckled nervously. "Is this normal for Bartholomew? Is this something we all have to live with?"

"He wasn't like this when he was married," Thomas replied. "But ever since his wife died, he has been going through some strange changes. I think after all that had happened, he actually truly loved his wife."

"How did his wife die?" Billy asked.

"She was shot."

Billy's eyes widened, and he straightened his back against the wall. "What happened?"

"A burglar," Thomas answered tartly. "There was a murder investigation."

"Did they catch the burglar?"

"No," Thomas replied. "They never caught anyone. The Sheriff tried charging Bartholomew with the murder."

Billy heard the floors creak upstairs and the door click open. One set of heavy footsteps sounded along the hallway, leading to the stairs.

"Was he acquitted?"

"Yes," Thomas answered simply.

Bartholomew descended the stairs quickly. "Thomas!" he shouted gleefully. "I was looking for you. Let's sign those documents."

Thomas straightened and followed Bartholomew to the kitchen, his eyes squinting back at Billy suspiciously. They would have to mold Billy Eastman to fit into their plans some-how. He gestured at Billy to follow. As the door closed to the kitchen, Bartholomew narrowed his eyes at Billy. "Do you know what we are signing today?" he asked, probingly.

Billy shook his head. "No, what are we signing?"

"An order to secure the assets of the Eastman Empire."

"I'll gladly sign that after I get my money."

Thomas frowned and stepped threateningly closer to Billy. "You will get your money."

♎

The afternoon sun shone fiercely on his back. A bead of sweat dripped from his forehead and trickled down his chest. It was so hot outside for the past two weeks that Jeremiah could barely even wear a shirt. It was covered with sweat and sticking to his back. He straightened, looking around cautiously, and pulled the shirt over his head. There was nobody around, and he was in a large thicket of bushes, so he concluded that it was a relatively safe risk to take.

Instantly, he felt a slight breeze on his bare chest and flung his shirt onto a nearby branch.

Jeremiah breathed a sigh of relief and raised the large metal rake once again. The tool hit the ground and snagged onto the weeds as he used the strength in his arms to pull them out. He worked tirelessly cleaning up the edges of the garden in the full sun. He bent down every so often, plucking the smaller weeds out with his bare hands.

He hadn't seen Georgina all day and was almost certain that she was not going to show up. It was getting late in the afternoon, and soon he would be all finished. He shouldn't have kissed her hand like he saw so many other gentlemen kissing women's hands. Jeremiah was unsure what to do now that he was a respected groundskeeper and living with Georgina every day.

He wanted so much more with Georgina than just friendship.

She was the most attractive woman he had ever set his eyes on. With her amber colored skin, dark eyes, and perfect long legs, she was a black man's dream come true. The first day when he had held her hand, he never wanted to let it go. But when he had been hired, he thought it was best to focus on doing the best work he could do. It was a very good job, and even though it had derailed his plans somewhat, it was a perfect situation to be in Philadelphia for the time being. He didn't want to scare Georgina away.

But it seems he had done just that.

He grunted and swung the rake as dirt flew up from the thrust. He was mad at himself for wanting her so badly. The bushes rustled nearby, and he looked up as a rabbit bounced out, scurrying across the lawn.

"Jeremiah," a sweet female voice called.

He looked up and instantly straightened. Georgina stood by the bushes like a goddess, her golden eyes roaming over his half-naked body. Jeremiah instantly felt self-conscious of his long, slim, and sweaty chest. Words wouldn't come to his lips, so he searched for where he had thrown his shirt.

Georgina watched him as he clumsily looked for his shirt. She giggled, "It's over there." She pointed to the bush, where the thin shirt hung on the branches.

"I apologize, Miss Georgina," Jeremiah mumbled awkwardly. "I didn't think you'd come. It was getting so late." He wiped the sweat off his gleaming chest as Georgina stared at him hungrily. He caught her eye and knew in that moment that she was the woman for him. He grinned and shrugged the shirt on, pulling it here and there over his muscular, sticky back.

Georgina tried looking away, but it was impossible. She finally looked down, then peered up again. "I was busy in the house and couldn't get away," she lied. Georgina had tried on several outfits, trying to find a suitable one for the garden that still showed off her curves. She had rushed to rub strawberries on her lips and buttered her cheeks lightly. She stood proudly with her riding boots and her large, flowing dress. It was much too hot outside for the dress, but it was a pretty blue color, and it looked fabulous on her.

Jeremiah pulled himself together and took two large strides towards her, grasping her hand and kissing it. "You look absolutely gorgeous," he murmured, careful not to bring attention to her obviously overdone appearance. Her lips were a dark red, and her gown was grossly out of place in the garden, but she looked ravishing. He smiled and pulled her hand into his. "Let's go for a walk," he said. "I need to show you those flowers and my plans."

They leapt together over the large plowed area he was working on and sauntered over to another overgrown garden. He pointed. "There it is."

The rose bushes were grossly oversized, reaching almost fifteen feet high and five feet in width. The thorns would have stopped any sane man, but Jeremiah loved problems, it seemed. His entire life, he yearned for challenges, things that kept him engaged and thinking. The physical work was hard, but it always left him somehow balanced, while his mind sought to overcome those challenges. But with Georgina, he was somehow vulnerable beyond reasoning.

His mind registered Georgina's warm, slender hand in his, and his heart soared with hope. Maybe this wasn't a foolish dream, after all.

They stopped near the bushes as a frown clouded over her face. "This rose bush?" she asked, astonished. "That overgrown bush has been here forever! The thorns are an inch long! Jesse talked about getting rid of it."

"Yes," Jeremiah commented. "It is a very old bush, probably almost 50 years old, and at the end of its life." He gestured with his hand as if the rose bush had taken over the entire garden. "But I will save it and cut the root into four, scattering red roses everywhere." He reached over and cut a small rose, handing it to Georgina. "It will recover and blossom into a beautiful lady, just like you. You'll see. I have done it before. Everybody takes cuttings and grows roses from that. I have always separated it from the roots. The plant will survive, maybe one might die, but there will be three more rose bushes to make up for it." He smiled broadly, his teeth lighting up his face with a strange work-induced glee.

Georgina smelled the single rose in her hand. "You can really do this?"

"Of course I can," Jeremiah answered. "I was in charge of one hundred trees in a massive orchard. We used large rose bushes, like this one, to discourage rodents and rabbits from entering the orchard. I separated many of these old rose bushes. A few died, but the strongest ones always lived. Similar to life."

"That's beautiful," she replied. "You are the best grounds-keeper for us. I'm so glad we found you."

Jeremiah caught the glint in her light brown, sexy eyes. He turned, grasped her chin, and lowered his voice to almost a whisper. "I'm glad I found you, too." He leaned closer and shifted his other hand to encircle her waist, nudging her body closer.

Georgina blinked nervously.

He knew that he had to take the risk. It was now or never. She could reject him, but at least he'd know. Jeremiah quickly leaned into her lips and kissed her gently. He pulled back to see her reaction.

Georgina leapt at his lips and kissed him back eagerly. Her soft mouth crushed against his lips, and it felt like he was floating into heaven. She liked him!

She stepped closer to him, and her body molded easily into his arms. Her mouth was eager and tasted like honey and milk. Jeremiah continued kissing her and trailed his hands lightly around her waist, trying to remain a gentleman.

Georgina's hands, on the contrary, were wildly out of control. Her hands roamed all over his muscular back and even gripped his back muscles in an effort to keep him closer. Jeremiah had not expected this. Georgina was like a tamed woman finally set free. She kissed him with an animalistic fury and groaned with a decade of longing from deep within her soul. Jeremiah tried calming her desires and pulled back briefly. His body was responding urgently, but he was certain that his actions could easily become misconstrued. He was afraid for his job and the tiny gains he had made on his journey to Upper Canada. Jeremiah did not want to lose everything in Philadelphia, but most importantly, he didn't want to lose her.

"Georgina," he murmured, trying to stop his erection from taking over his mind. "I have waited forever for this moment with you." He kissed her gently again as she almost clawed his back. "You are the most beautiful woman I have ever encountered." He gazed into her light brown eyes. "I want to take it slow with you, Georgina. You mean a lot to me."

She snapped out of the trance he had pulled her so willingly into. "Yes, of course," she mumbled awkwardly. "I wish the same." She stammered, licking her swollen lips. "I have never been with a man. Forgive me, I don't know how to act." She looked down bashfully.

Jeremiah reached his hand under her chin and raised her face to his. "You have never been with a man?" he asked, respectfully.

Her eyes searched his. "Never," she replied, shooting an embarrassing glance down at her toes. "My entire life has always been servitude for the Eastman home."

Jeremiah smoothed his hands along her forearms to stop her wandering hands. "But you are not a slave," he replied, searchingly.

"It is true, I was released from slavery when I was 19. But you must understand that the Eastman household is also my family. Jesse was always a half-brother to me. I had nowhere to go, so I chose to stay and take on a more managerial role with the servants. I am paid by the estate. Jesse said I will always be taken care of for as long as I choose to stay."

"I see," Jeremiah responded, shifting his body to her side and urging her to walk with him. "Well, I am honored to be your first man. I will make it my mission for it to be the best experience of your life." He grinned sideways, glancing at her.

She smiled demurely. "I would love that."

Jeremiah led her back to the house, and once they were within viewing distance, they unclasped their hands. "I want everyone to know how much I cherish you, but I fear anger from the white people. I don't want to be persecuted."

"Jesse would never persecute you!" Georgina stated loudly.

"Well," Jeremiah replied slowly. "I am from the south. It's much different there."

"I heard many people are fleeing to Upper Canada. Is that why you travelled up here?"

Jeremiah grew silent. He couldn't tell her, not now, at least. He wanted her heart first. "I travelled up here for many reasons," he explained. He pointed, changing the subject. "Look, it's Mrs. Zee on the sun deck."

She frowned with amusement. Zee was always out on the sun deck. Jeremiah's refusal to provide more details about his background was unnerving. She eyed him suspiciously, then caught a sincere, happy grin that had spread across his face. His eyes were lit up like twinkling stars. She realized that Jeremiah was truly smitten over her. Georgina smiled back. She would pry the information about his past sooner or later, but for now, she would just enjoy the glow she was basking in.

CHAPTER 5

Zee walked into the front foyer as her twin sons packed their hunting rifles and bags. She stared at them with a glint in her eyes.

James stopped and turned towards her. "We'll be gone for two weeks," James said, pulling on a pair of leather boots. "We will be back soon enough."

Scott hefted a large bag onto his shoulder and hugged his mom. "We'll bring back some wild turkey and deer from Buffalo."

Zee stopped in front of the entrance, blocking the large double doors. Both her sons eyed her suspiciously.

"Momma, what is it? Did we forget something?" James asked nervously.

Both sons knew that Zee was fond of the hunting cabin that the Eastmans owned in Buffalo. They had been there several times when Jesse and the family had travelled to and from Canada. It was always a wonderful stay and a convenient rest stop.

The property was much more than just a cabin. It was a rustic log building with over 1500 sq ft of living space, much bigger than their cottage on Lake Huron. The Buffalo cabin was situated in the wilderness outside of Buffalo, nestled quietly on 100 acres of thick forested land. The Eastmans often rented it to hunting parties to keep it from being overtaken by animals. But lately it hadn't been occupied, and her sons were eager to utilize it.

Zee leaned against the door and shifted her own bag onto her shoulder. Both her sons looked at her curiously. "I'm coming with you," she stated firmly.

"Mom," Scott replied gently. "It's a rustic cabin in the woods."

Zee straightened her shoulders. "Don't you lecture me about living in the woods!" she growled. "I raised you kids in the woods. I helped teach you both how to shoot!"

"Okay, okay," James countered, trying to diffuse his mother's wrath. "Did you talk to Pappa about it?"

"Somewhat."

"What do you mean somewhat?" Scott asked.

"I had told him that I wasn't happy stuck in this mansion," Zee answered, leaning onto one foot. She frowned and stared at her twin sons, preparing for a confrontation. "The cabin would be a wonderful outing."

"And when did you decide this?" James asked.

"This morning," she answered. "When I found out you were going hunting. You both turn eighteen in two months. I don't completely trust you brothers not to get into a whole lot of trouble. I will be coming with you."

A clatter of footsteps sounded against the tiled floor as Jesse approached the door, with Samuel and Xavier in tow.

Zee's heart melted when she saw him. Part of her wanted to jump into his arms, and the other part of her wanted to flee from this stifling mansion. She didn't want to hurt Jesse, but she needed to get out of the Eastman lifestyle and reclaim herself. She was right about stating that her twin sons always seemed to find themselves in trouble, and it was a convenient excuse to rediscover the old version of Zee Collard.

Jesse stared at Zee's baggage for several seconds, then slowly his eyes raised to her face. "Are you leaving too?" he asked.

The words hit Zee like a band of wild horses. She swallowed and reached over to embrace him. His body was stiff. "Yes, I'm leaving with Scott and James to go hunting," she replied, her lips lightly kissing his neck. "We'll be back."

Jesse slowly wrapped his arms around Zee and held her tightly. "I don't want you to go," he said, his voice cracking unexpectedly.

"I know," she mumbled back, almost whispering the words into his chest.

"I fear for your safety," Jesse argued.

"I will be fine," she replied. "Jesse, please, I need this time away. Don't stop me." Her nose snuggled into his clothing as her body stiffened, waiting for his rebuttal.

Jesse took a deep breath of her scent. "Is there any way I can convince you to stay?" he asked. "Maybe we can organize a hunting trip with all of us."

Xavier interrupted, noticing the sheer pleading in his mother's eyes. "Pappa, we need you here," he coaxed. "The Eastman Empire is not on solid ground. You know that. Let Momma go. She would be safer in Buffalo."

Jesse released her and looked into her moist eyes. "On one condition," he stated softly. "You must take the trail guide. Bemidii will ensure your safe journey to the cabin."

"Is he here today?" she asked.

"Yes," Jesse responded. "He has been working on clearing some land for us down by the oceanside." Jesse's hand stayed on her waist, trying desperately to keep the physical connection. His other hand shot in the air as he turned to Samuel. "Can you please fetch Bemidii from the port? Right away?"

"Will do," Samuel stated, running off towards the back entrance.

"I wish I could go with you," Jesse said slowly, turning back to Zee.

James and Scott stood solidly by their mother. "Why don't you come, Pappa?" James asked.

"You heard Xavier. I can't leave until this threat from Bartholomew is over," Jesse answered. "Billy has been gone for several weeks, and I've received several letters from Bartholomew threatening to take over the estate."

"I didn't know that!" Zee screeched, releasing Jesse's hold on her. "How can they do that?"

"They can't," Jesse stated solidly. "My lawyer said that the letters are empty threats."

Zee pulled herself straighter and smoothed down her old riding pants. It was easier riding with pants on, rather than a dress, she mused. Her heart thumped at the thought of being away from Jesse for two weeks, but she knew it was what she needed. She felt like she was deserting her husband when he needed her the most, but in reality, they hardly talked anymore. She sighed. "Do you have enough weapons to protect the estate, just in case?" Zee asked. "Should we leave some? We are only taking three rifles."

"If it comes to that, we'll be fine," Jesse answered, gesturing to Xavier and Samuel. "I don't think it will come to that."

Xavier hugged his mother. "We'll be fine," he said calmly. "We have 30 weapons, maybe more. Don't worry, Momma. It might be a good thing you are going away."

"Don't say that," Zee stated. "I would always stay and fight, you know that."

Jesse gazed into his wife's eyes. "I know you would." His eyes turned glossy and almost watery.

Zee swallowed and held onto her convictions. "We won't be gone for long. I trust you understand, Jesse." She gazed into his eyes and felt his hurt feelings shoot back at her. Zee slipped her hand into his and squeezed it tight. "Maybe we can arrange a hunting trip once things have calmed down."

Jesse knew a hunting trip was impossible at the moment and felt powerless to save his marriage right now. "We will definitely do that," he lied.

The back door slammed closed, and everyone turned expectantly.

"Luckily enough, I found Bemidii just heading back for more equipment!" Samuel announced.

A young, native American man walked in behind Samuel. Bemidii was young, no older than twenty years old, and had a slim, lithe build with dark reddish skin and a head full of black hair.

"Bemidii," Jesse greeted, slapping a firm hand on the man's shoulder. "We need a trusted trail guide for my wife and two sons to travel with them to the Buffalo cabin. They are leaving right now. Can you join them on such short notice?"

"I know that trail well," Bemidii replied in clipped English, nodding his head in agreement. "I can deliver them safely. That won't be a problem."

"Good man," Jesse replied. "You will be paid handsomely once you return."

Bemidii stepped towards the front entrance. "Yes, Mr. Jesse. Anything for you."

"Well," Zee said, slipping her warm hand from Jesse's. She adjusted her bag onto her shoulder. "Let's go, then."

James and Scott opened the large front doors and began packing the last of the hunting supplies into the waiting carriage. Bemidii helped with the loading. Two horses were attached to the carriage, and another two were being brought from the stable for Zee and Bemidii.

A large white mare joined the caravan as Zee hoisted herself up onto the saddle. She murmured to her favorite horse. "Princess," she cooed. "We're going on an adventure, my sweet."

Another brown gelding stopped in front of Bemidii. The native trail guide deftly hoisted himself onto the lead horse.

Scott and James climbed up onto the riding seats of the carriage and waved to the family collecting at the front steps. Bemidii started slowly trotting ahead of them, leading the caravan.

Jesse blinked and swallowed as Zee met his eyes. He smiled. "Stay safe, my dear!"

"I will, don't worry," she replied, blowing him a kiss. Zee waved as her horse jerked forward, following Bemidii towards the north trail. The carriage horses pulled Scott and James with a jerk, trailing the group.

"Bye, Pappa!" Scott yelled. "We'll be back soon!"

Jesse waved at his sons, then shifted his focus to Zee. Her long hair trailed on her back as the wind billowed it from the sides. She kept her eyes ahead of her, only glancing back once. Jesse blinked and swallowed his emotions again.

A sinking feeling churned in the pit of his stomach as he realized his wife was leaving for the first time in 20 years, without him.

♎

Jeremiah found Georgina in the kitchen, fretting over the bread. He had bathed and shaved, hoping to impress Georgina and spend more time with her.

She instantly turned as Jeremiah walked into the kitchen. She wiped the dough onto her apron and exclaimed happily, "Jeremiah, I have some sweet bread cooling on the rack. Would you like some?"

"I would love some," he answered, pulling a chair out at the servant's table.

Georgina smiled and cut two slices of bread, then grabbed the butter and a knife. She approached the table with a happy grin on her face. "You must be so tired from all this hot weather. Can I get you some weak beer?"

"That would be wonderful."

Georgina returned shortly with the weak beer and sat quietly across from him. Several moments passed as she gazed at Jeremiah with lust in her eyes.

He chuckled. "The bread is so good. Thank you."

Georgina laughed. "You are most welcome," she replied, wringing her fingers together. "Are you done for the day?"

"Not quite," he answered. "Why?"

"No reason," she replied, much too quickly. "I am finishing for the day in an hour or so."

"Oh, I see."

Georgina shuffled nervously on the chair. "If you aren't too busy, I'd like to show you the rest of the Mansion inside. I live in a separate suite on the west side."

"You have your own suite?"

"Yes," she replied demurely. "This is my home too, remember?"

"Yes," he replied. "That's right." He shoved the last piece of bread in his mouth and chewed it thoughtfully. When he swallowed, Jeremiah tilted up the cup of watered-down beer and then drained it. He gently placed the cup down and smiled at her. "I'd love to have a tour."

"Okay!" Georgina smiled and bounced up to standing. "I will meet you back here in two hours then."

♎

Samuel finished cleaning his pistol, then poured two whiskeys at the office bar. He left his pistol at the bar and brought the two drinks to the large wooden desk. He pushed one over to Jesse and nodded. He noticed Jesse's pistol still lay scattered in pieces on his desk. "Have a drink. You look like you need it."

Jesse grabbed the drink and sipped it graciously. He began assembling the pistol slowly and thoughtfully as Samuel sat across the desk. Jesse smiled weakly at his friend and cleared his throat. "Things have changed so much in the last few years," Jesse said, his mind swirling with erratic thoughts. "And I'm wondering why."

"We are getting older, my friend," Samuel stated, sweeping his hand over his bald head. "Remember when I had a full head of hair?"

Jesse laughed. "It's not just that," Jesse replied, sipping the amber liquid thoughtfully.

"What is it then?" Samuel asked, lighting a cigar.

Jesse mused, trying to find the right words to express the turmoil going on in his head. "I miss Zee already."

"Of course you do," Samuel replied, handing him a cigar. "Zee's been your wife for twenty years, and she left without you for the first time yesterday." He blew out a cloud of smoke and paused thoughtfully. "I remember when you first met her while we were fighting in the War of 1812. You both were inseparable."

Jesse lit the offered cigar, inhaled, and blew out a cloud of smoke. "I think that's what I'm missing."

"What do you mean?"

"I'm missing how we used to be inseparable," Jesse answered, tapping his finger on the table and lifting the whiskey glass to his mouth. "I lost my wife a long time ago, it seems."

Samuel nodded thoughtfully. "Well, that definitely poses a problem." Samuel drank the whiskey down swiftly and stood for another glass. He approached the bar and stopped, turning to face Jesse, and leaned back against the bar. "What are you going to do about it?"

"What can I do?" Jesse stated. "She's gone already."

"She said she was coming back, right?" Samuel asked, securing his weapon into his belt.

"Yes."

"Well," Samuel countered decisively. "It gives you two weeks to find a way to win her back."

"Do you really think she left because of me?"

"Yes and no," Samuel answered. "She's probably very lonely, but I think Zee just wants to go hunting." Samuel poured another whiskey and returned to the large desk. "Look, I have known you and Zee the longest around here. In case you forgot, she was a tough farm girl who was an animal doctor. Do you think she's done any of the stuff that she loves here at the Eastman household?"

Jesse rubbed his knuckles along his bearded chin. Specks of grey sprinkled throughout his trimmed beard. He leaned across the desk. "I suppose you're right. She hasn't done anything like that for many years." He drummed his fingers on the desk and pocketed his assembled pistol into his gun belt. "I'm still attracted to her, but I'm afraid of hurting her since the miscarriages." Jesse downed the rest of the whiskey and placed the glass down. "She's a good-looking woman. I wish I could tell her that more and be with her more."

"Then why don't you talk to her?" Samuel asked. "She still loves you. I can see it in the way she looks at you."

"You think so?" Jesse asked. "I'm not as handsome as I used to be." He stood and adjusted the pistol on his gun belt, pulling his suit jacket over it to conceal it. Jesse was slim and muscular, but so many things had changed since the years had passed. The lines on his face were evident.

Samuel scoffed. "You still drive the women crazy, Jesse. Don't be stupid." Samuel blew a puff of smoke out into the room. "I wish I had your looks. I'd probably be married like you." Samuel laughed and stubbed out the cigar. "To be serious, Jesse, I know the way Zee looks at you. She's a good woman, and she needs you to do something to fix this. It's in her eyes. There's a pleading in her eyes."

"You think so?"

"Yep, definitely," Samuel added, gazing out the window. They both sat in silence for a few moments, contemplating life as the sun lowered under the horizon. Samuel stared out the large bay window as the night slowly fell across the grounds.

Jesse's eyes wandered aimlessly across the enormous estate grounds. Words jumbled in his head, but nothing coherent seemed to form, so he kept silent. The moment seemed somehow surreal, like an impending change was about to happen. At any moment, a storm could blow from the ocean and change the serenity displayed before him. At any moment, his life could change for the worse.

After several moments, Samuel spoke again. "So," he said slowly, butting out the cigar. "I guess the real question is, what are you going to do to save your marriage?"

CHAPTER 6

Zee watched Bemidii enter the thick forest along the narrow horse trail. She knew a little about the young man's story. Jesse had employed him as a trail guide and forest clearer back in 1831 when he had found the boy destitute on the streets of Philadelphia. Bemidii didn't speak English at all back then, but quickly picked it up working on the Eastman property. His past was largely unknown, and she was curious.

"Bemidii," she called in front of her. "Slow down, the carriage is struggling to keep up." Zee glanced behind her as the carriage slowly lumbered after them.

"Yes, ma'am," he replied, pulling the reins back on his horse slightly.

"Do you think this narrow path is wide enough for the carriage?" she asked as they both stopped on the path, waiting for the carriage to catch up.

"Yes," he replied briefly. "It is wide enough. My ancestors used similar paths, and they had their entire homes to move. A small carriage will fit."

Zee blinked, intrigued by this strange man's story. "Where are your ancestors now?"

"In the ground."

"They're dead?" she asked incredulously.

"Yes, ma'am."

"All of your family?" she asked again, clearly not understanding. "Your mother and father, too?"

"Yes."

"What happened?"

Bemidii didn't answer and just looked back at the carriage, watching it slowly catch up.

"Forgive me for asking," she commented quickly, as her horse began to impatiently trot in a circle. She regained control of her horse and tried to restart the conversation. "My father and mother have both passed on as well. It was a long time ago when my mother passed. I was only twenty when she died." She paused, remembering the day when she had tried to resuscitate her mother on the floor of their house in Niagara. "It was a difficult time." Zee gathered her emotions and continued. "My father was at war, and my mother died believing her husband had perished. He returned back alive eventually, but unfortunately, it was too late. My mother had died of a broken heart." Zee swallowed. "My father lived a long, lonely life until my youngest brother, Sam, died. It was too much for my pappa. After the war injuries and everything he lost, my father, George, died eight years ago. It still seems like yesterday."

The carriage was catching up as the creaking and rattling wheels grew louder. Bemidii circled his horse around. "We continue now," he stated, trotting ahead of her.

Zee followed obediently, still curious about the young native's background.

Nobody spoke for several minutes as the forest grew closer around them. Scott and James steered the carriage into the woods expertly. Bemidii was right. The path was just wide enough.

"My parents and family all perished during the relocation," Bemidii stated solemnly. "I was the only one that lived."

"The relocation?"

"Yes, the US president ordered us out."

Zee knotted her eyebrows, trying to remember what Jesse had told her of the recent gold rush in 1829 and the resulting removal of natives from the lands. The details swirled in her mind until finally she remembered the name of the act passed by Congress. "Because of The Indian Act of 1830?"

"Yes," Bemidii replied. "We were forced to move west." He glanced at Zee briefly and continued. "My Ojibwe tribe was small and always on the move, so it wasn't too much of a change for us. We just left early before the rest of the larger tribes began moving." He wrinkled his nose in disgust. "A bad choice. Once we arrived in the wilds of the Northwest, we were exhausted and hungry."

"That's awful," she replied. "I'm so sorry that happened. How old were you?"

"I had just turned eighteen," he replied. "My parents died of hunger first. We didn't know at the time, but they were giving up their food for us." Bemidii paused briefly, then continued. "Once they had perished, my younger brother and sister were too weak to go any further."

"How did you survive?"

"I found some fur traders who traded meat with me for showing them the way into the woods." Bemidii tried his best to explain in his clipped English. "It took me longer than expected, a full two days. Once I was able to return, I rushed back to where my family was to bring them the meat, but it was too late. They were all dead."

"I'm so sorry, Bemidii."

"I buried them in the ground with my own hands," he said, showing his left palm. He gently lowered his arm and continued. "I didn't want the animals eating them. The spirit survives long after the body dies."

Zee contemplated this statement. "I sure hope there's something for us all after death," she commented.

"There is," he replied. "Many of my elders in the tribe were named after animal spirits."

The calmness of the forest settled around them as if to join them in mourning the dead. "Well, I am happy that my father and mother are finally back together in heaven. They really loved each other." Zee rode in silence for several minutes before speaking again. "So I guess that's the story of how you became a trail guide then."

"Mostly," he replied. "I ended up with another large fur trade expedition heading back to Philadelphia. I guided them back all the way and was paid generously."

"Jesse said he found you on the streets of Philadelphia?"

"Yes," Bemidii continued. "Mr. Jesse found me at my lowest. I was beaten for my money and left for dead near a garbage pile."

"Oh my Lord!" Zee exclaimed as they entered into a clearing. "I didn't know!"

"Yes, Mr. Jesse, he picked me up and brought me to a doctor, got me all stitched up." Bemidii sighed. "I probably would have died if Mr. Jesse didn't do that."

"My husband is a good man," she stated, lifting a hand over her hat to pull it off. The string that was attached around her neck held the straw hat onto her back as it flapped in the wind. "Thank God for the wind. The afternoon sun is so hot!" she cried.

Bemidii looked at her in confusion. "The sun was always good to us, no matter how hot it became." His eyes scanned the path up ahead. "Stay here. I'll be right back!" he shouted, trotting ahead of the caravan to check if the path was safe and clear of hunters. Several minutes later, Bemidii circled his horse and returned. "Everything's clear, Mrs. Zee. Thanks for listening to my story. I haven't told it to many people."

"But how did you end up working at the estate?" she asked, a knot of confusion on her brow.

"Mr. Jesse stayed until the doctor finished, then he asked me if he could give me a ride to my home." Bemidii remembered the day when his life had changed. "I told him I didn't have a home."

"What did he say?" Zee asked, genuinely fascinated with this man's story. Her heart filled with pride of her husband's actions and his warm heart.

"Mr. Jesse asked me what kind of skills I had," Bemidii answered. "I told him that I was a trail guide. He offered me a room and a job until I recovered completely."

Zee smiled, her heart glowing with pride. Jesse had helped so many people, and here she was, riding off to the Buffalo cabin without him. Her mind swirled in conflicting thoughts, and her stomach churned at her decision, but she continued along, pulled by some force she couldn't quite understand. "My husband is a good man," she said sincerely. "You are the best trail guide, Bemidii. Don't you ever forget that. You are one of the indomitable spirits on this earth. My husband just helped you to realize that."

CHAPTER 7

Georgina awoke, blinking in the darkness of her room. At first, she couldn't see a thing, but several seconds later her eyes adjusted. She looked around, momentarily disoriented, then immediately smelled Jeremiah beside her. The tour of the mansion went so wonderfully well that they had talked for hours and hours in her suite. The bond was incredible between them. So undeniably strong, in fact, that they had both succumbed to the intense sexual attraction rather quickly.

She glanced down towards Jeremiah and felt a strange mixture of happiness and disbelief. It was such an odd feeling having a man beside her after all these years of living a romantically solitary life. Part of her loved it, and the other part felt like it was a foreign path she was embarking on.

Georgina turned and heard the blankets rustle in the darkness. She was astonished to find him awake.

"You can't sleep?" she asked wondrously.

"Not when I have the woman I've always dreamed of naked in my arms," he replied, grinning in the dark. "It's a bit difficult."

She giggled and snuggled her head into his arms. "Well, I have to say that you know how to love a woman."

Jeremiah smiled and kissed the top of her head. "At your service, my lovely lady."

"I could get used to this," she muttered absentmindedly.

The night cloaked them in silence, urging honesty to the forefront. "So could I," Jeremiah added, kissing her hair again.

She had nothing to compare it to, but the sex with Jeremiah last night was absolutely wonderful. Her cheeks were warm, and her lower belly felt satisfied. Several questions popped into her mind, and she was astonished that she hadn't asked him earlier. Everything had progressed so quickly last night. "I don't even know how old you are, Jeremiah," she questioned. "I never thought to ask. Everything just happened so fast between us."

Jeremiah chuckled. "Yes, our attraction is undeniable," he replied. "I'm thirty years old."

"Oh, God!" she exclaimed, bolting upright. "You're nine years younger than me! I had no idea."

"Shh," he said, placing his two forefingers on her lips to calm her. "Age doesn't have any bearing on our attraction. You don't look thirty-nine, and I obviously don't look thirty." He calmly ran his large hands over her curly, messy hair. "I want to be with you, Georgina. You could be fifty and I wouldn't care."

She relaxed back into his arms. "It still disturbs me. I wish I'd known before."

"Before you had sex with me?" he asked, the hurt evident in his voice.

"No," she answered. "I didn't mean it that way." She pondered for a moment. Her attraction to him was like a magnet from the day she had first met him. Would she have changed anything because she knew that he was nine years younger than her? "You're right, I suppose it doesn't matter," she continued slowly, measuring her words. "I've never met anybody like you before. You're kind, strong, and gentle all at the same time."

Georgina paused, trying to form her thoughts into words. "And there's something that I have never felt before, almost a kinship or like I've known you for a long, long while. It's strange."

"I feel that too," he stated simply.

"I wonder if we knew each other before," she stated.

"That's probably impossible. You were born and raised in Philadelphia. I have never even ventured to the Northeast before."

Georgina mulled over this information. "You were from the south? Whereabouts? My mother was from South Carolina. She died when I was six."

"South Carolina?" Jeremiah responded instantly. "That's where I am from!"

"Oh?" Georgina replied, slightly alarmed. "I hope we're not related!"

"Did your momma ever mention the Jackson family?" Jeremiah sat up, intensely involved in the conversation now.

"The Jacksons!" Georgina exclaimed brightly. "Yes, she did! They were a group of orchard slaves in South Carolina who were close friends of the family where she grew up." Georgina pulled herself up on her elbows and tried looking into his eyes in the darkness.

"How did she happen to arrive in the Eastman household then?" he asked.

"She was bought as a slave by Bob Eastman," Georgina replied. "Bob was my father. He wasn't a good man."

"I'm sorry," Jeremiah added.

"No, don't be," she replied. "This is life. Things happen that you don't really have control over. I am proud to be an Eastman now, even though I am an illegitimate daughter." She kissed him softly on the lips in the dark. "And I'm glad I met you."

"So am I."

They kissed softly for several minutes until Georgina pulled away gently. "We should sleep. You have a long day tomorrow, and so do I."

"Yes," he conceded and relaxed back onto her pillowed bed. "As you wish."

Something continued to intrigue her about their conversation. She couldn't understand it, but something, a piece, was missing. "How did you know the Jacksons?" she asked innocently.

Jeremiah grew silent. He wasn't sure how to answer, but he knew that he had to. "Umm, please don't be angry with me," he said softly. "There is something I need to tell you."

"What is it?" she asked, a tingle running up her spine.

"Promise you won't tell anyone?" he asked. "Even your family?"

Georgina frowned. "I promise." She braced herself for the truth.

"My real name is Lewis Jackson," he replied quickly. "I am a runaway slave from the orchard plantation in South Carolina." He paused, watching for her reaction. "I joined the Underground Railroad. Many wonderful, kind people helped me to escape and travel to Philadelphia." He grasped her hand, kissing her knuckles softly. "I'm sorry for not telling you earlier. My name has been changed to protect my identity. I am now Jeremiah Williams. People call me Jeremy."

♎

"I want this Eastman business concluded now," Bartholomew stated irritably. "I'm leaving tomorrow, and I hate loose ends."

"Where are you leaving to?" Billy asked.

"Nowhere you'd be interested in," Bartholomew answered.

Thomas stood stiffly by his side. "He'll be back in a few weeks. We are seizing the Eastman assets before he goes. You have your money, Billy."

"I only received half of it," Billy protested.

"You'll get the remainder when we have possession of the asset," Bartholomew sneered angrily.

Thomas laid a commanding hand on Bartholomew's shoulder. Even though Thomas was an assistant, he was still a very strong man who could crush Bartholomew with his fists. One of the very few men capable of this. He felt an obligation to keep Bartholomew mentally stable. Nothing would turn out good if his boss lost his temper. He knew this all too well.

Bartholomew glanced at Thomas, and his eyes narrowed slightly. He looked at the group of ten men gathered in the small house. "Well, what is everyone waiting for? Let's get this business concluded. I want to leave this shit town."

♎

They had slept the rest of the night and had awakened to the dawn breaking, the purplish colors lighting up the white curtains. They had made love again first thing in the morning. Her body felt like liquid, absorbing every sensation and every touch. They kissed and curled into each other, talking in hushed tones. Georgina needed to know more.

"It was a very difficult thing to confess to you last night, Georgina," Jeremiah said, kissing her head. "I don't want to lose you. I have never felt this way about a woman before."

"I'm glad you told me," Georgina replied. "I knew you were holding something back."

"You knew?"

"Well, I suppose I sensed it." She wasn't mad that he hadn't told her before. She understood what it was like to be a slave. Some things had to be kept secret.

"Thank you for understanding," Jeremiah said, smoothing her curly hair. "I am still the same man, although I am still a fugitive. They may still come after me."

"I will never reveal your real name to anyone, Jeremiah. I promise." She snuggled into his arms and breathed in his scent. As she exhaled, a thought crossed her mind. "Were you planning on going to Upper Canada?" Georgina asked curiously.

"Yes, I was preparing to leave for Canada," he responded quietly, the room filling with a heavy silence.

Georgina inhaled sharply. "Are you still going?"

"No."

Georgina sighed with relief. "Why did you stay in Philadelphia for so long? You were here for several weeks before you started working at the estate."

Jeremiah slowly sat upright and grasped her hand in his. "When I had first met you at the Baptist church, I felt something. That kinship you talked about. I needed to know more about you. I couldn't keep my eyes off of you."

Georgina blushed as she gazed into his dark eyes. "You stayed for me?"

"I am staying for you, yes," he answered.

"Is it dangerous for you to stay?" she asked sincerely. "I don't want you to be in danger because of me."

"As long as no one knows my real name, I should be alright," he replied.

"I would never tell a soul."

"Thank you," Jeremiah responded. He bent forward, grasped her chin lightly, and kissed her swollen lips. The loving kisses after a night of sex was just what they both needed. It was confirmation that they were both committed to following through on this budding romance. Nothing could ever tear them apart.

They must have kissed for an eternity because the sun started streaking through the curtains and lighting up the room with a yellow glow. Georgina gently pulled away and peppered his neck with kisses. "We should get our clothes on," she stated. "I have a long day, and so do you."

He agreed and pulled his briefs and pants on, while Georgina slipped into a plain white dress. "Do I get to see you again tonight?"

"Of course," she replied. Georgina tied a blue apron over the dress and searched for her shoes. She looked back at Jeremiah as he was buttoning on his grey uniform shirt. He was muscular, lean, and a very handsome man. His hair was cut very short, and he had a tall, confident gait, like that of a warrior. She licked her lips and opened the bedroom door as several pops sounded outside.

Jeremiah slammed the bedroom door and held her hand. "Shh," he said. "Did you hear that?"

Georgina scanned her eyes towards the window and stepped towards it.

"No!" he said, grabbing her arm with an iron grip.

She stood in disbelief while confusion filled her mind. "What is going on?" she exclaimed, anxiety rising in her throat.

"I don't know," Jeremiah answered. "But I don't want you getting hurt. That sounded like gunshots."

Just then, an explosion shook the front of the house and reverberated into the guest quarters.

CHAPTER 8

Xavier and Samuel ran in a panic to the gun rack, pulling out several rifles and pistols. They latched two ammunition packs onto their backs as Jesse pulled his own arsenal on. Everyone in the house, servants and family, began running into the dining room. Ellen was there as well as Johnny. They both grabbed weapons just as an explosion rocked the front entrance. Several pictures fell from the wall and clattered onto the floor.

"Where's Georgina?" Jesse yelled in the ensuing chaos. "I don't see her!"

Samuel loaded two carbine rifles and handed one to Jesse. They had bought the carbines from a European settler and regularly imported the ammunition for sport shooting. "I didn't see her," Samuel shouted back as he crouched towards the blasted entrance way.

Jesse shoved a pistol in his belt, slung the strapped carbine over his shoulder, and carefully adjusted his waist belt containing three handmade grenades. The small metal tins were prefilled with nails and gunpowder and needed careful handling. "If Georgina doesn't show up soon, I'll have to go find her," Jesse shouted as he crouched towards the gaping hole in the large front oak door.

Several shots peppered towards Jesse and Samuel's direction as they approached the front door. They both ducked. Jesse waved a cautionary stop hand signal at Xavier and the rest of the family behind him. The shots flew wildly over their heads.

Three large masked men immediately crouched through the smoldering front door entrance. They looked around frantically, trying to assess the surroundings.

Jesse aimed and fired at the lead man. The bullet whizzed through the air, and the man ducked but still caught the bullet skimming across the top of his head. The man swung his firearm, momentarily not realizing that he was shot, then wiped a hand over his bleeding head. Xavier shot the man to the left in the chest. The man flew backwards in a heap. The lead man looked behind in surprise, then bolted into the house, hiding from view in the west hallway.

In almost the same instant, Samuel fired at the man on the right. The bullet went wild, hitting the iron knocker hanging on the ruined door, then ricocheted firmly into the thug's shoulder, swinging him around in a startled panic and sending his left arm flailing. The thug scrambled back outside, holding his rifle in a painful grip.

Another two men jumped through the ruined front entrance, crouching and running into the house. Jesse fired and shot one of the men in the abdomen, sending blood squirting against the wall. The man crumpled into a bloody heap, screaming.

While the grand front entrance was pierced by the wounded man's screams, Jesse shot the second man in the head. The deadly hit spun the man crazily backwards against the wall, red blood streaking against the wall, where the man died instantly.

Another man ran through the entrance and joined the bleeding thug in the west hallway. Samuel cursed as his shot was two seconds late and slammed into the opposite hallway wall. "Dammit," Samuel cursed. "I missed him."

"Watch your right!" Jesse yelled as a rifle barked from the injured man outside. The bullet flew through the hole, whizzed past Samuel's ear, taking a piece of flesh with it.

"Damn!" Samuel ducked, holding his bleeding ear.

"Are you alright?" Jesse asked, pulling Samuel away from the shooting, and nodded for Ellen to come tend to him.

Samuel removed his palm from his ear and stared at the blood. "I think I'm alright," he replied. "You never know with head shots."

Ellen crouched beside him and cleaned up the wound, inspecting it. "It looks fine. The bullet just grazed your ear. I'll wrap some cloth around your head to hold the bleeding until the doctor comes. I wish we had Zee here. She'd be able to stitch it up right away."

As everyone moved back into the dining room, there was a momentary ceasefire. Jesse strained his ears and heard a slight shifting of clothing from the hallway. He didn't like that sound. "Someone has to go back out there and cover us," Jesse commanded. "We don't want these maniacs getting any further into the house."

Xavier crouched and splayed against the far wall with his rifle ready. "I got this," he replied. One second later, a single shot reverberated from the far side of the house, and a muffled scuffle broke out inside the west wing of the house.

Jesse turned his head sharply. "What was that?"

Xavier looked in astonishment at his rifle. "It wasn't me. I didn't even fire yet."

Ω

Georgina walked silently to the hidden hallway gun cabinet with Jeremiah. She inserted her key and opened the left side of the ornately carved doors. She reached for the right door and unlatched a safety latch.

Jeremiah whistled softly. "What kind of family keeps this amount of weaponry in the house?" Jeremiah asked, his eyebrows lifting in surprise while Georgina opened the cabinet fully. An assortment of European carbine rifles, old muskets, and flintlock pistols gleamed back at him. They were oiled and ready for action. The ammunition boxes were labeled and separated according to weaponry.

"Battled soldiers from the 1812 war, that's who," Georgina replied, taking a carbine rifle off the rack carefully and handing it to Jeremiah. "Do you know how to shoot?" she asked.

"Yes," Jeremiah instantly responded.

"Good," Georgina said, shoving a box of ammunition into his hands. "We'll take two carbine rifles."

Jeremiah reached into the cabinet and removed a sharply curved hunting knife. "This looks like the exact hunting knife I used to have back home."

"Take it," Georgina instructed. "You might need it. We have no idea who is attacking our home, but if my guess is right, it would be Bartholomew's team. That evil man was intent on taking over the Eastman shipping business from the first day he appeared in Philadelphia. I can't imagine how he reacted when he found out that he can't do it legally."

Several shots broke out within the house ahead of them. The shooting filled the expansive home and echoed into the west wing of the mansion. Jeremiah and Georgina had entered the main house through the long corridor that attached her home to the central mansion. Jesse had built the small addition for her ten years ago, after Zee and his family had moved back from Upper Canada.

Another skirmish of shots sounded, coming from all angles. "We'll need to be careful," Jeremiah whispered. "Stay behind me."

Georgina nodded and was glad he was taking the lead. She had limited firearms experience, just some shooting practice Jesse had insisted she take over the years.

The west wing was massive, so it took longer than expected. They both ran silently through the hallways and kitchen storage rooms. Georgina noted that no servants were present. "Something truly dreadful is happening," she whispered. "There are no servants. Let's slow down and be careful with our next steps."

Jeremiah walked ahead silently towards another hallway and stopped abruptly. He heard grunts and several whispered exchanges. Georgina bumped into Jeremiah's raised arm, preventing her from advancing further. He held two fingers to his mouth to motion for her to be quiet. Jeremiah peered cautiously around the corner and was astonished to be looking at the backs of two armed men in black clothing. One had a bloody head but seemed to be only superficially injured, and the other was aiming his rifle towards the dining room area ahead.

Georgina nodded and aimed her rifle at the taller, bloodied man as Jeremiah crept closer. He kept his rifle aimed steadily at the uninjured man's back. When he saw the man ready to fire into the dining room, Jeremiah pulled the trigger.

The loud blast from the carbine propelled the bullet into the back of the unsuspecting thug. He fell instantly, but not before the thug's own shot slammed wildly into the floor and the gun clattered harmlessly beside him. The other injured man spun around immediately and was greeted with Georgina's bullet. The bullet slammed into his right arm. He dropped the rifle and grasped his arm, cursing. He was a big man. It would take more than one bullet in his arm to bring him down. He rushed at Jeremiah without hesitation.

Jeremiah tried to raise the rifle again, but the large husky man was already on him, reaching out with his fists. The man grabbed his collar roughly and tried dragging Jeremiah towards the shooting as a shield.

Jeremiah growled viciously and attempted to disentangle himself from the man's iron grip. Georgina was frozen on the spot, too afraid to shoot for fear of hitting Jeremiah.

"Shut up and be a good slave," the large, beefy man slurred angrily. He looked back and saw Georgina. "Tell your slave wife to lower her weapon."

"Georgina," Jeremiah said, winking at her. "Lower the rifle, honey, do as he says."

Georgina slowly lowered the rifle, peering at both men cautiously. In a blur of an instant, Jeremiah swung his fist at the man's bloody head, connecting with a right hook on the side of his ear. The large man spun and stumbled wildly but regained his senses remarkably quick. Before Jeremiah could step back and bring up the rifle, the man had grasped his collar again, pulling him in front of him as a shield. "Stop fighting, slave!"

Jeremiah lost his footing and slumped against the man. They both shuffled clumsily out into the open entrance way. Jeremiah immediately saw that the large front oak door had been blasted wide open. One of the large oak doors was lying on the floor with a gaping hole in it, while the other hung sideways with the iron knocker facing inside. Bullet holes were peppered all along the inside walls as he watched Xavier train the rifle on him and the beefhead holding his collar.

"You shoot and your slave gets the bullet!" the burly man sneered at Xavier. "Put the gun down, son."

Xavier refused to lower the weapon but didn't fire, waiting for a chance.

Down the hallway, Georgina aimed her rifle at the beefhead's back and tensed her finger on the trigger, waiting for the right moment. Then she noticed Jeremiah jumping into action.

He reached his long arm behind him and pulled out the hunting knife. With one swift movement, Jeremiah arced the knife into the husky man's neck, stabbing the sharp edge into the artery. Blood sprayed violently onto Jeremiah, but he refused to step away. He pushed the blade deeper in and twisted it several times, amidst the spray of slippery red blood coating his arms and face. He didn't let go until the beefhead fell limply from his grasp.

Jeremiah looked up and watched Jesse enter the entrance-way with an astonished look on his face. "Thank you, Jeremy."

"All in a day's work, Mr. Eastman," Jeremiah chuckled as Georgina started running down the hallway towards him. The look on her face was confusing. She seemed to be focusing on something else. Jeremiah bent down and retrieved the hunting knife from the man's throat and wiped it on his pants just as another 3-man assault came through the front doorway, aiming directly at Jesse.

Both Xavier and Georgina shot the attackers at the same time. Two were killed dead but one remained, aiming towards Jesse.

Jesse ducked and pulled out the flintlock pistol, shooting at the last gang member. The man spun briefly, then started running. Jesse raced after him like a predator in hot pursuit. The man sprinted down the stone steps, leaped over the last step, and propelled his legs frantically across the manicured lawn.

Jesse ran hard to catch up to the man, gaining momentum. The man leapt over a set of manicured bushes and tripped, falling hard on his face. Jesse pounced on his back immediately, punching him in the side of the head.

"Don't hit me!" the younger man yelled. "I surrender!"

Jesse grasped him roughly as the testosterone pumped through his veins. He wanted to kill the man with his own hands, but something told him not to.

Jeremiah ran down the steps, catching up to them both. Jesse stood motionless, trying to calm his temper. Gulps of breath rushed from his lungs as Jeremiah closed the distance. Jesse jerked the man to his feet.

The young man's eyes widened when he noticed the blood-soaked black slave come after him. "Call him off! I surrender, Mr. Eastman! Please! The savage has a knife!"

Jesse snorted at the ridiculous comment. "You are coming with us, kid," Jesse sneered and nodded at Jeremiah to grab one of the young man's arms. Together, they marched the young man back to the stone steps and interrogated him right there amidst all the dead bodies of his comrades. It seemed that the young man was the only survivor. "Who sent you?" Jesse yelled at the man, shaking his hold on the man's collar.

Jeremiah wiped the hunting knife onto the man's chest. "Answer Mr. Eastman's question!" he growled.

Xavier, Samuel, and the rest of the family watched from the shattered front entrance. The young man looked at the crowd forming. "You can't kill me in front of all these people," he whimpered.

"Tell me what I need to know, then I will let you go," Jesse said viciously.

"You will?"

"Yes," Jesse confirmed. "Now, who sent you?"

The young man looked around nervously, then caved, his arms falling to his sides. "It was Bartholomew, Mr. Eastman."

Jesse relaxed his grip slightly. "I thought so."

Jeremiah held onto the man firmly. "Are you really going to let him go after what they did to us?"

Jesse narrowed his eyes and pulled on the man's collar again, lifting him to within inches of his nose. He sneered dangerously at the young man. "Tell Bartholomew that Billy is no longer an Eastman. Billy was legally estranged from the family on the day that document was signed." Jesse fished into his pocket and retrieved a copy of the agreement that he had found on one of the dead men's bodies. He wrote on it, scrawling an ominous message in capital letters:

BILLY HAS BEEN OFFICIALLY ESTRANGED FROM THE EASTMAN EMPIRE SINCE JULY 14, 1833. HIS SIGNATURE IS INVALID AND AGAINST THE LAW.

Jesse signed it and handed it back to the young man. "We will spare your life, but on one condition," he spat angrily. "You will be the courier." Jesse's eyes glared in a menacing frown. "Take this back to Bartholomew and warn him to never set foot on Eastman property again. There won't be any survivors next time." Jesse pushed the man down the steps. "Run! Before I change my mind!"

The young man sprinted across the estate grounds with the message in his hand. He disappeared over the hill into the distance, not looking back once.

Chapter 9

Zee and her sons had arrived at the Buffalo cabin later that week. Bemidii had left back home, while the twin boys hefted the bags from the carriage. When Zee opened the door, the musty humidity wafted out like a cloud finally being let out of the cottage. It was a long trip, and she was happy to finally arrive, but the stale air was stifling.

She opened all the cabin's windows quickly, going into every room and getting air flow to clear out the staleness. After three hours, things started feeling more like home to Zee. Something didn't feel right. Her heart ached, but it was more than that; she was certain.

A flood of memories surged through her mind unexpectedly. Memories of the Lake Huron cabin during the last few years of the 1812 war flooded her thoughts. At the time, Jesse and Zee had escaped to the Huron area while she was pregnant with Janey. Jesse had built the cabin himself over four months. It was enough to shelter them through the stormy lake winter. Over the years that had followed, Jesse and Zee had fixed the cabin nicely into a welcoming home, all the while having more children and adding to their family.

It was fundamentally some of the best memories for Zee. They were both young and full of energy, optimism, and idealism. The world was theirs to shape and mold to fit.

Zee exhaled and climbed tiredly into bed. It had been a long day, and they still needed to go into Buffalo for provisions. What they had brought with them were the only things they had. It felt eerily similar to Lake Huron, and a chill ran up her spine. What was Jesse doing right now?

Her heart thumped in her chest as she thought about Jesse and the way their marriage used to be. A decade ago, she was beside Jesse every step of the way. She prayed that he was okay and the family would get through this. Moisture formed in her eyes as she fell deeply asleep, with treasured memories turning into tortured dreams.

♎

She awoke suddenly and was immediately disoriented. Zee threw the covers off her body and swung her feet out of the bed. It was already morning! She had slept solidly all night, barely even turning once. She glanced around the large bedroom and inhaled the fresh country air. The windows were still open, and the cabin smelled refreshingly like spruce and oak.

Zee stood and opened the large bedroom curtains. The sun immediately flashed a golden ray of light into her room as if welcoming her back to the woman she always was. Zee frowned at the analogy in her mind and stepped quietly through the house to the kitchen, wondering why she felt so unsettled when everything was so wonderfully peaceful at the cabin.

"Good morning, Momma," Scott mumbled as he lifted his gaze briefly from the Buffalo Gazette newspaper. He stuffed a forkful of food into his mouth from the half-eaten plate of eggs and bread hiding behind the newspaper.

"Good morning, Scott," she replied and kissed him on the cheek. "I can't believe I slept in so late. Where's your brother? We need to go into Buffalo for provisions."

"He got up early, went into town, and brought back food, newspapers, and supplies. He's back outside scoping the area for deer herds."

"Oh, that's wonderful news," she replied. "Saves me from going into town right away. Let's see what he bought." She opened the door to the cold room and rummaged through the sparse items. Zee grabbed a carton of eggs, bread, and bacon, bringing everything into the kitchen. She laid everything onto the counter, then knelt in the lower cupboard, pulling out a cast-iron pan, and placing it on top of the wood stove. "You have the wood stove burning already, too?"

"Of course, Momma," Scott replied.

She munched on a slice of bread and mumbled. "Good bread."

Scott nodded in agreement and watched his mother move about the kitchen. Something in her demeanor caught him off guard. "Anything wrong?" he asked curiously.

Zee whipped her head around, surprised that her son had picked up on her humdrum mood so quickly. "Ah, it's nothing," she replied. "I probably just miss your dad."

Scott finished eating and stood with his plate. "That's to be expected. I don't think I ever remember you two being apart. If you did, I don't remember it."

"We never did."

Scott tilted the coffee cup up to his lips and gulped down the remaining caffeine jolt. "Never?" he asked.

"Never," Zee confirmed, her left green eye and right blue eye twitched with uncertainty. "This is the first time we have lived apart since we met in 1813."

"Hmm," Scott replied hesitantly.

Zee fell into an emotional silence and broke the eggs into the sizzling iron pan. She added a few slices of bacon and mused about the emptiness she felt gnawing at her heart. "Maybe I just need to find myself again," she muttered openly, accidentally voicing her thoughts into words.

"This trip will be the right medicine then. We'll go hunting this evening at dusk."

Zee smiled for the first time since they had arrived. Scott was right. Hunting and living the simple life were the best kinds of medicine for her right now.

♎

Thomas strutted to the living room with the hunting knife in his hand. Frustration bubbled up his throat. Bartholomew had left up north, angry and vengeful, leaving the failed takeover in Thomas's lap. He was glad Bartholomew was gone. His boss's temper was uncontrollable, and it often led to disastrous outcomes.

Now Thomas was responsible for cleaning up this Eastman mess.

He roughly grabbed Billy from behind by the collar. The chair Billy was strapped into tilted crazily backwards by the force, almost falling completely backwards. But Thomas held the chair firmly in his grasp and sneered in Billy's ear. "Give me the money back!" Thomas growled, running the knife along Billy's throat.

"I swear on the Bible," Billy muttered, blood dripping from his beaten face. "I don't have the money anymore."

"Where did it all go?" Thomas yelled, impatience flooding his veins.

Billy swallowed and lowered his eyes towards the knife at his throat. "I spent it. I spent it foolishly." He swallowed again, hoping the lie would take hold. "Wine and women."

"I don't believe you."

"You must!" Billy begged. "It was Bartholomew himself who led me on this path of debauchery!"

Thomas loosened the hold on Billy's throat. Bartholomew was terrible with his money. Wine and women were all he cared about, it seemed. Thomas even wondered sometimes if this life of debauchery is what was causing all these deals to collapse. "You still owe us the money!" Thomas barked. "The Eastman sale is dead! You owe us that money back."

"I will give it back!" Billy begged, watching the knife slowly fall from his throat, and Thomas's hand sheathing the weapon safely away. "Give me a week." Billy swallowed again, searching his brain and trying to find another way. "The deal is not dead."

"There is no legal or illegal way to take over an Empire like that," Thomas replied, the frustration bubbling up again. "Seven of my men were killed. Only two survived. One of those men is severely injured in jail and may still die. The other one was sent back as a messenger!" Thomas felt his face turn red at the audacity of Mr. Eastman's threatening message back. "Jesse Eastman is a crazed lunatic! He still thinks he's at war or something."

Billy nodded. His brother was not a man to mess with. "This was not my plan originally," Billy replied. "It was Bartholomew who chose to knock on that warmonger's door."

"We didn't hear any warnings from you," Thomas sneered as his hand went angrily back to the sheathed knife.

"I underestimated the mental state of my brother," Billy replied, licking the blood from his swollen lips. "I knew Jesse had some problems when he came back from the war, but I didn't realize he had such an arsenal of weapons at the estate. He kept that from me."

"He never told you?"

"No," Billy lied. "I didn't know about the war chest of guns." He watched Thomas visibly relax and felt a trickle of nervous tension run down his spine. Billy was still alive. He had to find a way to beat Jesse. He had to find a weakness. His brother had been a thorn in his side since the war ended, and Jesse took over the estate. "Look, give me a week. I will find a way to make this deal happen."

Thomas laughed crazily. "If you think you can bring down Jesse Eastman, you should go try to kill him yourself then. I'm not losing any more men in another massacre."

"No, not like that," Billy interceded.

"Like what then?"

"I will find his weakness," Billy stated coolly. "I am his brother after all."

Ω

Scott and James crouched in the bushes as Zee hid beside a large tree to the left. They all held their rifles, aiming towards the group of bucks in the clearing. They had all agreed upon the smaller buck. It would be easier to haul back and less work.

At that instance, the juvenile white-tailed deer turned its head and looked directly at the hunting group. Something had spooked him, maybe intuition or maybe he smelled them. The buck sniffed the air cautiously.

Scott, James, and Zee all fired at once.

The guns' roars exploded into the calm dusk air as the group of bucks leapt to escape. Two bullets caught the smallest buck in the act. He crumpled to the ground and tried in vain to get back up as the rest of the herd jumped away, leaving him behind.

Scott and James rushed to the downed animal as Zee trailed behind. The deer died a few minutes later. One bullet had pierced his chest, and the blood began oozing out of the deer's mouth, most likely from a lung shot. Another bullet had entered his rump, crippling his back legs, and the other bullet had gone wild.

"Yes!" Scott exclaimed. "Deer meat for dinner. This one looks like the perfect size."

James sliced open the deer's belly. "I agree. He's the perfect size and age."

Scott knelt beside James, immersing his hands in the cavity. He located and cut the windpipe. Scott grasped it in his hands and pulled hard as the entrails followed out to the midsection.

Zee knelt beside her sons and helped with the field dressing. It took them almost an hour to get the carcass hung and completely skinned. They lay exhausted for several minutes, with their guns ready to protect their kill from wolves.

Scott drank heavily from his water flask. "Okay, let's wait another few minutes for the blood to drain, and then we'll get this carcass back home."

Zee smiled and drank from her canteen, looking up towards the treetops. "It feels good to be out here with you both."

"We're glad you came, Mom," Scott replied.

♎

Zee felt the warm bath water swish over her breasts and tummy. She had become so bloodied that she had to have two baths. The first water was all red and needed to be dumped. The second bath was soothing and exactly what she needed. Zee inhaled fully and exhaled in one long, peaceful breath. She watched as her breasts bobbed with buoyancy in the warm water. She grasped one breast and then the other, pulling them together. Zee felt her desire immediately surface. She hadn't had sex in almost three months now. Zee felt ashamed that she had been counting the days and weeks. Her body yearned for her husband more and more as each day passed. Her hormones seemed to be playing tricks on her. She had started noticing attractive men staring at her back in Philadelphia. The way their eyes slid down her shapely body.

It was enough to make a woman wonder what she had done that was so wrong in her marriage. Zee shifted her body gently in the bath and watched the warm water slide over her large hips. She wasn't the thin, tall lady from 1813 anymore. But Zee had grown to love her large hips and pronounced buttocks. Her waist was thicker, and that wasn't something she liked, but it was still quite smaller than her hips, creating an hourglass look. Her breasts had grown in size, too, and she was quite happy about that.

Zee was confident with aging and proud of the woman she had become.

She pulled her body gently from the bath and stepped out, looking in the bathroom mirror as she dried off. Her breasts hung heavily and majestically on her chest. The water droplets had curled her hair slightly, leaving a mess of waves cascading down her shoulders. She rarely wore her hair down and only saw the beauty in it after baths or when she was combing through it. At approximately 24 inches, Zee's hair was quite long. Her dark blonde hair had always been quite thick. Thankfully, it hadn't thinned that much, and Zee still normally wore it loosely braided, letting the bangs fall around her face.

But tonight, she loved the feeling of all her thick waves along her shoulders and back. The mirror reflected a beautiful woman in her middle years. She looked no older than 30, ten years younger than her real age.

She felt good about that.

Zee padded into her large bedroom and lay down naked on the large bed that she shared with Jesse so many times.

Her body was exhausted from all the hard work during hunting, even though her sons did most of the heavy work. Zee pulled the blankets over her body and curled onto her side as the blackness began to consume the night. She wondered what Jesse was up to at the estate. Zee hoped he was alright and the threatened takeover had fizzled out to nothing but a memory. An unsettling feeling still remained in her heart.

She let out a huge sigh as her heart hammered with longing for Jesse. Memories flooded her mind of all the times they had hunted deer near Lake Huron and all the moments they shared on this very same bed at the Buffalo cabin. The annual trips to visit family were the best memories of all. Zee wondered if she'd ever get the version of Jesse back that she had fallen in love with, so long ago. He had been strong and courageous, stubborn and dominant. Just the kind of man a defiant young woman like Zee needed. Jesse was always respectful, but in the same breath, set down clear boundaries too. Zee loved this about him, curiously. It gave her the freedom to be herself and not worry about the farm and cattle as much anymore. She could be feminine and delight in it, but still wear her hunting pants. Jesse had been a very handsome sergeant in his twenties. His dark brown, wavy hair and his strong arms always got her attention. He was slim but extremely strong and held himself to a higher standard than most.

She missed the man he was. Jesse Eastman still stole her heart every time she saw him, even with the thinning hair and the wrinkles that adorned his handsome face. She just wished for some of those memories to be real life again. Zee wondered if that was even possible. They were both different people now. Or were they?

She wondered what he was doing right now. Was he thinking about her?

Chapter 10

The entire week was devoted to rebuilding and cleaning up the Eastman mansion. Jesse had donned his old working shirt and leather boots. He felt more like himself than ever before. "Hand me that screwdriver," Jesse instructed, holding out a large hand.

Jeremiah handed him the screwdriver and hefted the new door upright without being asked. Xavier helped with positioning the hinges while Samuel was still working on rebuilding the door frame on the other side. Samuel had added a piece of lumber temporarily to fix the gunshot holes. The new door wouldn't arrive for another two weeks. The immediate repairs to the front entrance had taken the family a full five days to reconstruct, and it was finally coming together.

"Should we send a courier to Momma?" Xavier asked suddenly, as if the thought had just abruptly entered his mind. "We've been working so hard on rebuilding after the shootout that I plum forgot that she had left. She won't even know what happened!"

Jesse had been thinking about Zee nonstop since the shoot-out. He had tossed around the idea of riding out there himself, but he couldn't leave a broken front entrance like this behind. Jesse had a family and business to protect. He didn't trust Bartholomew to not come back once Jesse had left. His mind churned with the possibilities and dangers.

Jesse missed Zee terribly. At night, he tossed and turned before going to sleep, wondering what he needed to do to save his marriage. He felt it right down to his bones. Zee didn't need to say anything; he just knew. She wouldn't have left without him otherwise.

He pondered sending a courier so Zee knew that the estate had been attacked right after she had left. Bemidii had just arrived back, and he thought twice about sending him right back again. But something else tugged at him, a warning or something even more sinister. He was afraid that Bartholomew would somehow trace Bemidii directly to her. Jesse shook away the thought abruptly. It was most likely his paranoia from being a soldier. Regardless, Jesse wanted to keep his wife's where-abouts as private as possible. Sending Bemidii back and forth would raise suspicion.

"I think it's better that she doesn't know right now," Jesse lied. "She needs the time away more than anything. It will upset her. She would immediately come back. I know it." Jesse wanted her back with every cell of his body. But he knew some of this was the truth. Zee Collard was the woman Zee Eastman needed to find again. Nobody on this earth would be able to help her do that. It was something Zee needed to follow through on.

"Are you serious?" Samuel asked incredulously. "You're going to keep her in the dark about all this?"

"Not in the dark," Jesse responded assuredly. "My wife knows the estate was under threat of a takeover, and it wasn't taken over. We won. I don't see any reason to worry her further. We'll tell her when she comes back." He paused and examined the door project. Jesse eyed the hole for the massive steel hinge and worked the large screw in. He twisted the screwdriver with sheer brute force into the solid wood. Sweat gleamed on his brow as he twisted and twisted until the screw was mostly in. He grabbed another screw and immediately started working on the bottom hinge, lining everything up. "Besides," he muttered, almost to himself. "I don't want Bartholomew getting even a whiff of where she is at."

Jeremiah held the door steady as Jesse's forearms bulged with brute force as he worked on securing the bottom hinge. He grunted and swore as the wood resisted the long screw. Finally, it began to give way, and after the screw was in, he let go and tentatively stepped back. The door swung, firmly attached.

Jesse turned as Georgina came rushing over with biscuits and beer. "It looks good!" she exclaimed, placing the snacks on a folded wood table for all the men. She immediately went behind everyone and hugged Jeremiah. "How's your hand doing, darling?"

Jeremiah looked down at his left hand. There was an angry, swollen bruise across his knuckles. He had just taken off the bandages today, and it was healing nicely. Nobody had noticed during the shootout that he had broken a knuckle in the fight. Punching that large beefheaded man was like punching steel. "It feels better today," Jeremiah answered and kissed her on the forehead.

"Thank you for your service in defending the Eastman household like you did," Jesse stated for the hundredth time. "I wasn't expecting you to fight so hard."

"My future wife's family was at stake," he answered. "There was no question in my mind."

"So that's for certain now?" Jesse asked Georgina, searching her eyes for the truth. He was glad but also partially saddened to learn that she might be leaving the household. "You are getting married?"

"Yes," she answered confidently. "I am still not sure where we will live, but we are looking for a small, quaint home not too far away. I will still run the kitchen here daily, don't you worry about that." She laughed. "I couldn't leave all those poor cooks to deal with your bad Eastman temper."

Jesse chuckled at the jibe. "Well, I'm thoroughly happy for both of you," he replied. "Is there anything special you'd like for a wedding gift?"

"Just your presence, Jesse," Georgina answered. "And everybody else's in the family. That would be the best gift of all."

"Then it's done," Jesse replied, still wondering about the actual gift that he would surprise her with.

"I'll be there, too," Samuel stated. "I've known you like a sister as well." Samuel chomped the remaining biscuit and washed it all down with his beer. "I'm all finished framing this side of the door. Jeremiah, if you could hold the door again, we will position those hinges and get the alignment right before putting in the final screws."

Jesse nodded and watched Georgina fold up the table and take everything away. She was deliriously happy and full of new love. It gleamed in her eyes, and her step was somehow lighter. Jesse remembered briefly how Zee had been like that when they had run away into the woods of Canada. She had that love gleam in her different colored eyes.

The random thought hit him hard. Zee's eyes were so unique and lovely. He had really fallen hard for her. The way she had looked at him. It was priceless.

Jesse missed her. His heart thumped loudly in his chest. He would have to find a way to bring that gleam back in her eyes and his own eyes. Jesse hadn't known how much he was risking, until she had left. The estate needed him, but he needed his wife more. He would need to make some big changes soon.

"Hey," Jesse barked. "Xavier, grab those screws and let's get this done."

Ω

"Janey!" Jesse exclaimed as he spread his arms wide for a big fatherly hug. "Thank you for coming on such short notice." His suit jacket flew open as he hugged his daughter tightly. He released Janey, then led her into his office while Xavier followed them in.

"What is the emergency?" Janey asked, turning around as everyone followed her in.

"No emergency," Jesse stated, gesturing towards a chair in the office for her to sit. "Just a lot to discuss that I need you here for. My brother, Joshua, will arrive soon, and your grandma is coming down the stairs right now."

"What does Joshua have to do with this?" Janey asked. "Is something wrong with Grandma?"

At that moment, Ellen Eastman glided in. "Nothing is wrong with me, dear," she explained. "But something is wrong with Jesse's marriage." Ellen stared coolly at Jesse.

"What's wrong with Momma?" Janey shrieked, a worried frown creasing her eyebrows.

"Mother! Enough!" Jesse barked at Ellen and then turned towards his daughter. "Nothing is wrong with Zee. But your grandmother is upset that I want to be a good husband and take back some of my life from this insufferable Eastman Empire!"

Ellen's eyes widened. "Well!"

"Don't you, well, me, Mother!" Jesse retorted, his finger pointing angrily in the air. "I have worked hard for the past ten years resurrecting the Eastman Empire from the damage Billy had caused while I was away at war and living in Canada." Jesse sat down heavily in the leather chair. "I deserve some credit for that, and I deserve my life back."

Ellen pursed her lips shut, refusing to speak.

Janey looked from Ellen to Jesse. "What are you not telling me, Pappa?" she asked Jesse.

Ellen interrupted before Jesse had a chance to speak. "That wife of his ran away into the woods!" Ellen sneered. "Living in luxury seemingly is akin to being in a prison for her." Ellen scoffed and sat down harshly in one of the leather armchairs.

"Mother," Jesse warned.

Ellen lifted her chin up and smirked. "That's what you get for marrying a peasant Loyalist from Canada."

"Mother!" Jesse stood up sharply. "Now that will be enough!"

Joshua stepped into the office and closed the door. "What's all the shouting about?"

Janey hugged her uncle warmly. "Uncle Josh! Welcome to the family feud!" she laughed jokingly. "I am not completely sure what all this is about or why I am here either."

Joshua leaned down to Janey and patted her shoulder. "I think I have a bit of an inkling of what's happening."

"Why am I always the last to know?" Janey exclaimed.

Xavier spoke up. He had remained quiet through most of it. "I wasn't told much either," he added. "This seems to be something between Grandma and Pappa."

Joshua clapped his hand on Jesse's shoulder and half-hugged him. "It's good to see you again," Joshua said, smiling warmly. "I heard about the shootout. By the looks of the front entrance, you could barely tell that a bloody massacre happened."

Everyone laughed. The anger slowly dissipated in the room. The aftermath of the shootout had been difficult, especially dealing with the authorities and identifying all the men who were killed. The police were stationed near the front of the estate, and a full security detail had been hired. The Eastman Estate was a fortress now. No unauthorized people were allowed in.

"Would someone please tell me what is going on?" Janey asked. "I have a husband and two babies at home."

"You have a nanny, right?" Jesse asked.

"Yes," Janey answered. "Why does that matter?"

"It matters a lot."

Janey looked around in confusion.

It was Joshua who spoke up. "Let me take my educated guess," he started slowly. "Jesse wants to hand over the reins of the empire to Janey and Xavier. He's tired of doing this at the expense of his own family. And he's called our mother and me here to provide our endorsement." Joshua eyed Jesse. "Am I right?"

"Partially," Jesse replied.

"Well, then, inform us about the rest," Joshua urged.

"I want you, Janey, and Xavier to run the estate."

The entire room broke out in multiple retorts at once, with nobody able to hear anything. Jesse watched calmly as his family exploded in a chaotic blend of excited chatter before him. He sat down heavily in his chair and waited for the shouting to abate.

After several minutes, he could finally speak. "Let's address the issues calmly," Jesse spoke commandingly. "If there is anyone who cannot be respectful, they will be asked to leave." He eyed his mother, Ellen, with an unspoken threat.

"How am I expected to run this estate with twin babies?" Janey asked. She ran her fingers through her thick, dark hair and reclined back wearily.

Jesse spoke first. "That's why I am asking Josh and Xavier to be working controllers," he answered.

Ellen interrupted. "Xavier is not Eastman blood," she muttered.

Xavier rolled his eyes and defended himself. "Grandma!" he spat back. "I was raised as an Eastman all my life and never even knew my biological father."

Ellen pursed her lips in defiance. "Still, Collards are not Eastmans."

Janey shouted next. "So, are you saying that I'm not an Eastman either?" she barked. "I am proud of everything my mother had to overcome. She's the strongest woman in this household!"

Joshua raised a hand to quiet everyone. "Mother," he said firmly, pointing a finger at Ellen. "I agree with Janey and Xavier. All of Jesse's children are Eastmans, and Zee is a fine, strong woman." He leaned against the desk and crossed his arms over his chest. "You must get over this family rivalry. Father is not here to cause conflict anymore, thank God. The Revolutionary War is well in the past. We have been mostly accepting of the changes affecting the country now."

"Billy didn't accept loyalists," Ellen retorted back. "And neither did your sisters."

"Billy tried to liquidate the Eastman Empire for his own gain!" Jesse shouted angrily.

"That's right," Joshua agreed. "Don't you start with all this, Mother." He frowned at his mother and shook his head. "And don't speak for my sisters, they aren't even here."

Janey stood and brushed her dress down daintily. "Now, if we're done with this ridiculousness, I'd like to get on with my day." Everyone stopped to hear her next comment. "Good, now that I have your attention. I'd like to say that I will most certainly accept the appointment of being a director of the Eastman Empire. I could be the Secretary. If it helps my father and mother and the entire Eastman family, then of course I will do it."

Xavier nodded, speaking firmly. "Well said, Janey," he added. "I agree with Janey. If it helps the Eastman Empire, I will gladly do it." He gestured his large arm around the room to encompass everyone. "Besides, in the natural progression of families, the young will eventually take over the helm anyway. Whether it be today, in five years, or in ten years, it will happen. If it provides my father with more quality of life now, then all the better."

Jesse clapped his hand onto Xavier's shoulder. "You have been the closest and most involved member of the family throughout all the daily interactions. Xavier will be the strongest asset because he knows the most."

Ellen frowned. "What about Scott, James, and Johnny?" she asked.

"They are all too young," Jesse answered. "We can list them as advisors until they are twenty years of age, then they can become directors."

Joshua nodded. "That sounds like a sound plan to me," he answered. "I can include my own young children's names to that list, too."

"I'm in agreement with that," Jesse stated. "That's why I wanted you to be a part of this, too. Two families instead of one will provide more balance and less greed."

Janey spoke next. "But we need to have at least two key people in case everything breaks out into chaos. Too many people will often lead to indecision, I would think."

"True," Jesse confirmed. "I will appoint Joshua and Xavier as President and Vice-President, then Janey as Treasurer. The transition period will occur over the next year as I train everyone, and after that, I will remain on as a director, like you are presently, Mother." He paused for the information to fully settle in everyone's minds. "Monthly meetings will be held with all directors and advisors. As the children get to the age of twenty, we will discuss their roles then. If Joshua doesn't want the pressure five years down the road, we can all vote for a director to take his place." Jesse stared at his mother, Ellen, and his voice softened. "It is for the best, Mother. Like Xavier said in his youthful wisdom, the company will eventually be passed down to the younger family members anyway. It is the circle of life, Mother."

Janey, Xavier, and Joshua all nodded.

"Do I have everyone's agreement?" Jesse asked, pulling the lapels of his suit together firmly. "Raise your hands for yes."

Janey's hand shot up first, followed in quick concession by Xavier's hand, then Joshua's. Jesse raised his hand and glared at his mother. She slowly stood and joined the others, raising her hand stubbornly halfway.

"Is that a yes, Mother?" Joshua asked, clearly perturbed by his mother's tenacity.

"It is the circle of life," she muttered. "We all age, and I suppose we have to trust that we raised our children right." Her eyebrows unknotted and she exhaled wearily, then finally raised her right hand fully. "Yes, I agree."

CHAPTER 11

Georgina lifted her arms around Jeremiah's strong neck and whispered in his ear. "I love you." Her fingers danced over his muscular shoulders and down to his biceps. "Are you awake, sweetheart?"

Jeremiah's eyes blinked open, slowly at first, then fully. He gazed into Georgina's lovely face. "I am awake now, yes. What is it, dear?"

She fumbled over her words, trying to find a subtle way to tell him, but nothing seemed to work. "Sweetheart, I know it's early and we haven't known each other that long," she stuttered. "But there are always consequences to sleeping together." Her voice trailed off.

Jeremiah sat straight upright in bed, fully alert now. The dawn streaked rays of light through the heavy curtains, creating a golden glow to the room. "What are you telling me, Gina?" He said, using the cute nickname he had chosen for her.

Georgina blushed and swallowed, not certain how he would take this important news. "Well, I am not completely certain yet, but I know something has changed," she mumbled, touching his lips gently with her fingertips. "I hope you're not upset. I had no idea because I'm thirty-nine years old and it never occurred to me that it could be this easy."

"What is it, Georgina?" Jeremiah said hastily.

Georgina bit her lip, inhaled sharply, then spilled out the words in a torrent. "I believe that I may be pregnant. Now, sweetheart, I know it is too soon to discuss children and such, but my monthly curse failed to appear and my breasts have begun to hurt, oddly enough." She gazed down at her lap, clearly embarrassed. "There are many other signs, too. I am sick in the mornings." She swallowed and looked into his eyes, searching for any clues to his thoughts. "I'm sorry, I wish we could have discussed this properly without having everything thrown at us like this."

Jeremiah swung his arms around her like a beast and lifted her small body from the bed. He held her firmly against his chest and kissed her roughly on the lips.

The joy that spread through her body was like none other. Georgina squealed with delight. Her shrieks of joy were momentarily muted as they kissed for several minutes.

Finally, Jeremiah gently released her. He gazed into her eyes. "I am thrilled that you are having my baby," Jeremiah cooed seductively. "Nothing pleases me more, my dear. Nothing at all in this world."

$$\Omega$$

Zee swung swiftly onto her horse and snapped the reins. Her mare trotted confidently into the bushes. Zee travelled along the meandering paths until she found the narrow road winding towards the city of Buffalo.

It was a large city of approximately 15,000 people. After the completion of the Lake Erie Canal in 1825, the population had increased dramatically. It quickly developed into an important trading center for many goods traveling to and from the canal.

Zee was intent on stocking the cabin with enough supplies to last the entire week. They needed grains and vegetables as well as more coffee and weak beer. The road was narrow but became wider and wider as she neared Buffalo.

Scott and James were still sleeping when Zee had decided to go into town by herself. It was very early in the morning, and she wanted them to get enough sleep. They had worked hard on butchering the deer while she cooked. They deserved some extra rest, and she could surprise them with a nice dessert tonight.

As Zee neared Buffalo, the sounds and smells of a bustling city wafted into the air. More and more carriages and horses appeared, with some fur traders with pelts over their backs. Farmers with vegetables and craftsmen with wares.

She had an empty wagon behind her horse that she intended to fill with supplies before returning back home. Zee chuckled to herself. She was already thinking that the cabin was home.

Zee entered the market with a friendly smile on her face. Even though she was dressed like a man, several tufts of hair poked out from under her cap, and her aristocratic nose and jawline secretly revealed her femininity. She tried to nod and only spoke when necessary. Zee Eastman was in male territory after all. Most women did not venture into trading markets without their husbands.

She was never afraid of entering such situations. Zee held her head up confidently, and her shoulders were squared. If they found out she was female, then so be it. If they thought they could cause trouble, then they would have a taste of the knife she always kept in her boot or a quick bullet lodged in their skull. Her rifle was strung across her back, and both boots had knives hidden in handmade side holders. She was Zee Collard today and couldn't be happier.

She rode her horse right up to the trading market and then disembarked, leading her mount through the crowds. She stopped to drape a large ground cloth over the trailer and proceeded through the stalls and trading posts. Zee browsed through the inventory and found several pots and coffee before locating the supply store in the middle of town. She bought the pots and coffee, then hitched her mount outside the supply store and went in through the creaky front door.

Several people were in the store. It was a busier crowd than she expected. It was Saturday, after all, she told herself. Everybody needed supplies for the week ahead.

Most of the patrons were servants in clear uniforms or burly men. One man stood at the end of the line, and he stood out from the rest. He was well dressed with shined shoes and a manicured beard. His hair was slicked back, and he wore a double-breasted suit. She nodded politely at the well-dressed man and took her place in line, casually viewing the walls of merchandise. Zee started making a mental note in her head of all the items she needed to bring back to the cabin when a scuffle broke out near the front of the store.

Everyone turned their attention to the shouts on the boardwalk. Zee's adrenaline pumped as the shouts grew closer, and she braced herself, pulling her rifle around to her shoulder from her back.

The shouts increased in intensity until finally the body of a vagrant flew through the window and landed in the middle of the store.

Immediately, everyone began shouting at once. The store owner yelled. "Who's going to pay for this window?"

Another store employee picked up the vagrant by the collar. "You will be paying for this!"

The assailant shouted from outside and raised a rifle as everyone ducked, including Zee. She crouched against the back wall but had simultaneously swung her rifle to bear in the same motion. Several men were in front of her. Nobody could see clearly, and everything happened so fast.

The well-dressed man surprised everyone and pulled a pistol from his coat jacket, shooting the crazed man clearly in the shoulder. The assailant spun violently around like a spinning toy and then staggered to the left and the right as the vagrant pleaded with the store employee. "That man is a drunkard who tried to steal my wife! We are both here on a lengthy journey from Germany looking for work!" the vagrant shouted in a thick European accent.

"If this is the truth, where is your wife?" the owner asked.

"She is in the hotel cookhouse across the street!" the vagrant shouted. "We were minding our own business, trying to eat breakfast, when he tried to steal my young wife!"

The employee shoved the man towards the door. "Leave your hat, go get your wife, and come back here to work behind the counter helping us with all these customers! Your community service can pay for that broken window. Saturdays are the worst days to be starting fights!"

As the vagrant left the store, everyone began chatting excitedly. The well-dressed man glanced back at Zee and gestured his hand out to help her stand, but she waved him away.

She had her eyes glued to the assailant, who was recovering from his gunshot wound and swinging his rifle to bear. Zee squinted one eye and focused down the barrel of her rifle.

A large blast filled the small store, and everyone ducked again, except Zee. She stood up and checked to make sure she had hit her target.

"Boy!" the owner shouted at her. "You are a good shot! Much gratitude to you, my young man. I saw him ready to shoot a round into my customers! I reached for my rifle, but you saved the day!" He slapped a heavy arm onto Zee's shoulder. "Boy, you deserve a store credit! You can have fifty cents off your order. What name shall I write it out to?"

Zee lowered her voice artificially and croaked. "Zee, my name's Zee."

The well-dressed man scrutinized her and walked up to the shop owner, laying down two dollar coins. "You let this boy have anything," the man looked at her again, noticing the lashes framing her beautiful eyes. "Absolutely anything he wants. This boy saved our lives."

The store owner looked at the coins. "That's a large amount of money, sir!" he replied. "Are you sure?"

"Yes, I'm sure," the man responded, pulling Zee to his side. "This boy saved our lives."

Zee opened her mouth to speak and thought better of it. Her voice was ridiculously feminine, and she had a hard time lowering her voice. She was tall enough to pass for a boy, but her voice was sultry and so obviously female. Zee nodded and approached the counter as the well-dressed man stood behind her.

"What's your order?" the store owner asked, finally noticing Zee's eyelashes and blond hair poking out of her cap.

Zee lowered her voice and spoke. "I have a list to bring back for the family," she croaked, her voice pitching in an odd tangle of masked femininity. Zee handed the list over to the shop owner. As he read it, he began pulling items from the shelves.

She turned to the well-dressed man and pushed her hand out for a handshake. "Thank you, sir, for your generosity."

The man shook her hand. "The name is Barton. Pleased to make your acquaintance. Who taught you to shoot like that?"

"My father," she replied, telling the honest truth.

"You have a good father."

"He's no longer with us, but yes, my Pappa was a good man."

"My sympathies," Barton replied.

"It was his time, unfortunately," Zee replied, offering no further conversation. She didn't know this man, but was grateful for the distraction. Zee glanced at him one more time before turning her gaze back towards the counter. Barton was a strikingly handsome man, she noted. He was quite out of place in this city filled with trading posts, craftsmen, and farmers. She had only been to Buffalo a handful of times, and the population had exploded recently, so maybe he was one of the rich businessmen looking to buy merchandise from overseas. His dark hair was shoulder length and he was impeccably groomed, with a confident, commanding composure.

The store resumed its prior bustling chaos with more customers lining up for wares. The German vagrant returned with his wife and was immediately put to work as the Sheriff's aides searched the body of the dead assailant. The Deputy Sheriff approached the store's customers and began questioning everyone. Zee hoped they wouldn't take her to the station. She would have to reveal who she really was. Zee just wanted to get out of here and return back home by sundown.

As the store owner finished compiling her order, the German vagrant was tasked with loading it all onto her waiting horse-drawn wagon. The store owner refunded the balance to Barton and shook Zee's hand. "Thank you for being here at the right time." He handed her the handwritten credit. "You can use this the next time you're in town."

Zee nodded and croaked in an artificial boy voice. "Thank you, sir!"

Zee rushed to get out of the store, but she was too late. The Deputy Sheriff pulled her arm and gestured for her to join the crowd of law personnel. The morgue official had already arrived to take the body away. "You're the one who shot this man?" the Deputy stated. "I need a statement from you."

Barton stepped in. "I shot this man," he interrupted.

"That's not what the witnesses in the store say."

"I shot him first, hitting his shoulder and only injuring him," Barton said confidently. "When he recovered, he raised his weapon to shoot into the crowd of customers. That's when Zee shot him dead." He clasped a heavy hand on her shoulder, praising her. "This boy is a hero."

"I can take that as your official statement?" the Deputy asked.

"Yes," Barton replied.

"Let me take your name, and you can all be on your way," the Deputy waved for Barton to come.

Barton joined the officers and wrote down his name. The officer looked up at him in astonishment and shook his hand. "Have a wonderful day, sir, and take that boy back home."

Barton smiled charismatically and rejoined Zee.

"Thank you," Zee said in her normal female voice. "I appreciate that. I need to get back to my family before sundown. I really didn't want to waste time at the Sheriff's office."

Barton smiled. "I knew you weren't some random boy," he chuckled. "Your lashes can't fool me. You are a masked beauty, I can tell."

Zee blushed and expressed her gratitude again. She hadn't been complimented like that in decades.

"Don't be shy," Barton said, touching her waist lightly. "I will accompany you back home. Who knows, you may get into some more trouble." He chuckled. "We make a good team."

"Thank you for your offer," Zee replied, finding her voice. "But I don't need protection or anything. My sons are awaiting my return."

"You have sons?"

"Yes, twin sons. They are mostly all grown up. Another few months and they'll be adults."

"You don't look old enough to have adult children," Barton said appraisingly. "I am shocked."

A large throaty laugh escaped from Zee's mouth before she could contain it. "Much appreciated, Barton." She swung her leg onto the horse and mounted. "I have five children!" she exclaimed.

Barton feigned shock and laughed. "You are a special woman, then!" he replied. "How have you managed to look so young? I thought you were twenty-five!"

Zee laughed wholeheartedly as her horse began trotting away. "Twenty-five!" she yelled back. "That's an outrageous compliment if I ever heard one!"

Barton tapped his horse and galloped to catch up to her. He pulled the reins and slowed to a trot beside her as they travelled south along the road. "Either I am poor at guessing ages or you're just one of those timeless beauties."

Zee blushed and twisted in her saddle, looking sideways at Barton.

"I've made you uncomfortable," he immediately said. "I will stop. I will only accompany you to your home, and then I will take my leave."

"Okay," she replied firmly. Zee was conflicted. Part of her loved the attention and compliments, but the other part wanted this man to go away. Her instincts told her to be wary of this stranger, but everything was being drowned out by the chaos of the day.

She couldn't deny that the sudden male attention made her cheeks glow. Jesse had shown her so little attention in the past few years that some days she felt like she was a stone. She couldn't blame it all on Jesse, though. Throughout the last few days on her own, Zee realized how much of her former self she had given up. Zelda Eastman wasn't the same woman, and it pained her to come to this realization. Zee needed to let go of all the mothering she had focused much of her life upon for the past twenty years. Her children were all growing up into adults now. She was left with a hollowed-out version of herself. She needed to shift the focus to regaining herself and finding the real Zee Collard. But it was more than reclaiming her old self now. She had to somehow find the balance between the version of the old Zee Collard and the new Zee Eastman. Someone that she was comfortable with being, now that she was getting older.

The rhythmic trotting of the horses broke the silence. "You are deep in thought," Barton mentioned, glancing over at Zee.

Zee was surprised that she had let her guard down so easily. "Oh, yes," she mumbled, attempting to conjure up a small lie. "I was just thinking about my sons."

"What are their names?"

"Scott and James," she replied nervously. She didn't want to give this stranger too much information about herself. "Do you have children?" she asked, trying to steer the conversation away from herself.

"I did have one child," he replied quietly.

Zee's eyes widened, and she glanced at him with sympathy. "What happened?"

"My son died from pneumonia as a baby," he replied. "He was born in San Antonio, where we lived. But I needed to go up to Detroit for business, and my wife would not stay home. She brought our son. His small body could not handle the colder weather or the trip, I don't know which. He died at six months old."

"I'm so sorry," Zee responded empathically. "That's awful." Zee trotted into the more wooded area of the trail as their horses' hooves clopped against the dirt mixed with stones. "You never attempted to have more children with your wife again?"

"My wife died a year later," he replied stonily, looking into the distance. "She caught smallpox and perished while I was away on business."

Zee slowed down her horse and looked at him. "My sincere condolences," she replied sincerely.

Barton glanced at her, then gazed ahead in apparent deep thought. "This is life," he stated. "It doesn't always happen as you wish. All we can do is move ahead sometimes."

"This is true," Zee replied, gazing out at the sloping scenery. "We all have to go through pain. Sometimes it's a necessary evil." A beautiful summer meadow clearing appeared in front of them. "Look, meadow flowers!" she exclaimed. "The beauty of life is always around us. We just need to open our eyes and see it." She tapped her heels on her horse to increase speed as Barton followed her, galloping into the meadow.

The landscape opened up into a larger clearing, one mile wide and three miles long. Several hundred purple meadow flowers adorned the right side of the meadow, while pinker versions of a similar flower blossomed on the left side up ahead. "Isn't this so beautiful?" Zee cried out excitedly, stopping her horse to dismount. A small stream meandered through the meadow, and she led her horse to drink. She bent over and plucked several wildflowers into her hand excitedly. "I will bring these home for my sons!"

Barton was only a few steps behind her, plucking his own assortment of flowers. "Your husband would love to have the flowers lighting up the home," he mentioned casually. He straightened and awaited her reply.

Zee knew it was an unspoken question. Barton wanted to know if she was available. It was flattering and concerning at the same time. She inhaled the flowers comically in her hand and peered at Barton with her oddly colored eyes, trying to form her answers.

"Your eyes," Barton said, breaking the odd silence. "They are different colors."

"Yes," she gazed down. "I was born with this condition. One green eye and one blue eye has made me a freak of nature to some people."

"I think it is beautifully unique."

"Thank you," she replied graciously. "And yes, my husband would love these flowers in our home."

Barton straightened and handed her the extra bouquet of flowers he had picked. "He is a lucky man."

Zee smiled politely and accepted the flowers, bundling them all together with a straw string. "Thank you, but I suspect that I am not the easiest wife to behold. My husband deserves all the credit." She chuckled and turned back towards her horse, waving him on. "I must get back. It's still another 30-minute ride from here, and I'd like to get some deer stew cooking for dinner."

♎

Barton was a true gentleman and held up to his word. He helped her unload the supplies, met Scott and James, then took his leave, politely bowing and then disappearing into the woods, a stranger never to be seen again.

Zee had cooked the deer stew and made some dough for bread before going to sleep. Scott and James stayed up drinking beer as Zee relaxed in her large bed in her white nightgown. She mused about the day, the shooting, and meeting Barton. It felt exhilarating to be on her own, but a tiny part of her told her to be wary. She hadn't been alone in twenty years. Zee thought back and wondered if she had ever travelled alone in her life.

She had not.

Before she met Jesse, she was young, and her parents accompanied her on rare family trips. They all worked so hard at the farm back then that traveling was a strange luxury. When she met Jesse, he was her world, her everything. She had built a family with him, and they both constructed a world of togetherness. When they had moved to Philadelphia, it was a huge adjustment, but she was happy to be accepted into the family. Everyone had accepted her, with the exception of Ellen and Billy. The cool alienation from these two made her feel like an outsider over the years, and slowly began to erode the strings of attachment between Jesse and her.

She still loved her husband, but something was obviously wrong. She knew this now.

Zee had, for once in her life, experienced a strange phenomenon.

She felt appreciation for another man, other than her husband. Zee lay heavily on her bed and rolled over to the side, curling up. Her body was shaped like a C, with her breasts bobbing over her arms. She felt an old, familiar desire streak through her as her bosom brushed her arms. Zee cupped one of her heavy breasts and slowly squeezed it as sexual arousal raced through her body. She searched her mind for visions of Jesse when they were young, and a memory popped into her mind of the moment when they had met at the door of the Collard's farmhouse, right before he had taken it over as a military hospital.

The very first time she had laid eyes on him, Zee was immediately overtaken by his handsome, dark eyes and his confident stature. She murmured and smoothed her hands over her body lightly, dreaming of the first time Jesse had made love to her. She squirmed as Jesse's imaginary hands slid over her breasts, stomach, and thighs. His magic fingers hovered over the apex of her moist thighs when suddenly the image changed.

The man transformed into a darker version of Jesse with slightly darker skin and a manicured beard. His hands reached over her body expertly, like an experienced lover. He knew what to do and how to bring out her darkest desires. Zee stopped abruptly and lay on her back, breathing heavily, as an epiphany seized her. The sober knowledge struck her. This vision in her mind was no longer her husband, Jesse Eastman.

It was Barton.

♎

She had awakened early and decided to take steps to salvage her marriage. Her mind was appalled that she had fantasized about another man last night. Zee had not consciously made the decision; it just appeared out of nowhere from a man who had simply paid her attention. Zee felt somehow dirty. Her mind reeled with all possible conclusions and reached none, but one epiphany.

She must save her marriage and fix what was wrong.

Zee sent for a courier to go back to the Eastman Estate to ask Jesse if everything was alright, what was happening with Bartholomew's threats, and if he needed her back before the two weeks were complete.

She cleaned the cabin and spontaneously left to go swimming naked in the local lake. It was early morning, and the humidity hung in the air like a veil. The only sounds were the birds and the hum of insects flying in the forest. She quickly removed all her clothing and dropped them in a pile on a large rock. Zee walked quickly into the cool water, feeling the sand sinking in between her toes and the cool lake swirling around her. She felt exposed, so she dove right in, swimming languorously. She turned on her back and floated for several seconds as her eyes met the distant blue skies overhead. It felt wondrous and freeing to be one with nature. Her heart swelled with peace. At once, her body sank, and she turned back over, chuckling, then switched to a front crawl, swimming again through the cool water. She splashed like a toddler in a bath and submerged her entire head, swimming underneath for several seconds, then bobbed up for fresh air.

Zee had learned how to swim when they had lived at the Lake Huron cabin. It was the best way to relieve the stress of raising a house full of children.

Zee bobbed up once more and swam back to shore. She walked quickly out of the lake and dried off, swiftly putting her clothes back on, fighting against the protest of her moist skin. When she was finished, she towel-dried her hair and walked back home.

When she arrived, her sons were chopping deadwood. They both looked up, alarmed.

"Where did you go?" Scott asked.

"I went for a morning swim!" she answered jubilantly.

"You used to do that when we were young in Lake Huron!" James announced. "How was the water?"

"It was wonderful," Zee answered joyfully.

She laid down her towel and helped gather the firewood into the woodshed with her sons.

Several more hours went by, without Zee even noticing the passage of time. She had enjoyed a long, peaceful day with her sons. They cooked deer steaks for dinner, then retired back outside, sitting around a fire.

They drank beer and laughed at the old memories, bonding as a tight family.

"Momma," Scott stated, chuckling at the memories. "This is what I remember as a kid! You were so courageous and spontaneous when we were little! It was so much fun!"

James agreed, laughing. "That's right, I remember the trips to Philadelphia, too! Staying at this cabin with Pappa, our brothers, and our sister. We had a wonderful time together back then."

Zee felt her eyes moisten at the memories that seemed so far away but yet so close to home. "Your dad was a wonderful husband during those early years," she responded.

"But something changed after a while," Scott noted.

Zee became quiet and defended her husband as she always did with her children. "Jesse had a lot to deal with. Billy had almost ground the Eastman Empire into ruins. You know this." She waved a finger at her sons. "You should learn from him. Your Pappa is a hard-working man."

"Yeah, he is," Scott replied, choosing to stay silent.

Zee stood up to return to the cabin, looking away to wipe the tears from her eyes. "Let's go see if the courier has returned yet!" she exclaimed. "I am curious to know what has been going on since we left."

Scott and James picked up a log and threw it on the fire. "We'll be there soon. You go on ahead, Momma."

♎

The courier didn't come back for several days. The note he handed to her was scrawled with Jesse's handwriting:

My dearest Zee,

I love you and miss you with all my heart, sweetheart. Everything is alright at the estate. Some issues arose with Bartholomew, but we have dealt with it fine. Do not worry about us. We are handling everything well.

I will let you know if something else arises, but for now, enjoy your time away with the boys. I know you need it. I love you, my dear.

Sincerely,

Jesse

(Bring back lots of deer meat! We need it!)

Zee let the note float to the floor.
He wants her to stay at the cabin.
Her heart sank, and Zee shuffled to the kitchen in a haze.

CHAPTER 12

Jesse opened the door and walked tiredly into his office. He was torn whether he should have asked Zee to come back. He didn't want her to get worried about the attempted armed takeover. He tried to be sweet but as vague as possible in the letter.

Writing was not his forte. He had trouble expressing his emotions and, like most men his age, believed that it was not something to be terribly worried about. Deep inside his heart, though, something nagged at him. An instinct, a pang of jealousy, he wasn't sure what.

He wanted Zee back. Jesse had already been working on changes to himself as well as the estate. He was growing his hair, and it fell slightly past his ears now. He still slicked it back and wore suits, but he felt a change churning inside him.

Jesse wanted his wonderful marriage back to how it used to be. He saw how Georgina and Jeremiah were together, and it made him envious. Zee and Jesse could have that back if they tried.

But it would take time, and he needed to do it slowly. He would surprise Zee with news of his resignation and ask her if she wanted to move back to Lake Huron next year.

Jesse smiled up at the ceiling. He already knew the answer. It would be a wholehearted yes.

Jesse closed his appointment book as Xavier and Joshua walked in. Their training would begin today.

But another thought crept into his mind. He still had to somehow help Georgina organize a big wedding with little advance notice. It felt like an impossible task. Jesse had no experience with large weddings!

He sighed heavily and showed Joshua on the map where the port bays were situated. Xavier filled in the details of which ports needed repair and which ones were more productive.

Jesse's eyes faded towards the window. He could barely focus. Something tugged at him. Then a solution slipped into his mind that resolved both problems at once, and he smiled.

"Pappa?" Xavier asked. "Are you alright?"

"I'm fine, son," Jesse replied, as a small mischievous grin formed on his lips.

♎

Zee butchered another deer carcass that Scott had shot the day before. It was a large doe, and the meat was plentiful. She had on her butcher's apron, smeared red with blood. Her feet were tired from standing all afternoon, so she chopped a few more roasts up, thinking that she would rest soon. James and Scott were in the shed, plucking several wild turkeys.

A series of heavy knocks sounded on the front door.

At first, she was alarmed, then she thought maybe it was the courier coming back with something special from Jesse.

She wiped her hands and went to answer the door with a spring in her step.

When she opened the door, her heart sank.

"Hello, Zee," Barton said innocently, standing there with a bouquet of wildflowers.

"Barton," Zee said curiously. "What brings you here?"

"I was back at the store filling up with more supplies when I thought of you," he responded, handing the flowers to her. "I saw that you had purchased as much flour as you could, but they had run out that day." He gestured behind him. "So, I picked up several more bags for you today."

Zee peered out the door at his wagon and smiled. It was filled with four large bags of flour and mixed grains. "That's enough for an army!" she cried happily.

Barton laughed infectiously. "It's all I can do. You were such wonderful company when we were riding back."

"Come in," Zee said, opening the door further. "I can call Scott to bring in the flour."

"No need for that, I can bring the flour and grains in," he said. "Hold the door."

Barton rushed back to the wagon and effortlessly hefted the bags over his shoulder and brought them into the kitchen, one by one.

"How did you know?" Zee asked, smiling. "I was actually thinking of going back to Buffalo to get more flour."

Barton laid the last bag onto the wooden kitchen bench, surveying the bloody mess on the kitchen table and the blood-soaked apron Zee was wearing. He made a mental note. Zee wasn't the typical kind of woman he was used to. "Well, I know a good woman like you needs flour for daily bread," he answered, pausing. "And after what had happened in Buffalo the last time you were there, I would hope you wouldn't have to experience another shooting again."

Zee smiled politely. "Well, thank you, Barton."

Barton nodded, raking his eyes over her voluptuous body. The apron was tied tight around her waist, and her hair was fastened with hairpins, the strands pulled away from her face and the remainder flowing freely down her back. "You are most welcome, my dear."

Zee caught his eyes and felt unnervingly naked for a moment. A mixture of excitement and repulsion spread through her. She was uncertain whether to feel flattered or targeted. Then she remembered who she had fantasized about that one time and instantly felt embarrassed. Zee willed herself to say something. The silence was becoming unnerving. She looked up as Barton took two steps towards her and laid a large hand on her forearm.

"Would you like a coffee?" she muttered quickly, removing her arm from his touch and turning towards the cupboards.

"Yes, please," Barton replied. "I would love that. Do you have a bit of whiskey to add some flavor to my coffee?"

"Of course," she replied, grasping the bottle of whiskey and pouring a splash into his coffee. "Would you like cream as well?"

"Yes, please."

She poured a rich dollop of cream into his coffee and added a touch of honey, handing the cup to him. "How much do I owe you for the flour?" she asked.

Barton chuckled. "Nothing, my dear. A beautiful woman like you deserves to be treated well. I am happy to be at your service." He grasped the coffee cup and took a sip. "You should have a whiskey cream coffee with me. It's absolutely delicious."

Zee eyed him suspiciously, wondering what it was that he wanted from her. Finally, she relented and told herself it was fine to enjoy the friendship of a gentleman. Maybe he didn't have any motives other than companionship. Zee pulled another cup from the cupboard. "I think I will have a whiskey coffee. Your drink does look scrumptious."

Barton watched her fluid movements and sipped his coffee silently. "You are a very beautiful woman, Zee," he commented his thoughts out loud. "I hope you don't mind me saying. Your husband is a very lucky man."

She stopped stirring her whiskey cream coffee and turned around with her hands on the counter. "It seems you have just been influenced heavily by my odd ways," she said, chuckling with a nervous smile. "I am grateful for your help, Barton, and maybe I am the lucky partner, who knows. My husband is a good man."

"Can I meet him?" Barton asked pointedly. "I would love to shake his hand."

"He is not here."

Barton drank the rest of the coffee in one gulp and placed down the cup. "For heaven's sake, why would a man not be at a hunting cabin with a wife as beautiful as you?" Barton asked sincerely.

"Long story," she replied coolly.

"Well," he responded. "I know marriages are complex. I've been through it myself." Barton sat on the curved leather sofa chair with the empty cup in his hand. "That coffee was delicious. May I have another?"

"Certainly," she replied courteously and grabbed the cup from his hand. "Would you like something to eat as well?" She unwrapped the bloody apron and placed it aside. Zee's peasant dress was a blue-grayish color and badly needed a wash. She immediately felt self-conscious. Zee wasn't expecting to have company today.

Barton's eyes followed her movements and the swish of her hips as she walked. The dress revealed what he had thought when he had first met her. The boy clothes had hidden a very feminine and beautiful woman.

Her large breasts were pushed up, revealing a creamy white neckline, and her hips churned with the dress's movements. For a moment, he had forgotten what she had asked. He would agree with anything this woman asked of him, he thought, chuckling to himself. "Yes, of course, that would be lovely," he replied, not certain what he was agreeing to.

Zee tilted her head and glanced at him quizzically. He was an odd man, she concluded. A handsome man, but quite odd. She ladled several scoops of stew into a bowl and placed two slices of bread beside it, then set it on the side table. "Enjoy," she stated, returning to the kitchen to prepare his second coffee.

"Oh my, that smells delicious," he commented, grabbing the bowl. "Join me."

Zee pursed her lips and ladled a small bowl for herself and sat with him. She was surprised to see that her coffee cup was also empty. They both ate stew in silence.

Barton hummed his appreciation and chomped down the bread and stew, eliciting several mumbles of gratitude. "You are a most wonderful cook!"

Zee laughed. "My family would say otherwise!"

"Well, I don't know why," he countered. "Your bread is fantastic, and the deer stew is tender and just what I needed." He finished the bowl and placed it back on the side table. He held his cup up for a toast. "A toast to our chance meeting. I am grateful for our acquaintance."

She lifted her cup, realizing it was empty, and stood up. "Hold that toast," she said. "I will refill my cup." She poured more whiskey, cream, and coffee into her cup and returned. "A toast to our chance meeting."

They clinked cups and both took large swigs. The alcohol smoothed her apprehensions and left her feeling more at ease with this odd man.

"How long have you been married?" he asked. "If you don't mind me asking. I never had the opportunity to have a long marriage. God had other plans."

"I'm so sorry about your wife," Zee responded. "I have been married for twenty years."

"Twenty years!" he exclaimed. "My goodness, that's a long time." Barton fell momentarily silent, doing the math on his hands. "That makes you my age! I am forty-two."

Zee chuckled, warmed by the whiskey in her blood. "Yes, I am forty."

"Another toast to us both!" he exclaimed.

They clinked their coffee cups and drank the remaining drops. "Another coffee?" she asked, chuckling.

"I would love that," he replied, watching her leave back into the kitchen. Her movements were mesmerizing. She had this aura of sensuality that was difficult not to notice. "Please make yourself another one too."

"I will definitely do that," she noted, mixing their coffees again with whiskey and cream.

"That deer stew was delicious!" Barton exclaimed, dabbing his lips with a napkin. "How many deer did your sons catch?"

"So far we've killed four deer, three rabbits, and five wild turkeys," she replied proudly. "We're going out again tomorrow!"

"You hunt with them?" he asked incredulously.

"Yes!" she replied instantly. "That's why I came out here!"

"To hunt?"

"Mostly to hunt," she replied happily. "But also, for other reasons."

"What other reasons?"

Zee pursed her lips uncomfortably. His questions were becoming intrusive, she noted. But the whiskey had loosened her tongue. "I just thought coming out here would help me recover who I once was."

"And who was that?"

"I was Zee Collard before I got married and became an Eastman," she replied, her story spilling out in a torrent. "I was a farm girl. I worked hard on the land and with the animals, becoming somewhat of an animal doctor. Then the War of 1812 happened, and I met my husband. We escaped into the wilderness and lived as hunters, raising all of our children in a cabin just like this."

"You are from Upper Canada?"

"Yes."

"And you married into the Eastman family?"

Zee paused. She had probably revealed too much to this strange gentleman. "I married my husband for love, not money," she replied, curious at the obvious change in Barton's manner. He started shifting his legs uncomfortably, and a frown was forming on his brows. "We lived in the Canadian wilderness for ten years," she continued. "Then we moved to Philadelphia, and that's when things started changing."

"Your husband changed?" Barton asked, folding his fingers in a tent over his chin.

Zee stopped to mull over the question. "I suppose he did change," she answered. "I never thought of it that way." She handed him his coffee and sipped her own. "I always thought we had both changed."

"Why did you change?"

"I had to," she replied quickly. "I was eager for the Eastmans to accept me. I was a farm girl, after all."

"A beautiful farm girl," Barton quickly added. He stood and moved into the kitchen, looking at the unfinished deer carcass still strewn all over the kitchen. "Did you need help with quartering up this deer?"

Zee returned to the kitchen, grabbed her apron, and put it back on, handing him a new one. "I would gladly accept the help," she answered quickly. Zee hefted the chopping knife and began slicing roasts and steaks, cutting through bone and muscle. "If you could wrap these up and place them in the cooler." She pointed behind them to a latch door in the floor.

"I could chop them for you," he stated questioningly.

Zee slammed the butcher knife through a thick portion of meat, and the roast thudded to the side. It was a very large knife, and she was not going to let a stranger get his hands on a knife in her household. "Thanks for the offer, but I am already dirty and I enjoy it," she smiled wickedly, showing her teeth.

Barton chuckled and wrapped several roasts. "Whatever you say, Mrs. Eastman," he said chidingly. "You're in charge here."

"Don't call me that," she retorted immediately.

"Call you what?"

"Mrs. Eastman," she said. "I hate that title. Just call me Zee."

"Okay, Zee," he stated calmly. "You're not happy with being married?"

Zee felt her blood run cold for a few moments. Was she miserable being married? Was it true? "I suppose after twenty long years, things change," she answered slowly. "I still love my husband, if that's what you're asking."

"Why didn't he come with you then?"

"You ask a lot of questions, Mr. Barton," she answered, wiping the bloody knife.

"I apologize," he replied quickly. "I just find myself captivated by your story. You're right, I shouldn't ask such personal questions."

She slammed the cleaver down onto another section of bone and muscle. This time, it got stuck halfway through the bone. She hefted the roast and slammed it down on the counter violently. The roast fell into two pieces. "I wanted to come out here to rediscover myself, Barton, that's all. I would have loved for my husband to come, but I knew he was too busy with his business affairs."

Barton chose to stay silent for a short while, wrapping another few roasts and then carrying them all towards the underground cooler. Zee rushed over and hefted the latch door open for him. Barton nodded and climbed down the ladder into the dark, cool storage area. He laid the roast on a shelf with the others and climbed back up, thoughts churning in his mind.

Barton returned to the table and wrapped the remaining roasts and steaks, helping Zee to clear up the final butchered meats. They drank two more whiskeys each and were beginning to feel the effects of the alcohol.

"Thank you so much for helping me with all this meat," Zee exclaimed. "I will give you a roast to return home with."

"That would be lovely, thank you," Barton replied, removing his apron and stepping closer to Zee. He was undeniably attracted to her. She was like a string of fire that just kept moving, dangerous and mesmerizing. His hand reached up to her chin, and her eyes met his.

Scott opened the side door and slapped three turkeys on the cleaned table. "Hi, Barton," he said. "I didn't see you arrive. What a nice surprise!"

Zee moved back from Barton and looked at the turkeys with a frown. "I just finished cleaning up the deer with Barton! Now I have another mess!"

"Well, maybe we can have some turkey for dinner for a change," James hollered as he walked inside with another two turkeys. "I will put these in the cooler, Momma." He walked past Barton and nodded politely. "Barton," he said. "Will you be having dinner with us?"

"I would love that."

Zee smiled. "I guess it's turkey for dinner tonight then."

♎

The night grew darker as the evening went on. Barton stretched out comfortably on the sofa, his long legs draping over the opposite edge. Zee watched him curiously as he chatted with her sons, engaging them in meaningful conversation. Scott and James were also falling under Barton's charismatic spell. Something inside Zee's heart told her to be wary, but she quickly stamped out the fear, rationalizing that they spent little time outside of the estate.

Scott stretched and stood. "Well, I'm going to bed," he said. "That was a delicious dinner, Momma." He turned his head, addressing Barton. "Will you be staying the night on the sofa? It is growing quite dark."

"If that is okay with you men," Barton replied politely. "I would appreciate that. It is not pleasant travelling in the darkness of night."

James nodded. "That's alright with me," he confirmed. "There are no other guest rooms here. I'll be going to bed as well. See you in the morning."

James and Scott walked down the hallway and disappeared to their rooms, leaving Zee and Barton alone.

Barton leaned forward and immediately grasped her hand. "I always dreamed of having a wife like you, Zee," he mumbled, his voice thick with sleep.

Zee bolted upright. She turned sharply and began busily loading up the plates to take into the kitchen when she felt his sudden grasp onto her waist.

"Wait," he said thickly. "I want to thank you for the wonderful evening." He quickly closed the distance between them and kissed her on the cheek.

Zee flinched and pulled away. "You are welcome, Barton," she replied, pausing. "Remember, Barton, I am a married woman. You must remain a gentleman or else we cannot be friends."

"It was just a kiss on the cheek."

Zee nodded, moving to the wash basin and began scrubbing dishes. She could feel him following, and her senses went on high alert.

Barton shuffled closer behind her. Something strange told him to stop, but he wasn't sure what it was. He had never experienced a woman like her before. She was beautiful, refined but yet willfully stubborn and dangerously savage with a knife. He took two more steps behind her and stopped. "I apologize," he calmly said. "I won't attempt to kiss you again. It was bad manners. You are a happily married woman after all."

She turned her head halfway with her hands still in the sink. Her blue eye glared at him in the darkened room.

"I don't understand you, Zee," Barton said, clearly confused at the sudden change in Zee's behavior. "You are the most complex woman that I think I have ever met." He let his hands go slack to his sides. "Why would your husband discard you like this? It is beyond my comprehension."

She twirled around instantly, with a wet utensil still in her right hand hidden behind her back. "My husband did not discard me!" she seethed, an angry frown creasing her brow. "I walked away for a few weeks. That's all, nothing more and nothing less. My husband is a good man, and I love him dearly."

Barton stepped back and stood firmly rooted to the floor, a curious change happening across his face. He grinned, then almost chuckled at her. Finally, his grin faded, and his previous demeanor returned. "I am most grateful for your hospitality tonight, Zee Collard," he said, deliberately slow. "I am sorry if I offended you. It was not intentional." He turned and walked quickly towards the sofa, then lay down fully, stretching his legs. "If you could be kind enough to bring me a blanket, that would be most considerate of you."

Zee watched his every move, then gradually released the sharp knife in her hand back into the sink. "I will get you a blanket," she muttered, almost angrily. "After I am done cleaning up. Good night and sleep well, Barton."

♎︎

Barton had left in the early morning hours, before anyone in the house had even awakened. Zee padded into the kitchen and looked around at the large open room to make sure everything was in its normal place. The small pistol she held in her hand was cool to the touch. She couldn't understand why she felt so defensive around Barton sometimes. He was a gentleman who truly enjoyed her company. Even her sons got along with him quite easily. She blinked rapidly and felt tears moisten her eyes as a sudden rush of emotion filled her heart.

Barton had said that Jesse had discarded her.

She knew it wasn't true, but the words still stung.

Barton didn't know anything about her and Jesse. He was just a lonely widower looking for female companionship. His comments about her relationship were idle observations from a lonely man.

Zee lifted her chin up and wrapped a thin coat over her body. She walked to the door and pulled on a pair of boots. She slipped the small pistol into her coat and stepped out into the fresh morning air. Zee immediately checked to see that Barton's wagon and horse were gone. She then settled down into a large wooden chair on the front porch.

She stared out at the rising sun and wished Jesse could return to being the man whom she had fallen in love with so many years ago. She knew it was an impossible request. Jesse would never be twenty years old again. They would never live in Upper Canada again. Their lives had become interwoven, and so many things had changed over the years. Even Zee was not the same woman.

The clouds parted and revealed the sun glowing over the horizon. It was 6 am. Barton had left in a hurry, she mused. She was glad he left. Zee was feeling very defensive after his remarks about her marriage. She mused whether, deep down, she really did feel discarded.

Maybe something would change soon. Maybe Jesse and her just needed a change.

A horse whinnied in the distance.

Zee sat up, the pistol in her pocket ready. If Barton came back forcefully, she would shoot him. Zee's brows frowned determinedly, and finally she stood with her right hand in her pocket, gripping the pistol.

The horse galloped closer and closer. But it had no wagon, just a lone rider. It wasn't Barton. It was someone else. Could it be Jesse? She loosened her grip on the pistol.

The rider came more and more into view and, sadly, it wasn't Jesse.

It was Bemidii.

Zee smiled, stepped off the porch, and approached Bemidii as he held out an invitation. "Hello again, Mrs. Zee! Your presence is requested at the wedding of Georgina Eastman and Jeremiah Williams."

Zee grasped the note and opened it. It read:

To my beautiful wife,

Georgina is getting married at the end of this week! I need your help to organize the wedding, guest lists, food, and everything.

I also miss you.

Please come home for a few days.

Love,

Jesse Eastman

Happy tears fell from her eyes, and she looked up at Bemidii. "Tell Jesse that I will return home today for a few days. I will bring lots of deer meat for the wedding." She reached out and hugged Bemidii. "Go on!" she instructed happily.

"Do you want me to escort you all back?" Bemidii asked politely.

"No, it won't be necessary," she responded. "I would rather that you travelled back and let Jesse know that we are on our way."

"Yes, ma'am!" Bemidii circled his horse and left for the long journey back to the estate.

Zee turned on her heel and rushed back into the house. "Scott! James! Get up! We're going home for a wedding!"

CHAPTER 13

Georgina and Jeremiah kissed under the flowered archway. They both smiled as the pastor declared them husband and wife. Turning towards all the guests, they beamed proudly, and the crowd cheered. Over fifty people had attended. All of the Eastman family and relatives were present, as well as half the congregation of the Baptist church. Georgina felt her heart burst with joy. Jeremiah was the man whom she had dreamed of her entire life, and most importantly, Jesse approved.

Georgina grasped Jeremiah's hand lightly and walked into the crowd of well-wishers. Flower petals and rice landed on their heads for good luck and fertility. Almost every relative and friend were throwing handfuls of the confetti. Georgina smiled and eyed Jesse standing with Zee near the front. She had originally thought Zee and the twins couldn't come because the wedding plans were such a rushed surprise to everyone. Georgina and Jeremiah had agreed to marry by the end of the week. Georgina's pregnancy wouldn't wait much longer without people noticing.

Jesse smiled and walked behind the couple with the rest of the immediate family as they ventured out of the church into an awaiting carriage. The reception dinner and dance would be held at the estate, with local musicians. Jesse and Zee had successfully put together a quick celebration for the wedding. He was thrilled that Zee had returned home so quickly. Jesse kept his hand wound around her waist, like he might lose her if he let go. The joy of seeing her return filled him with a loving glow that he hadn't felt in close to a decade. He leaned over and kissed her cheek, whispering in her ear. "You look absolutely stunning, my dear."

"Thank you," she replied, beaming.

"I hope Georgina loves her surprise wedding gift," he added.

"Oh," Zee replied, grinning. "You know she will, my dear."

They all watched as Jeremiah helped Georgina into the awaiting carriage. The crowd cheered as the newlyweds left to the reception.

Once the carriage started lumbering further down the street, Jesse and Zee leapt onto their horses and rode ahead, aiming to reach the estate in plenty of time.

As the air rushed past him and his horse kept pace with Zee's, his heart leapt with love. Jesse was thrilled that Zee was here, and his heart melted every time he laid eyes on her. She had stayed for five days so far organizing everything. Scott and James attended the hastily planned wedding, also. Only one more day, then they'd all be leaving back to the hunting cabin. Jesse was glad to see all the relatives in one place. But most of all, he was completely smitten with his wife. He had barely left her side. Every day, he grasped her waist, whispered in her ear, and kissed her freely. She was the light in his soul, and he wondered why he had left it to dim for so many years.

Something began to change profoundly inside Jesse. His heart burst with joy when she had prepared everything for the wedding, and he couldn't take his eyes off of her. She was dressed in a pink gown with hidden riding britches underneath! He chuckled to himself. That was his wife, the spunky woman he remembered.

The entire day had taken on a dreamlike quality. Jesse felt like his life was shifting in a different direction. When he had witnessed Georgina's heart filled with new love and happiness, something changed inside of him.

Jesse wanted that same uplifting feeling of love back in his life. He wanted his wife back and his marriage fixed. Jesse whispered to himself that he would do everything possible from this day forward. Earlier in the week, he had already begun training Janey, Xavier, and Joshua with the daily operations of the business. But somehow, in his heart, he knew it was still not enough. He needed to somehow fix the emotional and physical divide that had become wedged between himself and Zee. There were many years of neglect, and he had to accept his involvement with this. But there was something else, too.

Jesse felt that he needed to woo Zee again. His heart somehow demanded it. As he galloped back to the estate with Zee trailing behind him, Jesse's mind ventured off into a thousand different directions on how to win her back.

The rolling hills of Pennsylvania glittered in the distance with a bright, moist green halo, as if telling him everything would be alright. He glanced back to ensure Zee was still following safely. Zee's riding figure looked like an angel as the morning mist settled around her and billowed with every gallop. He smiled at her and continued on at a good speed.

The scenery became smaller and smaller as they both travelled closer to the Atlantic Ocean. It reminded him of the day so many decades ago when he had journeyed back from the Northwest, starving and his body badly battered from living in the wilderness with the Overland Astorians.

He shook his head. 1811 was a long time ago. Back then, Jesse didn't think he would live to see another day.

But instead, he had grown into a man, fought in a war, fell in love with a beautiful woman, had a family of his own, and then returned to rescue the Eastman Empire from ruin. He had accomplished all of this in the last twenty years, with his wife by his side.

Jesse glanced back again and gazed at his lovely wife. She was riding confidently on her horse, holding the reins tightly and lurching forward.

He had to believe that he could win her back and change the direction his life was taking.

His future depended on it.

♎

The dinner reception was a lovely gathering of relatives, friends, and good food. After dinner, Jesse stood and spoke to the gathering.

"As everyone knows, Georgina has been my half-sister and confidant since I could remember, as a small child." Jesse gestured towards Georgina and waved around the room. "We were born only six months apart, so we grew up very close within a strained family. We often hid our childhood play games from our parents in fear of the racist slurs that so often plagued families during that time." Jesse gestured for Georgina to stand and smiled broadly. "I am proud of you, Georgina."

Georgina stood and tried folding her hands together, but began involuntarily reaching up to her eyes, dabbing the imminent tears. Her voice felt choked up, and her emotions threatened to let go at any moment. All she could do was nod.

"You have been a wonderful sister, servant, and a valuable asset to the Eastman Estate household." Jesse rummaged his fingers in his pocket aimlessly. "I wish in all my heart that you could continue to supervise the household staff, because, honestly, I do not know of anyone who could take your place." Jesse smiled and tapped Zee on the shoulder, nodding. Zee rose and took his hand on cue. She smiled mischievously. Zee had helped Jesse finalize the plans for the wedding gift. It was a miraculous feat, considering the magnitude of the gift, that they had managed to keep the whole thing a secret.

Jesse and Zee pulled their chairs out and walked around the table to Georgina, as Jeremiah shifted in his chair. The entire room was hushed, curious about what was happening.

"I knew that one day, Georgina," Jesse stated as he drew near. "You would find a husband and a life of your own." He stopped and gazed emotionally into his sister's eyes. "And now, here we are." Jesse waved Jeremiah to stand.

As Jeremiah stood, his height dwarfed everyone, but it was his demeanor that mattered the most. He held his head high with a kind tilt to his head and a gentle smile. "Jesse," he started.

Jesse interrupted him. "Jeremiah, you are everything a brother would want for his sister to marry," Jesse said, as he reached out his hand for a handshake.

Jeremiah grasped his hand strongly. "You are a good man, Jesse."

Jesse nodded and stepped back, turning his attention back to Georgina. "My sister," he started. "I have a gift for you. A gift for your wedding that I know you will cherish and enjoy forever." Jesse rummaged in his pocket again as Zee beamed with a huge co-conspirator smile.

Georgina seemed confused and glanced around for the mysterious giftbox, wondering what was going on. Jeremiah was equally confused.

"Forgive me," Jesse stated. "I could not wrap it or bring it here. It is too big."

Georgina frowned in puzzlement, then smiled jokingly. "What have you done, Jesse?"

He played with the item in his pocket and began to pull it out. "Hopefully, I have made your future a bit brighter," he said, pulling out the object in his palm.

Georgina watched in astonishment at the item in his hands. Her puzzlement grew into confusion, then awareness as she began guessing at what it could mean.

Jesse dangled the keys from his fingers and hung them up for everyone to see. "These are the keys to your new home."

Georgina gasped in surprise, and both hands flew to her gaping mouth. "Oh my Lord, Jesse!"

Jesse handed the keys to Georgina as she gently grasped them in her hands.

"It is the property next to the estate down the hill towards the market," Jesse stated. "It is a small house, but it has four acres of land and plenty of space for your future family." Jesse nodded and grasped Zee's hand tightly. "The beginnings are tough. I know, Zee and I experienced it too. We lived in nothing but a hand-built log home for ten years. But we were happy, very happy." He kissed Zee on the cheek and then focused his attention back on Georgina.

Georgina was weeping fully now. Tears streamed down her face and dropped onto her gown. She tried wiping the tears, but it was futile. She tried speaking, but what came out was little more than a choked-up sob. "Jesse."

Jesse reached over and hugged Georgina warmly, whispering in her ear. "I want you to have a good start."

Georgina managed to speak. "Thank you, Jesse."

"Thank you for being a loyal member of this family since day one," Jesse replied. "It's the least I could do."

Jeremiah reached out and shook Jesse's hand. "I won't disappoint you, Mr. Eastman. I love Georgina deeply."

'I know you do," Jesse replied.

$$\Omega$$

The night was over, and Zee was exhausted. After the trip back home and the rush to find a gown, then organizing all the food and cooking, it was all she could do to keep an eye open. But the energy she felt in her heart made her feel hopeful for the future.

Something was changing with her husband. Jesse was attentive, and his hands had been all over her for two days. Tomorrow she would return back to the cabin, and she didn't want to go, but they still needed to collect the remainder of the meat and bring it all home. Jesse had told her about Janey, Xavier, and Joshua taking over, and she was thrilled that something tangible was actually happening.

She began to realize that Jesse felt the same way as her! He didn't want to live at the Eastman estate anymore. He had never wanted to!

Her heart fluttered with desire as the door to her room clicked open.

Jesse stood there in his nightclothes and soundlessly clicked the door shut behind him. "My beautiful wife," he whispered provocatively.

Zee's heart hammered in her chest at the sight of Jesse in his nightclothes. He was still the most beautiful man in the world to her. His hair had thinned, and he had wrinkles on the sides of his eyes, but all she saw was the man she had met 20 years ago. "My handsome Jesse," she responded, her voice thick with desire.

Jesse took two large strides and scooped her up effortlessly in his arms. "You are the same woman I married twenty years ago, and my love has never wavered," he whispered, then kissed her lips, walking towards her large bed.

Zee's eyes twinkled, and her heart melted at his words. "Jesse," she replied simply, any coherent thoughts no longer coming to her brain.

"I'm going to make love to you," he whispered, a grin creasing his face. "I will be gentle, but I will make love to you all night. Over and over again. Just like I used to."

As he laid her down on the bed, Zee's mind crumbled into a hormonal mess. "Yes," she moaned.

He removed her nightgown gently and pulled down her undergarments, revealing her pale flesh. Her breasts glittered in the moonlight, and his penis grew rigid at the sight. He spread her legs and ran his hands lightly along her inner thighs, edging her legs even further.

Zee grasped the pillow behind her with one hand and stretched her body out to greet him. Her hips involuntarily arced upwards, and an intense warmth spread throughout her entire body. Her blood raced into her groin, and she shivered in anticipation.

"It's been too long, my dear," he said thickly. "You're my angel of desire." He lowered his head and kissed her inner thigh. "You are my dessert, my craving, my everything." He kissed her opposite thigh as her hips involuntarily twitched towards him. "Even your skin tastes like honey."

Zee whimpered and lost all of her coherent thoughts. "Please," she pleaded.

Jesse danced his fingers lightly over her vagina, brushing the sensitive skin. He moved his fingers under her buttocks and squeezed lightly. Her body convulsed in his grasp as little whimpers escaped from her lips. "I will be gentle like I promised," he murmured, kissing her intimate lady parts gently, driving her mad with desire.

She writhed and grasped his shoulders, wanting more. "Please, Jesse," she pleaded. "I can't take it. I need you inside me."

Jesse smiled. "I am going to take my time, sweetheart," he murmured. "Every touch, every taste." He kissed her hip and gently moved his lips down her leg, licking her skin lightly. "You are my dessert tonight."

Zee cried out in desire. "I don't need you to be gentle. I need you to take my body and claim it. Make me your wife again, just like you used to."

"I don't want to hurt you."

Zee opened her eyes and gazed down at Jesse. "Jesse, look at me," she said slowly. "You don't need to treat me like I'm fragile. I am not."

"But the miscarriages," he mumbled uncertainly.

"You won't cause another miscarriage," she replied. "Just pull out when you're ready."

Jesse raised his head up, a dawn of understanding coming over him. "It's that simple?"

"Well," she replied. "We can certainly try."

Jesse smiled. "I will do whatever you wish, my sweet." He kissed her vagina lightly and stepped back, pulling down his night pants.

Zee watched in a trance as his penis jumped out, rigid and glistening at the tip. She licked her lips. "Jesse," she pleaded again. "Please, I need you now."

Jesse stared at her pale body stretched out on the bed. Her nipples were rigid, and her vagina was already glistening with moisture. He could smell her. It was an exquisite smell. "You smell so good." He pulled his shirt off and stripped completely naked. "My beautiful wife," he murmured as he lowered himself on top of her, his weight satisfyingly pressing onto her hips.

Zee moaned and wrapped her arms lightly around his back, pulling him to her. "I can't wait any longer," she pleaded. "It's been too long, Jesse. Please now. Enter me now." She shuddered with anticipation. "Please."

Jesse propped his elbows up beside her shoulders and gazed down at her face. "I love you," he mumbled and kissed her full lips. The taste of honey flowed onto his lips as her tongue suddenly entered his mouth urgently. He groaned and began sucking on her tongue hard. His hand fluttered down to her vagina as he inserted a finger into her wetness. She moaned underneath him, and the sound reverberated into his mouth. His penis grew painfully rigid, and he knew it was time. He arched his back briefly and positioned his hips above her entrance, guiding his penis with only his hip movements. The moistness touched his penis, and he felt momentarily like he would lose control right away. He sighed and began kissing her again.

She writhed towards him urgently, her hips pushing upwards.

"My sweet," he said thickly, smiling. "You missed me."

Zee exhaled heavily and moaned out the words. "Yes!"

Jesse pushed down with one gentle thrust, and his penis poked into her entrance. He stopped and kissed her lips again, gazing into her eyes. "You will tell me if it hurts?" he asked.

"Yes, I will," she replied quickly. "I promise."

Jesse slid slowly inside her, inch by inch, eliciting groans from his own throat as well as hers. Her vagina gripped him and moistened his penis as he continued the deliberately slow action of penetration. "Zee," he groaned into her lips as he pressed his penis fully into her. He felt his penis throb with excitement and tried to calm his mind as he slowly reversed for another thrust. He slid back into her again, the wetness leaking out onto his scrotum. Jesse inhaled roughly, trying to control his orgasm. It was all he could do to keep from ejaculating. He stopped at her entrance and exhaled.

"Don't stop," she begged, pushing her hips forward.

His penis glided back into her wetness again. Jesse groaned with frustration as he felt his imminent orgasm threaten to explode. He tried breathing and refocusing, but nothing would work. She was right, it had been too long since they last had sex.

Jesse groaned heavily. "Honey," he cried, pulling out instantly. His penis jerked and suddenly ejaculated everywhere. The cum shot onto her stomach, her breasts, and even the tip of her chin. Jesse grasped his penis to try to stop the ejaculation, but it was of no use. His penis had a mind of its own now. Another spray hit her stomach as he shuddered and knelt above her. "I'm so sorry," he mumbled. "It's been too long."

Zee smiled wickedly at the explosion scattered all over her body. She gazed up at him while he held his twitching penis. "I love it," she chuckled, dipping her fingers in the creamy white trail. She swirled her fingers in it, then was suddenly gripped by mischievousness. Zee licked her lips and sucked on her wet fingers, one by one. "You are my dessert now," she chuckled playfully.

Jesse watched her in a trance for several minutes as she licked up everything. His penis miraculously began growing again at the sight. He touched himself to test whether he was still sensitive and noticed that his penis was ready again. "My dirty lady," he mumbled and grabbed her hips, tossing her body to the side.

He bent her right leg, tossing it over her left leg, then wrapped his arm under her waist, gripping her in a full spoon hug. Jesse grasped his penis and thrusted into her vagina from behind, sliding effortlessly into her wetness. He rhythmically thrust into her, full of renewed energy and stamina. He circled his right hand around her and rubbed the top of her vagina, massaging the hard nub until her legs began to vibrate. He kept the steady rhythm until she hastily took over and began rubbing herself.

Jesse grabbed her hips and continued his steady thrusts into her vagina as sudden yelps of pleasure erupted from Zee's mouth.

Her breathing changed into heavy gasps of rising desire until they reached a crescendo, and a final long moan released from her mouth. "Jesse!" she cried with pleasure. "Oh my Lord! Yes!"

Jesse felt a gush of wetness release onto his penis, his scrotum, and everywhere. But he was relentless with his thrusts, not missing a beat. The moisture slapped between their bodies as he continued driving his penis into her lake of wetness.

Zee writhed and squirmed as another orgasm gripped her. Jesse didn't change his rhythm, nothing. The thrusts continued like a drum of his favorite song. He would not stop until he claimed her again and again.

Finally, his orgasm felt imminent, and he pulled out just in time again. His penis erupted and sprayed all over her buttocks, like a geyser. He watched as her buttocks jiggled and gently squeezed one as his cum emptied onto her body. He shivered and collapsed beside her.

His breathing slowed as he let his muscles melt in the moment. Sweat dripped from his forehead, and his brain felt slightly foggy. He relaxed his grip on her and kissed her shoulder, hugging her from behind. He aimlessly licked her ear as her body continued shaking from the fading orgasms. "I'm not done yet," he whispered in her ear lovingly. "I need a little sleep, then I will love you again and again."

She turned and faced him. Her chest was flushed, and her hair was a grand mess. She smiled and kissed him slowly. She turned fully around and faced him. "Are you making up for lost time?" she teased.

"No," he replied, snuggling her into his chest. "I'm just reclaiming my beautiful wife."

$$\Omega$$

The morning came too quickly, and the caravan was leaving back to the cabin to pick up the remaining deer meat. Jesse watched as Zee and his twin sons left the estate grounds. He wanted to go with them, but was forced to stay for the possession date of Georgina's new house purchase.

As he watched his wife turn to wave goodbye happily, Jesse pondered what it was that kept him from telling her they were moving back to the Lake Huron cabin next year. It may have been a mixture of intense pleasure clouding his mind and a bit of jealousy.

He had asked what she had been up to since she had been gone. Zee had mysteriously responded that they were just hunting mostly. Normally, Zee would include details of their trips to others and use her delightful, colorful language to pepper the conversation. But this time, she hadn't said much. Just hunting.

Jesse stood and waved back at her. After twenty years, he trusted her decisions. Although something still gnawed at him. An intuition, maybe that things still weren't entirely right? Or just a pang of jealousy? He didn't know, but it bothered him to feel like this.

They had the most wonderful sex last night, and his body was satisfied completely. His heart and faith in his marriage were restored.

He no longer wore suits. Jesse had made the decision this morning to wear only his working shirts, riding pants, and leather boots. His hair had begun growing, and his wide-brimmed hat perfectly hid his thinning hair on top. The longer tufts of hair stuck out on the sides, framing his handsome, bearded face. But most importantly, he felt on top of the world.

But something was still wrong. Jesse could feel it.

Jesse turned on his right foot and headed back into the estate, his leather boots tapping soundlessly on the marble floor. He passed by a hallway mirror and saw his reflection. He stopped and analyzed himself. The sandy brown leather boots matched the color of his hat, and his dark hair sticking out of the sides of the hat somehow framed his chiseled jawline. He surprised himself. He looked good.

He was a unique man, Jesse knew this. There weren't many other men like him, if any. There was a time in his life when he was a wild, untamed man. He had changed into a different man over the years, without even knowing it. He needed to reclaim himself, just like Zee was doing.

He stuffed his hands in his front pockets and sauntered through the mansion, planning what he was going to do next.

Chapter 14

They arrived back at the cabin several days later, and Zee was exhausted from all the travelling. Her thighs and buttocks still ached in that wonderful way after sex. Her heart fluttered with love and hormones. She felt much better about her marriage and felt torn about going back to the hunting cabin. They were only here for a few more days to pack up everything and bring it back. They had even brought two extra packhorses.

Zee removed her clothes and washed herself by the washstand. The water had been warmed, and the washcloth felt soft on her skin. She cleaned her face, breasts, and her lady parts. She mused about her conversations with Jesse and why she had omitted any talk of Barton.

She knew that she wanted to deal with this mess herself. Zee Eastman was a strong, grown woman, and she would eradicate Barton from her life by herself. It wasn't a huge task, she told herself. She didn't want to trouble Jesse with this silly business. He had other, more important things to deal with. Zee looked down and finished cleansing her vagina as a wave of memories of her husband rushed to her brain.

A satisfied sigh escaped from her lips as she put down the washcloth.

Zee wrapped a dry towel around her waist and began rubbing herself dry.

A sudden distant noise sounded through the log walls. It was like there was some kind of movement outside. Zee quickly pulled the nightgown over her head nervously and let it fall loosely over her sides. She peered through the window. Her eyes searched the blackness and couldn't find anything abnormal. The night was silent. She must be hearing things, she mused.

Zee knelt softly on the floor at her bed and placed her palms together in prayer.

"Please, God, ensure that I do not get pregnant," she prayed aloud. "And thank you for everything. I'm so happy that Jesse and I are back to being a loving husband and wife. I don't know if the way we made love will work, but please, I beg you, let this method produce no pregnancies. I desperately need to feel intimacy with my husband. I cannot live without it." She paused, trying to form her next words. "I don't know what Jesse is planning, but let it be a happy future for us. I don't want to live at the estate anymore. I love Jesse, but the estate suffocates me. Give me the courage to find a better way, for me and my husband."

Zee nodded her head down in silent prayer, then lightly said, "Amen."

She straightened and then climbed into bed, her head swirling with thoughts. Jesse had made love to her two more times that night, and it was the most wonderful physical sensation to be loved like that. He had set out to reclaim her, and he did exactly that.

He still confused her though. He had told her about his eventual retirement from the Eastman Empire, but talked about it being a year away from now. Zee understood that he still needed to be involved for the smooth transition, although he hadn't mentioned what would happen after that year was finished.

He had simply mentioned that things would get much better in one year. Then he asked her to trust him.

Of course, she trusted him!

It was ridiculous to think otherwise. But it still left her bewildered about their future. If she knew more, then she might feel better about living at the estate for another year. But if he wanted her to remain living at the estate with him permanently, then she would need to somehow tell him that she just couldn't do it.

Tears escaped from Zee's eyes as she considered moving back to Upper Canada to the Collard farm. Even though she would love to see her sisters, brothers, and nephews, Zee felt that it would spell the end of her marriage.

She didn't want that.

Zee wanted her husband back and their old life back. But was it possible?

She didn't know.

Her eyes began to flutter closed when she heard a slight knock at the front door. At first, she thought it was her imagination, but then she heard it again. Zee bolted up in bed. She had retired early to bed, so it was still only 9:30 pm, but who would be knocking at this hour?

Zee pulled on a nightcoat and rushed towards her bedroom door. She opened it soundlessly and peered into the main living area as Scott suddenly stomped angrily to the front door.

The door opened, and Barton stood there with flowers.

Scott glared at him angrily. "It is quite late for you to be dropping by."

"I apologize," Barton said. "I was worried and just wanted to know that everyone had gotten back alright." He peered into the main living area, searchingly. "Is Zee here?"

"My mother has already retired to bed, Barton," Scott responded stonily.

"Oh, I see," Barton replied. "It is still early, so I thought maybe she would still be up."

Scott moved the door a fraction of an inch and squared his chest. "She's tired from the trip. Come back tomorrow."

His brother, James, appeared in the hallway with a rifle. "What's going on?" he barked angrily. "Who is at the door?"

Barton glared at the rifle and frowned. "Not to worry. It is only me, Barton. I was checking to see that your mother had returned safely. No need to murder me in cold blood." He turned to leave and shot an angry glance at James. "I will be on my way." Barton threw the flowers down onto the floor. "Give those to your mother."

Scott kicked the flowers inside and closed the door, latching the locking arm across.

James lowered the rifle. "What was all that about?" he asked.

'I don't know," Scott answered, picking up the flowers and laying them on the table.

Zee watched in the dark from the crack of her bedroom door, and a chill ran up her spine. It took thirty minutes to travel from Buffalo to the cabin. How did Barton know they had arrived back? Did he have people on the trail watching them?

She turned her head towards the window and suddenly didn't feel safe. Was Barton following her? Had he been watching her clean herself?

A moment of indecisiveness crossed her mind, and she now wished that she had told Jesse about Barton. Her sons had spoken about Barton in casual conversation, but Zee never elaborated. She now doubted her decision to keep silent. Maybe she was wrong, and the situation had grown out of her control. She was a strong woman, but not stronger than a fully grown man.

Zee frowned and wished Jesse was here. She should have told him about the nervous close encounters she had with Barton. She should have let Jesse know all about her fears.

A tendril of worry snaked through her nerves. Zee was afraid that she had underestimated Barton's tenacity. She inhaled deeply and walked to the closet, loading her pistol quietly. She padded lightly back to the bed and stuffed the pistol under the opposite pillow. Then she lay down to sleep.

♎

Jeremiah and many of the church members helped Georgina move into their new home. Jesse had signed the purchase documents, and everything was legal. They had their own home! Jeremiah was delighted.

The day was filled with moving furniture and wooden boxes. Georgina had a lifetime of household goods to move.

"My dear," Jeremiah exclaimed jokingly. "I had no idea that you had so much stuff!"

"I have lived here my entire life!" Georgina shot back. "Besides, our new home is only a few acres away."

"That is true," Jeremiah agreed.

"I have instructed the cooks to bring us over some dinner," Georgina mentioned.

"That's wonderful," Jeremiah responded. "I look forward to getting settled into our new home."

A burly church member grabbed one of the boxes and smiled at them. "Congratulations to you both!"

Georgina turned. "Pastor Brown!" she exclaimed. "How lovely for you to join us in moving to our lovely new home!"

Jeremiah shook the pastor's hand enthusiastically. "I had no idea you were here helping!" Jeremiah shouted. "I would have offered you something."

"Don't you worry about that. I just arrived, Jeremiah," Pastor Brown replied. "I am here to help my followers in Christ."

Georgina hugged the pastor warmly. "We are grateful for your assistance! We couldn't have done all this without the congregation's help," she said, gesturing to the crowd of people volunteering. "However can we repay you? If there is anything we can do in return, please let us know!"

"That won't be necessary," Pastor Brown replied. He hefted a wooden box full of canned goods. "Where do you want this?"

"Just put it on one of the wagons, along with the rest of the items," Jeremiah answered. "There are four wagons awaiting in the front. Wherever it fits is fine with me." He grabbed a box and showed Pastor Brown the way. "Just follow me." It was a long walk to the front of the estate. Georgina's suite was an entire separate addition to the right of the sprawling mansion. Jeremiah and Pastor Brown walked along the pathway leading to the front. The flowers and manicured bushes along the way reminded him of what a lovely improvement he had been to the Eastman Estate. He had worked tirelessly, trimming and re-sculpting the entire yard. Now, it was just the monumental task of maintaining the grounds.

"What a lovely pathway!" Pastor Brown acknowledged. "Look at all these beautiful flowers, and the bushes are so eloquently trimmed! A modern paradise."

"I did all that," Jeremiah commented quietly, trying not to sound too boastful.

"You did all of this?"

"Yes," Jeremiah replied proudly. "Gardening has always been a passion of mine." He stepped down several stone steps towards the entrance. "Helping God's beauty to flourish is my purpose in life, one might say."

"Well, you certainly do a wonderful job at that!" Pastor Brown exclaimed. "Mr. Eastman must be so grateful."

"Mr. Eastman is a good man," Jeremiah stated. "He pays me well, and I get to do what I enjoy. You can't ask for much more than that in life." He guided the pastor through many twists and turns in the flowered pathway until finally they emerged facing the long expanse of the front gardens. A melody of bushes, small trees, and flower gardens dotted the landscape. "As you can see, I have much work to do just to maintain everything."

"Yes, I see!" Pastor Brown replied. "Keep in mind, that you must store some of that energy for your new home and your family now."

"Have you seen the new house yet?" Jeremiah asked, his eyes glowing with pride. He pointed in the distance towards the wide road.

"No, I have not," Brown replied, shielding his eyes from the strong summer sun. "Is that the house over there?"

"Yes!" Jeremiah stated. "Let me take you! The first wagon is already full. You can ride with us." Jeremiah placed the boxes on the second wagon and gestured for the pastor to join him.

Georgina bounded down the walkway with several bags over her shoulders. "Hold on!" she shouted. "I need to go with you! I have some clothes I need to bring to my new room!"

"Hop on, sweetheart," Jeremiah replied and patted the seat between the pastor and himself. He grabbed the bags from her shoulders and helped her up onto the riding seat. After a few moments, he snapped the reins lightly, urging the horses to move, and the trio slowly lumbered towards the new William's family home. The wagon ride was rougher than he would've liked. "Are you okay, my sweetheart?" he asked Georgina, his eyes showing concern for the baby inside his wife's belly. "How are you feeling?"

"Everything is fine, Jeremy," Georgina smiled, her face lighting up with a pregnancy glow. They didn't want to tell anyone of the pregnancy yet, afraid of people finding out that the marriage was consummated before the ceremony. "Don't worry." She placed a gentle hand on his arm as the wagon pulled them towards the curved road.

They all sat in reflective silence, jostling with the wagon as the large horses pulled the group. It was a hot summer day, and they all soon began to sweat. Georgina wiped her brow and tried piling up her hair into a bun. Within minutes, they were halfway down the road.

Pastor Brown pointed at the white house down the road. "Is that it?" he shouted exuberantly.

"Yes!" Georgina replied happily. "It is the quaint family home that I have always dreamed of."

"You deserve it, Georgina," Pastor Brown stated as the horses pulled them closer to the front entrance of the white wooden house. "I'm excited for you both. You must show me your new home."

When they were close enough, Jeremiah stopped the horses and climbed out, holding his hand out for his wife. She disembarked as the pastor jumped out on the other side. "Grab a box, Pastor!" Jeremiah slung all three of Georgina's bags over his shoulders and grabbed a lighter box, handing it to the pastor. "We can move some items in as we show you the house!"

The pastor accepted the proffered box as Jeremiah grabbed a heavier box for himself. Georgina tried to grab a box, but Jeremiah stopped her. "I don't want you carrying too many things, my sweet. Just put it on top of my box."

Georgina didn't argue and just happily led the way into the house. She swung the front door open, and they all entered, standing in the large foyer. The interior was scattered with a few random pieces of furniture, and boxes were piled up by the door. "Let's put these items in the kitchen, and I will show you my very own cooking area!"

Pastor Brown followed as the couple initiated a tour of the new house.

Georgina showed him the new wood stove and marbled cooking counters. "You must see this!" she smiled gleefully, waving them towards the latch door. "Not too many houses have such a large cellar! You must see this! I am so excited."

Jeremiah lifted the heavy wooden floor door up, and a waft of cool air emerged into the kitchen. "She's right. You have to see this!" Jeremiah gestured for the pastor to join them in the cellar.

Georgina went first, climbing down backwards on the newly replaced wooden ladder. "It is the best part of our new home!" she exclaimed happily.

The pastor followed down into the cellar. "Oh my! This is larger than I expected!"

Lastly, Jeremiah climbed down. It was a large area, spanning over 20 feet in each direction. Several shelves dotted one wall, and the other wall had several supporting beams keeping everything stable. It was very cool and a perfect room to preserve different foods. "Isn't it wonderful? Georgina loves this the most about the house," Jeremiah added.

"It is the biggest cellar I have ever seen in such a small house like this!" Georgina exclaimed.

Pastor Brown walked around the large room curiously, inspecting the supporting beams. "This is almost a livable space!" He turned around to face them with a strange, enquiring look on his face.

"It is!" Georgina smiled delightfully. "And you wouldn't even know!"

Pastor Brown quietly ran his hand along the stone walls, something obviously going through his mind. "This is over 20 feet!"

"Yes, it is," Jeremiah confirmed. "Before us, the property was owned by wine enthusiasts. They had grown some vines and started to produce their own wine."

Georgina frowned and wondered what the pastor was thinking as he inspected the stone walls. "What do you think, Pastor Brown?"

Pastor Brown slowly turned to Georgina and Jeremiah, with a thousand thoughts swirling through his mind. His black eyes glittered in the darkness of the cellar. He gently approached Georgina and grasped her hand, then grasped Jeremiah's hand as well. "You both are truly blessed to have such a large hidden space like this."

Georgina and Jeremiah looked at one another, clearly confused by the pastor's intense interest in the cellar.

"Jeremiah," the pastor stated slowly. "You had both mentioned earlier, if there was anything you could do for the church." His voice trailed off.

"Of course!" Jeremiah interrupted. "Anything to repay for the congregation's help."

Pastor Brown looked from Jeremiah to Georgina, then his eyes settled back on Jeremiah. "Does Georgina know about your origins, Jeremiah?"

Jeremiah coughed slightly and hugged Georgina. "Yes, she knows how I arrived in Philadelphia, Pastor Brown. She is supportive, understanding, and a wonderful woman."

Pastor Brown lowered his voice and looked around at the empty room. He addressed Georgina. "So, you know about the Underground Railroad?" he whispered.

Georgina blinked. "Yes, it isn't really a railroad, though. Or is it?"

"No, it is not," Pastor Brown answered. "We only use that terminology to hide the existence of the movement. We cannot be discovered. Not yet. Not until all the slaves have been freed and the laws have changed everywhere."

"I am grateful to the Underground Railroad," Jeremiah whispered. "I wouldn't have met my lovely wife otherwise."

"So you won't be moving on to Upper Canada?" Pastor Brown asked curiously.

"No," Jeremiah replied. "I have a new identity and a future family with Georgina. Don't tell anyone, please, but we have a child on the way already."

Pastor Brown nodded to Georgina. "You are the best thing for Jeremiah." His eyes roamed around the cellar again, thoughts clearly churning in his mind.

"What are you thinking, Pastor?" Georgina asked boldly.

Brown turned his head abruptly to address Georgina. "May I speak boldly?"

Jeremiah straightened. "Please do, we can handle the criticism." Jeremiah clenched his jaw, preparing for the sermon about unwed fornication, but it didn't come. Jermiah looked down at the pastor, surprised. "What is it, Pastor?"

"Well," Pastor Brown started, turning towards them as his hands ran along the walls. "It may not be as you were thinking." Brown stopped and took two large strides towards them, pulling both their hands into a prayer position. "Philadelphia, as you may or may not know, is one of the stations in the underground railroad. Many slaves are indeed dependent on us to provide for them on their journey of freedom to Upper Canada. This city is one of the most important stops. It is the gateway to their new lives, living free from slavery in Canada."

"Yes," Georgina nodded. "Jeremiah has informed me of the significance of Philadelphia. But what does this have to do with us? He's staying in America, with me and our growing family."

"Sometimes," Pastor Brown spoke, his voice taking on a strange sermon quality. "Our own family goals and necessities are secondary to the entire world's needs. Often, God can call upon normal citizens, just like you, for a stronger, more worldly purpose."

Georgina and Jeremiah looked at one another, clearly confused.

"I will get right down to it," Pastor Brown stated finally. "The Underground Railroad needs more stations, stations that are secure and hidden. These places need to be close to ports or entry points." Brown let go of their hands and gestured around the large cellar. "This area is perfect. The cellar is perfect and the port is nearby to receive many newcomers." He turned around in a circle to emphasize his words. "Do you understand what I may be asking of you?"

Jeremiah nodded. "You are asking us to be one of those stations, right here in our cellar."

Georgina looked up at him in surprise, her mouth falling open slightly.

"Yes," Pastor Brown continued. "This is exactly what I am asking of you." He gently grasped Georgina's hands. "I know it is a surprise to you, Georgina. I only request that you deliberate with your husband. We cannot proceed without your approval." Brown smiled warmly. "Your life, Georgina, has been in a constant whirlwind of change lately. I know. You went from a closeted existence, devoting your entire life to the Eastman Empire, to meeting a wonderful man, getting married, owning a home, and having a child in your belly. It is a lot to consider." Pastor Brown walked towards the ladder, then stopped once more to assess the cellar. "This would be a perfect place to house black men and women on their journey towards freedom." He nodded and started ascending the stairs. He stopped on the third rung. "Think about it, Georgina. Discuss it with your husband. Jeremiah will let me know what you both decide upon. God bless you both." Pastor Brown ascended the remaining stairs and disappeared into the upper kitchen.

Jeremiah turned to Georgina and held both her hands, kissing her knuckles. "We can discuss it more once we are fully moved in, dear. Don't let this worry you too much." He gently lowered his head and kissed her fully on the lips. He straightened, then softly kissed her forehead. "I will always be your faithful husband regardless of your decision."

Chapter 15

The early morning was moist and refreshing. Dew collected on the bushes and glittered in the morning sun as Barton approached the cabin. He knew that he must make things right between himself and Zee. Whatever happened last night was an error, a mistake of timing. Her sons were simply overreacting. He knew this.

Barton tied his horse to the post and walked gently up the porch stairs to the front door. He must not lose Zee. She was the best thing he could have ever hoped for. Zee Collard was a hardy, strong, and amazingly beautiful woman. Barton chuckled to himself and wondered why it had taken this long for him to find the right woman.

The circumstances weren't ideal, but he could make it work. He must! There were no other women who could provide the same level of happiness for him that Zee could. She was the rough diamond he had been searching for.

The way they had met was so random and uncalculated. He had never experienced any such thing in his life before. She had shot a man right before his eyes. Something about the dangerous side of Zee pulled him in fiercely. Barton felt drawn to her like a moth to the fire. He could not stay away if he tried. She was the catalyst that had ushered in the moment of realization that everything in his life had meaning. Zee Collard was his angel from up above. She was the most dangerous yet sweetest woman. Perfect for a man like him.

He stopped abruptly as the words churned in his head.

It was true that he had not been the best man in his life. He had done things that he had regretted, but Zee was changing all of that in him. The devil inside him was ready to repent. Barton could be the man he was before his wife died. He could be anything, with Zee Collard by his side.

She had broken into his sinful life and gave him kindness, without ever wanting anything back. She was dangerous with a gun and a knife. She was not just beautiful; Zee Collard was gorgeous.

Barton exhaled heavily, looking at the front door, as realization took over his mind. Zee Collard had stolen his heart, without him even knowing it.

He strode to the door and knocked softly three times.

♎

Zee brought the coffee cup up to her lips and felt a shiver run up her spine again. She had awoken at 5 am suddenly and could not go back to sleep. Something, she wasn't sure what, had deeply disturbed her.

Obviously, seeing her son Jacob pull a rifle on Barton was most likely the first sign of trouble. Maybe her son's intuition was better than her own. Zee had only feared Barton that one time when she had been washing the knives and he had tried to kiss her. She had dismissed the instinctive reaction as an alcohol fueled response.

But was she missing something?

Her entire body had been so consumed with her desire to be loved by her husband again. She wondered if maybe Barton had somehow picked up on that sexual energy. Zee hadn't meant to attract other men. It certainly wasn't her intention.

Zee exhaled and looked up to the ceiling. "I wish you were here, Jesse," she whispered at the log beams.

Several soft knocks sounded on the front door.

At first, she thought she was hearing things. It was still very early in the morning. The sun had just risen. She dismissed the sound and continued sipping her coffee.

Then she heard it again.

Three knocks.

Zee stood abruptly. Fear was her immediate reaction, and her hands shook, almost dropping her coffee. Then, as quickly as the fear had filled her mind, a fierce motherly protection snaked into her blood. She calmly placed the coffee down and checked for the knife in her boot. Zee felt the smooth wooden handle, and it calmed her nerves. She was in charge of this household, she told herself.

Zee turned and raced to the bedroom. She picked up the pistol, stuffing it in her apron dress pocket. Her mind jumped to several conclusions, and she tried valiantly to calm the anxious thoughts.

Her sons were both still sleeping. She could wake them or just be calm and address the person knocking on the door.

She knew who it was, of course.

It was Barton.

She could feel his persistent presence.

Zee squared her shoulders, drank the remaining coffee, and stomped towards the door. She opened the door softly and looked right into Barton's wild eyes.

"Barton," she said simply.

"Zee," he replied, his hand running nervously through his hair. "I wanted to apologize for being here so late yesterday. I was concerned about you. It was a big trip going to Philadelphia and back. I was worried."

Zee narrowed her eyes slightly. Her entire body was stiff, and her hand was prepared to pull the gun out quickly. The unexpected apology caught her off guard. He was not here to fight or cause trouble. "I was quite tired from the trip," she responded stiffly. "I had gone to bed early. I didn't even know you were here." Zee let the lie slide out of her mouth. She didn't want him to know that she had seen everything last night.

"Oh?" he replied. "Well, your sons weren't too hospitable."

"Is that so?" she asked, using her body to block the doorway. "What did they do?"

"Scott was irritable, I think," Barton replied. "Then Jacob surprised both of us by pointing a rifle at me." Barton threw his hands into the air. "I hadn't done anything."

"Oh?" Zee replied. "I can't comment on what my sons do. They were probably just protecting me, as they should. I am their mother after all."

"Protecting you?" Barton chuckled. "Why? I am not a threat. I never was, Zee. I care about you." He let his arms fall to his sides. "I was only making sure you had made it back safely. You had been gone for several days. I was concerned, like any man should be."

Zee inhaled sharply and tried to calm her nerves. The man was apologizing, she told herself.

"Can I come in for a coffee?" Barton asked, peering into the cabin cautiously. "I need to talk to you. So many things have happened to me since you have gone."

"Has something bad happened in Buffalo?" she asked, instantly alarmed.

"No, nothing like that," he replied. "But some things have definitely changed since you went away."

Zee exhaled and opened the door wider. She grudgingly relented and accepted him into her home. "I have just brewed some fresh coffee. Something had awakened me early as well."

Barton stepped into the cabin, searching for the two sons. When he was certain they weren't around, he visibly relaxed. "I hope nothing bad has happened to awaken you so early."

"No, nothing like that," she replied, pouring him a coffee. She handed the coffee to him, staring intently at his strangely crazed expression. "Barton, we will be packing up the deer meat and leaving back home in two days. I thought you should know, since a group of hunters will be here to rent the cabin after us. You won't find me here anymore." Zee watched his face change from the strange appearance to visibly upset. "I hope it isn't too much of a concern for you. Jesse wants me back home, and I want to be there. Our hunting trip is coming to a close."

Barton's mouth dropped open, and his forehead began to sweat. "Just like that," he replied slowly.

"What do you mean?" Zee asked, a sliver of fear racing through her gut.

"You're just leaving," Barton answered. "Without as much of a thought for my feelings. Just like the deer you butchered."

Zee narrowed her eyes at him and squared her shoulders. She stayed eerily silent and felt the urgent desire to put a bullet in his head. Her right hand palmed the pistol in her pocket. Her heartbeat quickened considerably, and she fought with her mind to assess the correct response.

"I'm sorry," Barton said slowly. "I shouldn't have said that."

"That's right, you shouldn't have." Zee clenched her jaw tightly. "You should leave, Barton. You know I'm a married woman. Whatever help you have offered me during my stay in Upstate New York, I appreciate it, but it was something you wanted to do voluntarily, Barton. I never asked for your help."

Barton tensed his shoulders and nodded. "I helped you because I wanted to, Zee," he replied slowly, his voice softening unnaturally. "I have unfortunately fallen under your spell." He looked down at his shoes, uncertainly. He shuffled his feet, then looked up to the ceiling in exasperation. His gaze finally fell and locked onto Zee's eyes. "I started caring about you, Zee," he said, his voice breaking.

Zee froze, then had a sudden urge to hug him. She knew it was simply a normal empathic response, and she restrained herself. Zee could see the hurt etched across his face. "I had no idea," she responded.

Barton leaned on his left foot and looked at the door, then locked eyes with Zee again. "Can we sit down and talk?" he asked.

Zee clenched her jaw and remained silent.

"Give me at least this much," Barton begged, pulling a wooden chair out. "Sit, please."

Zee relented and sat in the offered chair.

Barton sat down opposite her, visibly relieved. "You know, I have never met a woman like you."

"I know, you've said that before," Zee spat back, palming the pistol in her pocket.

Barton laughed. "See? That's what I mean!" He palmed his hair flat against the side of his head and then nodded incredulously. "You actually produce a fear response inside of me sometimes. I can't make sense of it because I have never feared another man before, let alone a woman." He reached across the table with open palms. "Please hold my hands for once."

Zee stiffened. She did not want to remove her hand from the pistol. "No, Barton. I told you before. I'm married. I'm not sure what you don't understand about that."

"Okay," he relaxed back against the chair. "I understand." Barton picked up his coffee and took a few long sips, staring at her the entire time. Finally, he placed the coffee cup down on the table and spoke. "I don't think you know how simultaneously attractive and dangerous you are."

Zee stared blankly at him.

"Your eyes, they mesmerize me," he continued. "And it's not just your eyes. You are capable, strong, tall, and at the same time, so beautifully feminine. You are a unique woman, Zee. Contradictory, caring, and amusing, at the same time." Barton shuffled his feet under the table. "I know you're married. I wish you weren't." He laughed at the absurdity of the statement.

"I don't see what is funny about that."

Barton tilted his head. "I am laughing at myself for falling for you," he replied. "I know you cannot understand how a man can fall victim to a beautiful woman, but neither can I. I don't normally have this kind of response to women. I missed you when you were gone, Zee. I worried about you. I thought maybe something had gone wrong. Then I realized I was fretting over you, Zee. A grown man, like me, fretting over a married woman. I came back to the cabin as soon as I could to make sure you made it back safely. That's when I realized I was falling for you." He placed both his hands on the table and wrung his fingers together. "It hurts me to know that you will be gone from my life soon." He blinked, his eyes moistening at the declaration.

Zee inhaled deeply. "I don't know what to say. I'm sorry if I have hurt you, Barton. It was never my intention." She shifted in the chair and stared into his eyes. "I appreciate the friendship we have had, but I am returning to my husband and my family in Philadelphia. I love my husband. I never stopped loving him. You know how it is when you've been married for a while, things ebb and flow, sometimes things get worse, and then they get better. It is all part of the journey of a marriage. I think maybe you just somehow got caught in the web. I was always faithful and truthful to my husband. I always will be. He's the love of my life."

Barton sat forward in the chair, something obviously disturbing him. A change came over his face, and his eyebrows pulled together in a knot. "Then I will go and leave you alone."

"You can stop by and meet my family and husband in Philadelphia sometime," Zee added happily.

Barton chuckled. "No, I won't be doing that," he responded, pushing his chair out and standing up stiffly. "The Eastman family are not friends of mine. Zee Collard was becoming my friend, not the Eastmans. I will just accept this as my fate. Maybe one day you will be freed from your marriage and you will realize my worth to you." He turned and walked across the large living area towards the front door. He grabbed the door handle and opened the door, turning back to look at Zee one more time. "I will miss you." Barton lowered his head and exited, closing the door quietly behind him.

Part II

THE UNDERGROUND RAILROAD

CHAPTER 16

Billy paced up and down the hallway in the small house they all shared. He had just found out about Georgina's wedding gift. Jesse had bought the neighboring property for Georgina, but left Billy with nothing but the clothes on his back! And worse, it was a large house with four acres! Billy wished his father was still alive, then this mess would have been all sorted out with a firm hand.

Billy stopped pacing abruptly and stared out of the front window. Why couldn't he take on the role of his father? Was he too weak to act like Bob Eastman? He was even called Billy Bob by his parents when he was a boy. He could be the man that his father was. Billy ran his thick hands over his beard. What was holding him back? Was he scared of Jesse?

Billy stomped to the front door as he saw Thomas climbing up the steps. Billy yanked open the front door. "Thomas," he said simply. "When's Bartholomew coming back?"

"I don't know," Thomas answered. "He hasn't contacted us for the last two weeks. It doesn't matter. He put me in charge. I make better decisions than him anyway."

"Well, when do you think we can assemble another team to take over the Eastman estate?"

"We aren't," Thomas responded, blankly staring at Billy. "We lost that fight. I'm not going to lose more men. I told you that before. You didn't return the money, so you work for us now. We own you."

"I have been working! I'm putting together some information about the new property that the Eastman Empire has purchased," Billy replied sharply. "I have my own spies. I will have enough information by tomorrow. A lot more is going on than Bartholomew thinks."

Thomas lifted his chin and stared at Billy commandingly. "The Eastmans purchased a new property? What kind of information are you talking about?"

"I'm not saying much more right now," Billy answered. "I want to be certain and have everything ready to brief you, but I need a team of men, preferably the kind of men who don't take kindly to black slaves being freed so they can infiltrate our society."

Thomas laughed. "I know plenty of men like that."

"Then bring them together tomorrow," Billy stated. "I should have everything ready then."

♎

Jeremiah lifted the cellar latch door open and started climbing down the ladder. Georgina handed him a basket of food to take down. "Thanks, darling," he said, threading his arm through the basket. It smelled of fresh bread and cheese. He climbed down the remaining stairs and entered the cellar. Dim oil lamps glowed in two corners, revealing several black people lounging on the chairs and sparse furnishings. Another five black people were standing against the wall, clearly stressed about their plight out of America.

"Here's some lunch for everyone," Jeremiah declared, placing the basket on a large table.

A young woman stepped forward with her husband. She had rough hands, and her hair was matted from several days of travelling. The couple had just arrived this morning. They looked weary and beaten, but a flash of hope shone in her eyes. "Thank you, Mr. Williams," the young lady said, gently grabbing a warm slice of bread from the tray. Her husband curled his arm around her waist protectively and selected a slice of cheese from the tray, shoving it in his mouth hungrily.

The young black woman frowned at her husband, then stared up at Jeremiah questioningly. "Mr. Williams, can I ask a few questions? I am uncertain about what our next steps are."

"Yes, please ask any questions, that is why we are here," Jeremiah replied.

The young woman hesitated. Her husband nodded for her to continue. "Mr. Williams, my husband and I have not decided whether to flee to Canada or stay in Philadelphia. I know some former slaves are staying in the northern freed states, and some are going to Canada. What options do we have in Canada? It is a different country, after all."

Jeremiah smiled at the young couple. The woman didn't look any older than 20. She was most likely just recently married. "Good question," he responded. "I know that you arrived here from another station in Virginia. Canada is much closer to here than Virginia. It is still a long journey but we can help you arrive there."

The young woman raised her eyebrows in joy, hugging her husband.

"The biggest difference between Canada and staying in America is that you will be leaving to a different country." Jeremiah inhaled sharply. "I personally chose to stay because I met my lovely wife here in Philadelphia, but I was originally planning to flee to Upper Canada." He paused and gestured with his hands to the north. "In 1793, Upper Canada introduced a piece of legislation called the Act to Limit Slavery. I don't know that much about it, but the story that's told is about a woman named Chloe who resisted being tied up and sold in Upper Canada. The event came to the attention of onlookers and the government. Upper Canada introduced the legislation shortly after." Jeremiah ran his fingers over his eyebrows, trying to remember all the details. "There is some kind of provision in the legislation which states that any enslaved person who reaches Canada becomes free upon arrival."

A collective gasp sounded from the entire group of former slaves.

The young woman's husband spoke, his voice cracking insecurely. "But don't the states of Pennsylvania and New York offer the same?"

"There is an Act for Abolition of Slavery here in Philadelphia, yes. But many slaves are still being held until they are 28 years old." Jeremiah let his hands fall to his sides.

The young woman's face froze in fear. "I am only 18 years old," she whispered out loud.

"Then this is something for you and your husband to consider," Jeremiah replied. He wasn't about to explain his personal situation any further. He, himself, still faced the unspoken threat of his former masters finding him. "It may be better for you to escape to Canada then. For the rest of you, any enslaved blacks staying in Philadelphia or New York can live mostly free lives, but the country as a whole has not declared it as such, like Upper Canada did. Some former masters may send parties to find you."

A collective gasp rippled throughout the group of people.

"That is the worst possible scenario," Jeremiah added. "We need to think positively. Many good things will happen once you are free to live on your own."

The young woman smiled for the first time. "Thank you, Mr. Williams," she replied warmheartedly. "You are a good man for allowing us to stay at your home. We are grateful for your sacrifices and helping us to be freed."

"You are most welcome," Jeremiah answered. "As a devout Baptist and a former slave myself, it is the least I could do."

The young woman's husband reached out his hand for a handshake. "We are truly grateful," he said, shaking Jeremiah's hand. "Without you, who knows what may have happened to us?"

Jeremiah smiled. "Just tell me what each of you has decided, and I will facilitate the next station for each of you. The next station to Upper Canada from here is in Upper Canada itself. A ticket agent will help to arrange travel."

"Will we be travelling by train?" another black woman asked.

"Not likely," Jeremiah answered. "The Underground Railroad is a choice of words to covertly hide the network of travel agents, safe houses like this one are called stations or depots. Stick to speaking in these terms so people know. You are officially passengers on the Underground Railroad, and my wish is that you all safely arrive at your destinations."

♎

Georgina brewed another pot of coffee and placed another three loaves of bread in the stone oven. She heard the front door open and then close quietly. She knew it was her husband by his slight movements. "Jeremiah!" she yelled in greeting. "Come here, darling."

Steps sounded lightly through the hall until finally his tall stature appeared in the kitchen archway. "My beautiful wife," he murmured. "How's the baby?"

"Oh, I don't even feel anything yet," she replied. "A bit of stomach upset." Georgina laughed.

"Oh my," Jeremiah walked over and smoothed his hand along her flat belly. "Well, soon we will have a child. We will be parents."

Georgina grinned broadly. "Yes, we will be parents in eight months if everything goes all right."

"Of course it will," he replied sharply.

"I suspect it should," Georgina answered, a worried frown forming on her forehead.

"What is it, sweetheart?"

"Oh, it's nothing to do with the baby," Georgina replied. "It is one of the passengers."

Jeremiah's instincts came to full alert. "What's happened?"

"Oh, nothing has happened," Georgina replied slowly. "A young woman has enquired about getting a ticket agent today. I know so little about all of this, Jeremiah." She threw her hands up in frustration. "I have been baking and cooking around the clock to feed everyone. That's all I do, it seems. I barely have enough time to check into the Eastman kitchen."

"I thought you didn't have to start working at the Eastman Estate for another week until we got all settled."

"This is true," Georgina replied, wiping her hands on her apron. "But I cannot remain cooking and baking for a dozen people in the cellar for much longer."

"Then we will just limit the number of people who use this depot at any given time." Jeremiah searched her eyes. "We can do that."

"We are called a depot now?" Georgina asked incredulously.

"Depot or station, yes," Jeremiah answered. He inhaled sharply and hugged his wife. "It will be alright, my sweet. We can only do this temporarily, if that makes you feel more comfortable." He kissed her forehead and smoothed her hair. "I suppose the young woman and her husband have decided on continuing to Canada."

"How did you know?"

"She was asking questions last night."

"Well, you need to speak to her, Jeremiah," Georgina stated. "Her name is Sarah."

"Come with me," Jeremiah said, kissing her hand. "It will give you an opportunity to learn more." He walked to the cellar door and swung it open with one hand. "Come, my sweet."

Georgina relented and followed her husband into the cellar. Once they had climbed down, Jeremiah addressed the passengers. "Sarah?" he called. "We can discuss your travels now. If any others are choosing to reach Canada, please join us."

Sarah and her husband appeared from the dark recesses of the cellar. She spoke calmly and surely, grasping her husband's hand firmly. "We have decided on leaving to Canada today, if possible."

"Unfortunately, the ticket agent will not see anyone until tomorrow," Jeremiah answered. "He will secure your travels into Canada then. You will most likely need to wait another day or two so they can arrange horseback and a boat."

"A boat?" Sarah asked, her eyebrow lifting in surprise.

"Yes, you will be crossing the Niagara River on a ferry into Canada, with many others. A station there will be your last stop on the Underground Railroad. They will help you to integrate into the new country."

Sarah looked at her husband with hope and anticipation. "We can get there in a few days?" she asked, her eyes shining with joy.

"I am not certain on the actual number of days," Jeremiah answered. "I will contact the ticket agent today and let him know. He will come tomorrow to see you."

Sarah grinned broadly while her husband curled his arm around her shoulders. She turned to her husband with a sparkle in her eyes. "We'll be free," she spoke to her husband and kissed him lightly on the lips.

Georgina smiled and felt the joy emanating from Sarah. She started feeling better about the task she had been set with. These people needed her. These people needed freedom. Georgina had been a slave herself and was just finally understanding now that her life was not solely dedicated to the Eastman Empire. She squeezed Jeremiah's hand as he began to speak to the others, explaining the next steps in their journey.

"I will let you all know tonight when the ticket agent can speak to you tomorrow," Jeremiah concluded. "If anyone needs a wash basin and a change of clothes, please let me or my wife know. We can provide you with some warm water and clean pants."

Several people nodded, and a few stepped forward, asking for clean clothes. Once Jeremiah had settled which ones to serve first, he turned to Georgina and grasped her hand. "We will get the wash basins ready, and I will step out shortly to tell the ticket agent. Your future starts here."

Georgina followed her husband up the ladder and emerged in the clean kitchen. The smell of baking bread wafted into their nostrils. Jeremiah closed the cellar door gently. "My gosh, that smells wonderful," he said. "Let's get the wash basins ready, and then I will run out to summon the travel agent. He lives close by. I won't be long."

Georgina kissed him and grabbed a small wash bowl from the counter. "Who's the travel agent?" she asked nonchalantly.

Jeremiah winked at her. "It's Pastor Brown, of course."

Chapter 17

Billy gestured for the men to take a seat. A large table had been set up for the meeting. Thomas had found twelve men to attend the meeting, each with their own private agendas. Several were former slave owners who had lost their slaves mysteriously and were intent on recovering them or getting new ones. Three men had just arrived from Tennessee and Virginia, the others were more local landowners.

"Have a seat," Billy announced, waving his arm towards the large table and chairs.

"I hope this all goes according to plan," Thomas scoffed. "It better not be anything like the last attempt." Thomas ushered another fellow in and then turned back to Billy. "I just received a courier from Bartholomew saying that he will be travelling back soon, maybe within the next few days."

"Oh? Well, that's good news," Billy replied. "Where is he?"

"Buffalo, apparently."

"Well," Billy added. "I am certain that Bartholomew will love our plan."

"Well, if what you say is true, then it should be a fitting plan for everyone involved," Thomas replied. "Once the authorities find out that Jesse Eastman is linked to the black slave network, then we can take over the empire from the ruins. And it won't cost us anything."

Billy and Thomas waited for everyone to seat themselves before closing the door and commencing the meeting. "Hello everyone, and thank you for arriving here on such short notice!" Thomas addressed the men around the table. "I would like to introduce you to Billy Eastman."

Gasps and murmurs of surprise rippled through the crowd at the Eastman name.

Billy lifted a hand in greeting.

"Billy will describe the details of our plan," Thomas concluded, sitting down at the table.

Billy cleared his throat and started. "As you all know, this gathering is something very important to you all. Everyone here has something in common. You are mostly slave owners, either looking for more to buy or trying to recover some lost ones. Some people are here for other reasons, but everyone has a common goal." Billy tapped the table loudly to get everyone's attention. "And that's what I'm here for."

He waved his hand behind him to encompass the area of Philadelphia. "In the city of Philadelphia, very close to my home at the Eastman empire, there was a recent purchase of a property. My spies have been watching the property for days now, and it appears that a large group of blacks are being housed there. Rumor has it that most are runaway slaves."

Several men at the table grunted loudly, and a disgruntled shout sounded.

"Quiet, please," Billy said, motioning with his hands. "I know you all have been upset with your runaway slaves or are looking for a new addition, but please hear me out. This plan must go accordingly for us to get the slaves out and back on the market." Billy winked and felt pure glee in his heart as he thought of Georgina being taken as a slave again. "There are a few women as well. They will be sold at a higher price."

Several men chuckled. One spoke. "They'd better know how to cook and clean. No reason to pay more otherwise."

"Trust me," Billy said. "The women are valuable, and one in particular is beautiful."

A large beefy man stood. "I'll take her. When does the bidding start?"

Billy motioned with his hand for the man to sit down. "We will have time for bidding once the plan is executed. There is a lot to discuss before that happens." Billy unrolled a large parchment paper and laid it out on the table. On it was a crude drawing of a house and the surrounding property. "We don't know in which room of the house all the slaves are being hidden, but we do know for certain that there are between 10-14 people in the house, including the home's owners. They are all blacks." Billy pointed to the house on the map. "As Thomas has discussed with all of you earlier, your involvement with us includes your commitment and your strength. We will supply all the weaponry and ammunition, if necessary."

A small, wiry man stood. "I have explosives. I have brought them with me. We can use that as well."

Billy turned to eye Thomas's approval.

Thomas nodded.

"Well, I suppose that would be helpful," Billy replied. "Please have it all loaded onto a cart, and we will make sure that we can include it in our plans."

The wiry man smiled devilishly and sat back down as Billy continued to address the men. Several men sat in the chairs stiffly, as if expecting to be thrown into action at this very moment. Billy smiled and concluded that Thomas had chosen these men well. He pointed at the map and described the steps of the plan. Billy had devised most of it himself. It was incredible and ingenious. Billy was proud of himself, and it showed. He stood taller and stronger, almost like his father. He was the second son of Bob Eastman, after all. He had the Eastman spirit in his blood, and he would make Jesse pay for his mistakes.

Billy coughed and addressed the group again. "Please make sure everyone is ready. We start early. If you're taking weapons, please ensure that you pay for it first. You'll be refunded once the weapons are returned."

Thomas sat back in his chair and watched as Billy concluded the meeting with all of the men. The slave masters nodded in agreement and took whatever weapons and ammunition they needed from the hallway tables, leaving cash in a large box. Thomas curled his fingers into a fist and released his clench several times, rhythmically.

Billy noticed and sat down beside Thomas as the men began filtering out of the room. He tapped Thomas's knee. "It will all work out according to plan. And you don't have to worry about losing any of your men this time."

♎

Pastor Brown showed up unexpectedly in the evening. Jeremiah closed the front door quietly and walked into the house with the pastor trailing behind him.

Georgina replied happily. "Pastor Brown! You made it here early!"

"Yes," Pastor Brown replied. "A ferry to Upper Canada leaves next Thursday morning. It is several very long days of horseback riding before they reach the last stop of the Underground Railroad within the United States. Then they must cross the Niagara River. The US ferry port is a journey that needs to be scheduled right away. We must make sure they leave first thing in the morning. It is imperative that they start their journey in time before the ferry leaves."

"Come, tell them yourself!" Georgina beamed joyfully. "I'm sure they will be delighted to hear this. Especially, Sarah."

Jeremiah grabbed the cellar door and lifted it open.

Pastor Brown descended the ladder into the cellar with a spring in his step and a firm purpose from God in his heart.

Chapter 18

Barton shoved his feet into the stirrups and kicked the horse into a trot along the forested path. He slept horribly, tossing and turning all night. Barton kept reasoning that there wasn't much he could do about Zee leaving back home to Philadelphia. She was married, after all, and her return to her husband was inevitable. She would decide things on her own. Maybe the future would turn out much differently, and Zee would come back to him.

He told this to himself a hundred times.

But his heart would not listen.

He felt like someone had twisted a knife in his heart and left it there.

Barton finally gave up trying to sleep, watched the sun rise through his bedroom window, and decided upon some action.

He would confess his love to her and make her understand. He dressed quickly, then left through the back of the hotel. Barton mounted his horse and rode out of town. He resolved to turn his thoughts into actions. Zee Collard was the woman he had been waiting for his entire life. He couldn't just let her walk away without another word! He had to try.

Barton's rational mind kept fighting with his heart. He felt the back of his head tingle in warning. It felt like, somehow, this woman could be the death of him. But it twisted his guts up every time he thought about losing her! His mind was consumed by her. Barton was plagued by random visions of them together, hunting, then making love afterwards. They would live in a small hunting cabin and escape from the restraints of his miserable life.

He would change his life entirely and make it a happy life! Barton gazed down at the beaten horse path, listening to his horse's feet rhythmically crunching against the dirt path.

Sometimes, he felt like the devil inside him could never let go of his soul. But he knew better. Barton was once an innocent young man with a head full of optimism.

And Zee Collard brought that young man out in him again.

"I will make you mine, Zee Collard," Barton muttered into the wind. "You are my salvation! Only you." Barton cried into the gusts of wind swirling around him. He had never felt this strongly about a woman before. It could only mean one thing. They were destined to be with each other. "I cannot just allow you to exit my life, Zee."

An evil chill ran up his spine as he trotted towards her cabin. His eyes stayed glued to the path ahead of him. He could not turn back now. The trees curled over the path, creating the illusion that he was being sucked into a tunnel, leading right to Zee Collard.

And he didn't mind. She was his beautiful poison. The only one who could save him from himself.

♎

Zee awoke early again, a tendril of fear mixing with urgency lacing holes through her heart. She was a kind woman who truly cared for others. She never intentionally hurt anyone.

The look of suffering on Barton's face, when he had left, was devastatingly clear.

And she was responsible for that. She had hurt him somehow.

Zee was confused as to why he was so incredibly hurt. She had never offered him anything else but friendship. She had stood firmly behind her marriage vows and kept reminding him of this. She had even invited him to the Eastman estate!

Barton wouldn't have any of it.

Part of her was angry that he made her feel like the villain. It wasn't right, she thought. His insistence towards her was wrong, regardless of whether he had developed feelings for her or not. She cannot be held responsible for another man's feelings.

Zee had been very close to shooting Barton until he confessed his feelings. Now, she felt sympathetic towards him and somehow responsible. She exhaled heavily and thought about going back home to Jesse. Her heart fluttered at the thought of her husband. She realized with a striking clarity that she would not miss Barton at all, and that was how it should be.

Jacob and Scott had mostly packed everything up, and they were almost ready to go, so it would be soon.

But there was one thing she wasn't looking forward to. Living life at the Eastman Estate again. Zee was thrilled to be closer to Jesse again, physically and emotionally. She was optimistic that they had resolved many of the issues surrounding their marriage woes. What the future held, she did not know, but Jesse was the love of her life, and she gambled that their future would turn out better if they worked together. Jesse did not say what would happen once he completely retired from the Eastman Empire, but Zee no longer cared. She trusted her husband's judgement. Zee's heart was filled with love again; she could feel it physically in her chest. Her mind suddenly yearned to feel Jesse's naked skin against hers again.

Zee would walk to the ends of the earth for her husband!

Why couldn't Barton see that?

Zee shook her head and almost jumped when she heard three soft knocks on the front door. Her first inclination was to awaken her sons. But they had tirelessly worked yesterday, packing all the meat up and clearing the debris of leftover bones and skins, burying it back into the forest. Her sons needed to sleep longer than her.

Zee pulled a coat over her nightgown and squared her shoulders, stomping to the front door. She would resolve this situation with Barton herself. She stopped abruptly, back-tracked, and grabbed the small pistol, slipping it into her coat pocket. Zee turned on her foot and walked quickly to the front door. She grasped the handle and swung it open harshly.

"Barton," she said strongly, staring into his wild eyes.

"Zee," he said softly.

"What is it, Barton?"

Barton pursed his lips and shook his head sadly. "There's no reason to be like that, sweetheart," he calmly retorted. "I'm here to make peace."

"The only sweetheart I have is my husband," Zee spat back. "I feel like if I repeated that a hundred times, you still wouldn't hear me."

Barton pushed open the door and stepped in. "I don't want to fight with you, Zee."

Zee stepped back, momentarily stunned by his physical push into the house. She pushed her right hand into her pocket and grasped the pistol. "I didn't ask you to come in, Barton," she warned.

"I know," Barton said calmly, waving his hand down. "Calm down, beautiful. I am only here to let you know something before you go."

Zee stood firmly, squaring her shoulders, and felt an anger rising up into her chest. "Then say your peace," she said smoothly. "You have nerve, I give you that." She tilted her head back and stared angrily at him. To think, just moments ago, she was feeling horrible for breaking his heart. Barton had a certain way of invoking a protective anger in her. "So, speak your peace, Barton." She thumbed the trigger in her pocket.

Barton eyed her strangely, like seeing her in a completely different light. "You're angry," he said, his eyes creasing in feigned laughter. "So, I do evoke emotion in you! I knew that you felt strongly for me. I knew that it wasn't all a lie." He smiled viciously.

The anger bubbled up into her throat, and Zee fought to contain it. She stared blankly at him, without uttering another word. The man was crazy, she realized.

"You're done talking now?" Barton asked, chuckling.

Zee nodded, her face set in stone.

"Okay, now that I have your attention," he began. He waved his hands around the room. "You have all of this in your life. You are a good woman. I know this, but I could give you even more. I have not told you before, but I am wealthy, very wealthy, just like your ungrateful husband, Jesse Eastman."

"He's not ungrateful," Zee responded firmly. "I love him."

"You love him?" Barton stated questioningly, his eyebrows arching comically. "Even when he neglects you?"

Zee blinked hard.

"He neglects you, Zee," Barton stated knowingly. "You feel it, you know it. Everything else is more important than you, isn't it? The Eastman Empire, his family, friends, everything. You always take a backseat to everything he does." Barton's lips curled into a grin, knowing that he had hit a nerve in her heart. "That's why you're here, Zee. To get away from him. That's why you started falling for my charms. I didn't get caught in your web, Zee. You were looking to get away from your husband. You were looking for me." Barton straightened and smiled devilishly, knowing he had won.

Zee responded immediately. She struck his face with the palm of her hand, slapping him hard. "How dare you say such things about me and my husband!" she shouted, anger bubbling up into her head, threatening to make her lose her mind.

Barton felt the burn on his cheek and turned away from her briefly, hiding his smirk. She didn't like to hear the truth, he mused devilishly. "Zee," he said calmly, hiding his face. "I'm sorry. I didn't mean to create a fire of anger in you, but I needed to see that you have feelings for me. Now, I know." He turned back to her astonished face, his eyes quickly growing wide.

Zee had pulled the pistol out and was aiming it at his head. "Take one more step, Barton," she hissed. "And I will fill your head with lead."

Barton froze and inhaled sharply, raising his hands up slowly in surrender. "You can't shoot an unarmed man, Zee. That's murder."

Zee's eyes narrowed. "It's self defense, Barton."

Barton felt his blood run cold. She was going to kill him. "Look, Zee," he started, trying to reason with her. "Could you please put down the gun, so I can tell you why I came here?"

"Tell me now!" Zee shouted, placing her finger on the trigger. "And do it fast."

"Okay," he reasoned, exhaling nervously. "Zee, I don't know how else to say this. It isn't easy for me."

"Say it!"

"I love you, Zee."

A sharp sting sliced through her heart at his words. Her anger deflated, and she felt oddly remorseful, like she was again responsible for his misguided romantic inclinations. She needed to say something, but no kind words came to her lips. Several moments of uncomfortable silence filled the room. Finally, Zee found the words. "I'm sorry you feel that way, Barton. I didn't mean to cause you any hurt."

"Can you put the gun down, please?"

"No," she responded firmly, still aiming the gun at his head. "We can talk like this."

Barton chuckled. "Alright," he said slowly, trying to calm himself and get her to a better state of interaction. "I don't want you to go. It will tear me apart, Zee. We can get married, and I can take you anywhere in the world that you wish to go. I will give you anything. Stay with me, Zee." He heaved and felt decades of emotions threatening to moisten his eyes. "I would do anything for you, Zee."

Zee held firmly onto the pistol and waved it to the front door, then back at his head. "Leave my house, Barton," she said firmly. "Step slowly and don't make any quick moves."

Barton stood firmly, his eyebrows arcing incredulously. "I spill my heart to you, and you tell me to leave? That's it?"

Zee exhaled and softened her tone briefly. "Barton, I am not staying with you. I am leaving to go back home. I do not love you. I love my husband." Her eyes hardened with a steely resolve. "I am sorry that you feel that you have fallen in love with me, but it is misguided. I never gave you any reason to think otherwise."

"Jesse Eastman doesn't deserve you."

Zee narrowed her eyes. Something bothered her about that statement, more so than just the protective anger it produced in her heart. "Do you know my husband?" she asked. "I don't believe I ever told you his name."

Barton blinked, as if caught in a lie. "Jesse Eastman is well known as the heir of the Eastman Empire. Everybody knows who Jesse Eastman is."

Her heart hammered in her chest. He was clearly lying. Something else was going on that she truly had no knowledge about. "However, you know my husband, Barton, I need you to understand that I will protect him and honor him at all costs." She glared at Barton with murder in her eyes. "I would kill for him."

Barton stared back at her for several seconds until finally his eyes dropped to the floor and his voice wavered. "I will leave now. If you will allow me to exit, that is."

"You know where the front door is," Zee responded stiffly, following his movements with the gun aimed towards his head.

Barton slowly stepped towards the door and opened it. "I still love you, Zee. No matter what you do or say. It won't change my feelings for you." He stepped through the doorway and closed it softly, leaning his head against it in relief. "I would never hurt you, my darling," he muttered into the thick wood.

Zee lowered the pistol and felt a shiver of anxiety ripple through her arms as she heard the mumbled words through the door.

She had almost killed a crazy man in cold blood. Maybe she should have.

Chapter 19

Jesse's eyes fluttered open as his heart hammered in his chest. He looked around in the early morning darkness of Zee's bedroom. Something had awoken him. He sat up in bed and wondered for a brief minute where Zee was. His sleepy mind was somehow thinking she had been here with him in the bed last night. He could still smell her womanly scent on the sheets.

His mind slowly started returning to reality. Zee had left back to the cabin a few days ago. She was due back at the end of the week.

Something bothered him. Maybe it was a deep yearning for her, or maybe it was something much more insidious. Jesse flung his legs over the bed and stood up in the dark with only his undergarments on. He had an unnerving connection with Zee, like she was somehow calling for him.

He quickly shook his head. It was ridiculous to think she could be calling from that great of a distance. He must be losing his mind.

Zee was going to be back home soon, he told himself. There was no need to worry. He wondered if he should go out to the cabin and help them return with all the meat and belongings.

Jesse worried about Zee coming back safely. He sat back down on the bed and blinked into the darkness. Jesse tried to calm his mind and go back to sleep, but he could not stop his brain from worrying.

What had awakened him?

He was sleeping deeply then just awoke suddenly, with his heart hammering in his chest. Was it a dream? Was he just worried about Zee? Or was it something else?

He lay his head back down, then heard it again.

A faint crash in the distance.

That's what had awoken him!

Jesse bolted out of bed, tugging his pants on and pulling them up in a flash. He ran to the west-facing window and pulled the heavy draperies aside. A bright orange glow lit up the early morning horizon. At first, he thought it was only the sun, but then quickly realized it was something much more horrifying.

He unlatched the window, wrestling with it briefly, and finally opened it. He stood there with his naked chest tingling from the cool morning air. His pants were on. He was half-dressed, sniffing the air.

It was smoke. The orange glow flickered in the distance.

Then he heard a distant shout.

Jesse grabbed a shirt and bolted from the room, scrambling down the stairs, shouting for everybody in the house to get up. "Fire!" he yelled frantically down the hallways. "Get up, everyone, quick! There's a fire!"

Jesse yanked open the front door and gasped as he realized which direction the smoke was coming from. A moment of hesitation gripped him, and he ran back into the house, shoving a pistol into his belt and slinging a long-barreled rifle over his shoulder. He stuffed ammunition into his belt pouch as Xavier and Samuel appeared in the hallway, rubbing their eyes.

"What's going on?" Samuel asked, scratching his bald head.

"There's a fire!" Jesse shouted.

"Where?"

"It looks like it's in the direction of Georgina's house," Jesse replied solemnly. "We have to be prepared. Who knows, it might be another attack from Bartholomew."

Samuel grabbed a few firearms and handed some to Xavier. "Go! We'll catch up!"

Jesse ran out the front entrance and bolted down the dirt driveway, running at full speed. He turned back briefly and shouted as loud as he could. "Xavier! Bring blankets and buckets!" Jesse watched Xavier nod at the front entrance and disappear back into the mansion.

Jesse resumed his run and plowed through the fields to shorten the distance. He had to be careful of the uneven ground in some areas and jumped to the side nimbly. He heard more shouting, and he urged his legs to run impossibly faster. "Georgina! Oh Lord, Georgina!" Jesse shouted out loud, his emotions spilling out in words. He hoped he was wrong and the fire was somewhere else, but as he got closer, the smoke grew thicker.

As Jesse crested the hill, his fears were confirmed. Adrenaline pumped through his body as he gazed wide-eyed through the flickers of orange and yellow flames engulfing what looked like Georgina's house at the bottom of the slope.

His heart skipped a beat.

Then he heard another shout.

"Take your hands off me!"

A burly man shoved Georgina out the back door. They both stumbled onto the field grass. Georgina jumped nimbly up as the burly man swung a rope towards her. He was trying to wrestle the rope around her neck! She ran, but he managed to grab her arm.

Georgina kicked frantically, and a blow caught the man in the midsection. He stumbled back from the force briefly, but came at her again. She scanned the house, hoping to see Jeremiah running out. The flames were flickering out of the windows on the east side of the house. Their bedroom was on the west side. When she had awakened, Jeremiah was gone, and this burly man was dragging her out of the house like she was a slave!

Georgina narrowed her eyes at the man. "Who are you?" she shouted angrily. "This is my house!"

The burly man chuckled, waving back at the house quickly being overtaken by flames. "Not anymore! You are mine now!"

"You can't do this!" she shouted at him, her words tumbling out in a panicked rage. "I am an Eastman! I'm Georgina Eastman! And I'm a married woman. Where is my husband?" She frowned angrily at the man, her nightgown blowing in the coastal winds.

The man paused briefly, indecision clearly on his mind. He eyed Georgina and opened his mouth to speak.

Before he could say anything, another man grasped Georgina from behind and began dragging her to the horses. "She's a liar! No black woman is an Eastman! You're coming with us, you lying slave!"

Georgina tripped from the unexpected force and was mercilessly dragged by the collar of her nightgown. She heard it tear with the weight of her body and squinted her eyes shut from fear. But only momentarily. All the years of slave beatings came back to her, and she became paralyzed with fear. Her body momentarily froze, allowing these men to haul her away swiftly.

The burly man ran behind them and finally caught up, trying to catch his breath. "Maybe what she says is true?" he asked, hoarsely. "She is not as dark skinned as the rest. Damn beautiful girl, you are, Georgina." He blew a kiss towards her.

"It's all lies! We can get a lot of money for her. Besides, Billy would have told us!"

"Billy!" Georgina shouted in anger, struggling anew. "Billy is behind all this?" Her past fears quickly dissipated and were replaced by a festering anger.

"You know Billy?" the burly man said, looking at Georgina with wide eyes.

"He's my brother!" she shouted viciously. Georgina whipped her arms over her head, reaching towards her assailant. She struggled briefly but finally found his arms and dug her nails deep into his forearm. Georgina let out a primal yell and gripped her nails until she felt blood oozing onto her hand.

The man yelped in agony and let go. "You crazy witch!" He grabbed his arms, seething from the sudden pain.

The burly man grabbed her waist and threw her over his shoulder. "If what you say is true, we will let you go. We will be hanged for kidnapping an Eastman." He grunted from the weight of her body on his. "But you're still coming with us until we figure this all out. I sure hope it isn't true. I wanted you all to myself. I like black whores the best."

Georgina looked up as she hung mercilessly on his back. The flames in the distance were quickly engulfing the entire east side of the house. Then she noticed a tall man running out of the back door. It was Jeremiah!

Another tall man was running across the fields directly towards her. She couldn't make out who that man was.

She had to get out of this man's grasp! She tried struggling, but the man's grip just became firmer. Her head was hanging over his back, and the blood was rushing to her head. Georgina looked down for something to grab onto. All she could find was a chubby roll of fat along the man's waistline. She let out a visceral scream and chomped her teeth hard on his love handles. She bit down as hard as she could until she tasted blood, then began smashing her fists into his kidneys.

The burly man screeched and instantly dropped her. "Jesus, woman!"

Georgina landed like a cat and bolted back towards the flaming house.

"Where the hell are you going, woman?" the burly man shouted after her. "You want to burn in flames? That house is going to collapse!" He yelled hysterically, then ran after her.

A gunshot rang through the air, and the burly man dived onto the ground, looking this way and that, not sure which way it was coming from. "What the hell?" he shouted into the dirt.

Georgina ran as fast as she'd ever run in her life. She bolted and pumped her legs hard, not looking back once. Bullets filled the air behind her, and she prayed they weren't aimed at her.

Jeremiah raised his weapon, then quickly realized it was her and started running to meet her. "Oh my, sweet, Lord!" he shouted as Georgina caught up to him and collided into his arms.

"What happened?" he asked, breathlessly. "Who were those men? I was trying to fight the fire. Didn't you hear me shouting for you inside?"

"They thought I was one of the slaves!" she cried into his shoulder. "They were going to take me away and sell me."

Jeremiah's left eye twitched. "I will skin them alive!"

"No!" she cried. "Leave them! Billy is behind all this! Did they steal all the slaves out from the basement? Where is everyone?"

Jeremiah's eyes misted over. "That's where I was," he said, straightening as another man ran towards them. He moved her aside to raise his gun. "Stand here, honey. I don't know who this is."

Georgina let Jeremiah protect her but placed a cautionary hand on his arm. She squinted to see the man running towards them. As the man came nearer, she noticed the familiar gait. "It's Jesse!" she shouted happily. "Don't shoot!"

♎

Jesse saw the entire fight but couldn't shoot at the burly man while Georgina was wrestling with him. Jesse kept running, then stopping to aim, then running again. He couldn't risk it. They were too close together. He knew his weapons didn't shoot accurately at this distance. All he could do was keep running to close the distance.

He whooped loudly when Georgina freed herself. "That's my sister! Give 'em hell!" Jesse turned and ran towards the house to meet Georgina, then stopped briefly, assessing the previous threats. He squinted at the burly man in the distance, then crouched, aimed, and fired. The shot went wild, but the gunfire still dropped the big man to the ground. From this distance, Jesse didn't know if he had hit his target or if the man was just diving for cover.

Jesse fired another shot towards the other wiry man, aiming better this time. The bullet caught its mark, thudding into the man's side, and stumbled the assailant to the ground.

The burly man started crawling along the ground and crouching in a run towards Georgina. Jesse squinted in the lightening skies as the smoke began to waft over the fields. He aimed at the burly man and fired again, his bullet missing and whacking into the dirt.

Jesse could hear Xavier and Samuel catching up behind him now, the ground kicking up from their urgent steps and the buckets clanging against their knees.

He fired again at the crouched man. A heavy grunt sounded across the field as the man was hit. The man groaned and held his leg.

Jesse turned his attention back to Georgina and was relieved to see her safe with Jeremiah. He ran to greet them as several masked men ran out of the house behind them and slightly to the right. Jesse stopped and aimed his weapon as Georgina shouted his name. Jesse waved his gun in the air frantically to try to warn them.

Jeremiah quickly swung around to the threat from behind as bullets pierced the air.

Georgina shouted. "Down! Jeremiah, down!"

Jeremiah was too late. A bullet tore into his shoulder, sending him spinning to the ground. Georgina crawled hysterically towards him. "Honey! No! Sweetheart! Talk to me!" She lay on her belly, searching his body with her hands. "Don't you die on me! Jesus, God, save him!" Georgina raked her hands all over his prone body until she found the sticky blood oozing from his shoulder. She kissed him on the cheek. "Honey, are you okay? Say something!"

Jeremiah groaned, but no intelligible words came out of his mouth.

"It'll be alright, honey," she whispered. "It looks like you've got a bullet in your shoulder. You'll be fine, honey. Stay with me! Keep your eyes open! I will wrap it up, until we can get you to a doctor." She tore a strip of cloth from her nightgown and started tearing the clothing away from his shoulder. It wouldn't budge, so she searched his belt for the knife she knew he always hid there. She unsheathed it happily and cut the clothing away from the wound as several shots fired overhead. Georgina concentrated, knowing that they were both concealed in the tall grass.

She sliced and removed his shirt from the wounded left shoulder until finally the wound was visible. She wrapped the linen around the wound tightly and pressed hard to stop the flow of blood. Blood soaked the thin fabric easily. "Jesus Christ." She ripped the entire bottom of her night gown off in one large circular strip, then sliced the end off with the knife.

Georgina wrapped the wound tightly over and around his armpit until the wound was firmly contained. She smoothed her hand over his cheek and cuddled with him in the field as his eyes fluttered closed. "You can't die, honey."

An exchange of gunfire reverberated across the field.

Jesse, Xavier, and Samuel crouched in the tall grass, shooting towards the masked men. Several gunshots fired back as more men emerged from the house. One shouted, "Where are the slaves?"

Another shouted, "I checked the entire house! We were lied to! There are no slaves except the two that got away!"

Jesse aimed and shot the first man in the throat. The man reeled from the sudden impact, grabbing his throat, then fell to the ground with a thud.

Xavier shot another man in the chest, the bullet piercing a hole through his heart.

The remaining masked men scattered to several different locations, some trying to escape, some staying and fighting.

A cluster of retaliating shots launched towards Xavier and Samuel's positions. They both dropped to the ground, hiding in the tall grass.

Jesse ducked into the safety of the grass as well, his brow sweating from the heat of the flames licking towards the tall grass. "We need to get some water on this grass! It'll all go up in flames!" Jesse glanced towards the well to the left and the masked men to the right. "Xavier! Throw me a bucket!"

A bucket sailed through the air, landing ten feet away from Jesse. He scurried over to the bucket and started crouching into a run towards the well. "We have to stop this fire!" Jesse cried as Xavier scrambled behind him with Samuel providing cover. Several shots rang over their heads as they ran for the water.

Jesse and Xavier arrived at the well and hurriedly filled their pails as Samuel's shots continued. They ducked as the shots quieted and then scrambled towards the house on the east side that was burning the most. This side would quickly grow into a wild grass fire over the hot summer fields if left unchecked. Then they'd have even bigger problems.

"Wet the tall grass around a perimeter of the house! Don't just dump all the water in one place, sprinkle it evenly in a line. We want to create a buffer so this fire doesn't catch all over these fields." Jesse tilted the bucket and crouched backwards as the water dribbled out. "We will try to save the house after we have soaked the fields sufficiently."

Xavier nodded and followed his father's instructions, sprinkling the water the same way as Jesse but in an opposite line from Jesse so they both formed a perimeter. When they were out of water, they ran back to the well with the buckets banging against their knees.

He saw Georgina lift Jeremiah's rifle up over the tall grass and wondered if Jeremiah was okay. Jesse jumped down for cover as bullets cascaded towards him. Georgina fired, smiling, as she shot down one of the masked men. Her head bobbed back down into the grass. Jesse sighed in relief and continued towards the well.

Samuel shot down another masked man, then the shooting ceased. An echoing silence sounded as several men ran away into the distance.

Xavier and Jesse returned with more water and wetted more of the house's perimeter that was raging in flames.

Samuel ran towards the wounded, burly man, who was still moaning on the ground. Samuel kicked the man's hand as he reached for his weapon. "No," Samuel warned. "You're not going to touch that gun, Mister." He picked up the man's pistol and pointed his rifle at the burly man. "Get up, now! I don't care if you have to limp on one leg."

"I can't," the man groaned in pain. "I have a bullet in my leg! Do you know how painful that is?"

"I can end your pain for good if you don't get up."

"Don't shoot!" the burly man shouted in reply. "I'll get up." The man grunted and shifted until he was standing on one foot, seething through the pain.

Samuel pointed towards the burning house to the left. "That way! Move!"

♎

Georgina ran towards the house with her own bucket of water. "Those bastards!" she yelled.

Jesse met her at the back door and grabbed her arm roughly. "It's too dangerous to approach the east side of the house. It's fully in flames now!"

"I'm going in!"

Jesse tightened his grip on her arm. "No, you're not!"

Georgina eyed Jesse. "Look, my husband might die, and my house is burning down. I'm going to do everything I can!"

"No, Georgina!" Jesse yelled commandingly. "We fight this fire from the outside."

"There are people inside!" Georgina yelled, her voice pitching in a frenzied panic.

"Who?"

"It's a long story, Jesse!" Georgina explained briefly, her eyes wide with fright. "We have a dozen slaves in the cellar waiting to escape to Canada!"

"Is that who those men were after?"

"Unfortunately, yes," Georgina answered and prepared to run into the burning house.

Ω

Jeremiah heard his wife's panicked voice. She was yelling something. He woke up in a start and sat up, confused, looking up at the purplish predawn skies. Jeremiah turned his head and sighed as their house burned down, a section of wood supports collapsing right before his eyes. Half of the east wall crashed down into the flames, sending sparks into the yard. His eyes combed the back entrance to the house, then he spotted his wife. Georgina was talking to Jesse with a bucket of water in her hand at the back door, ready to charge in.

"Georgina!" Jeremiah shouted with all his might.

Georgina stopped and looked into the field, running towards where she had left Jeremiah. "Honey?" she cried, her eyes moistening with hope, running straight to her husband. "Are you alright?"

"I'm hurt, but I'll live," Jeremiah answered, trying to stand up. "Listen to me, Georgina. The slaves are all dead, honey." He paused and swallowed hard. "That's where I was when you woke up in the middle of the night. I was trying to free them, but the kitchen was fully in flames." He gently rose to standing as Georgina rushed over and grasped his arm. "Sweetheart, the wooden trap door was on fire, and it was quickly spreading to the walls. I tried going in, but my clothing caught on fire. I rolled on the ground and tried again. It's hopeless, honey. You can't go in there." Jeremiah shook his head sadly. "They are trapped in the cellar. Who knows, they might survive? But it is too dangerous. Trust me, I almost died trying. It is in God's hands now."

Georgina opened her mouth to say something, but nothing came out. She cried out loud. "God!" Georgina fell to her knees and prayed with both her hands. "God help us all!"

♎

All the servants from the Eastman mansion arrived shortly after. They all joined together to help douse the flames. They stopped the flames from reaching the west side of the house, and together they kept the tall grass watered down. Fourteen people, including Georgina, Jesse, Xavier, and Samuel, kept up the firefighting efforts until the flames burned down into smoldering ashes. A light rain had steadily fallen during the team effort, aiding the firefighters. They looked up to the sky in gratitude, watching the full storm approaching.

The east side of the house had completely collapsed. The entire east wall was gone, and part of the north wall had collapsed as well. The west half was intact, and the south backyard facing wall was still standing. The black ashes smoldered, and a thick, heavy black smoke rose into the clouds, mixing with the dark approaching rain clouds. The clouds circled towards them, sending each raindrop sizzling onto the smoldering ashes. Some of the fields had burned slightly, but the watered perimeter and the rain had kept it largely contained.

Samuel dragged the wounded, burly man to a wooden outdoor chair and tied him to it, as Jesse and Georgina attempted to access the cellar through the ashes. Several servants poured water on the ashes, and a few started digging through the debris with shovels, trying to find the kitchen access to the cellar.

Jeremiah was in no shape to help, so he stayed with the captured slave hunter, leveling his weapon at the burly man, while the others tried desperately to free the black people trapped in the cellar.

No sounds came from the house. The smoky sunrise echoed back with an eerie silence.

The rescuers worked tiredly, shoveling and saturating the ashes with multiple human trains of water buckets. After several frenzied minutes, the cellar access was cleared. Geogina shouted into the black, charred hole. "Say something if you are alive down there!" she shouted, tears streaming down her face. "Please God!" She turned to Jesse and waved for him to come along. "We're going in!"

Jesse stared down the hole to the old stone cellar. "The wooden ladder is gone," he declared ominously. He pointed towards the wreckage of collapsed house walls. "Is there anything in that pile that we can use as a board to get down into the ground cellar?"

Samuel and Xavier ran to the collapsed pile of walls and sifted through the debris for several minutes as everyone hung on a thread of hope.

Xavier pulled a six-foot plank out. "Will this work?"

"No, it needs to be longer," Samuel answered, hefting several long pieces of floorboards out, then discarding them. "It needs to be at least eight feet long to reach the cellar. Does anybody have some nails and a hammer?"

Georgina shouted and pointed at the intact shed. "In there! There are tools in the shed!"

Several servants ran to the shed and returned with nails and a hammer.

Samuel and Xavier hefted a long floor plank out of the debris. They grunted as the thick, twelve-inch-wide wood floor joist was stuck underneath something. They both pulled and felt a bit of give, but it wasn't enough.

Jesse ran and helped with several others as six men tied a rope to the floor joist and pulled it completely free from the debris. They sat exhausted on the wet grass, looking at the ten-foot-long wood floor joist. It was the right size in length. Samuel waved his hand at the servant with the hammer. "Hand me that hammer and let's find some small wood pieces to hammer into this plank for steps. We need about five to ten steps. Each piece of wood needs to be this size!" He pulled a small, twelve-inch-long, partially blackened wall stud. "Everyone help! We will nail these in."

Samuel took the footlong piece and nailed it approximately 18 inches from the top of the wooden plank. He hammered the nails in, securing the piece of wood so it reached from one side of the plank to the other, providing a secure step footing for the rescuers going into the cellar. Another piece was handed to him, and he nailed that one in approximately 18 inches lower than the first one. As the pieces of wood scraps came to him, he nailed those in, too. Sweat dripped from his forehead as the sun fully rose and blanketed the site with a brief yellow ray of sunlight. Shortly after, a crackle of thunder sounded as rain started to fall again.

After several minutes, Samuel and Xavier hefted the large makeshift ladder towards the cellar opening. As they got closer, Georgina saw that the cellar access was much bigger than the original size. The cellar door was gone, and the surrounding areas were charred. She inspected the rest of the kitchen, and it appeared that the walls and roof were destroyed, but the floor looked mostly safe. A small section towards the back of the house appeared to be the only area completely unaffected.

The men maneuvered the plank ladder into place and threaded it into the cellar entrance.

"Clear some more of this debris!" Jesse shouted. "I want to make sure the floor will not collapse into the cellar while we are in there." He picked up a shovel and started shoveling the debris off the blackened kitchen floor. Several broken dishes and black pots clanged as the workers sifted through the rubble. "Be careful with the floor! Be light on your feet. It's very wet, but we don't know what's underneath all of this."

A crack rippled throughout the floor as several rescuers jumped from the site. "Get off the floor!" Jesse shouted as another crack rippled through the debris.

The workers stood, sweating and exhausted from the physical effort, leaning on their shovels. Georgina leaned on her shovel and looked at Jesse. "What do we do now?" she cried. "We can't just leave them all down there. Alive or dead, we need to get the bodies out."

Jesse surveyed the soaked destruction of the kitchen as a wind blew in his face, pelting him with rain. He pulled his hat lower over his forehead and wiped his wet hands on his pants, trying to find the best solution to the dilemma. He waved his arms in a straight line. "The floorboards go along the length of the house from east to west. They will still be supported from the west side of the house." He waved to the intact side and then pointed to the cellar opening. "One of us needs to go down there and support the floor with a few of these planks, standing them up like beams, holding everything up. We can thread in some additional floor boards to provide more support."

Several of the servants volunteered, hefting the large beams down into the cellar as the rain continued to sprinkle down on the site.

After continuing with hard work and ingenuity, the rescue site was secured. "That should be safe enough, boss!" a male servant shouted up towards Jesse. "You won't like what we found down here, though."

Jesse and Georgina climbed down into the cellar and gasped. A pile of bodies was clustered together on the far side of the cellar, towards the back side of the house. Georgina's heart fluttered then dread filled her heart. "They're all dead?" she asked.

"It looks like it, Mrs. Georgina," the male servant responded gravely.

"Let's take a look and make sure," Jesse said, grasping Georgina's hand. "We didn't come here for nothing. We will give them all a proper burial."

Georgina walked with Jesse to the huddled pile of bodies. Tears streamed down her face at the grisly sight. Her hands began to shake.

"Stay here, Georgina," Jesse said. "I will bring some of the bodies out. Samuel! Come and help me!" He shouted at the ceiling.

Several seconds later, Xavier and Samuel were there, removing the bodies one by one with Jesse. They laid them close to the makeshift ladder as several other rescuers lifted the bodies up through the cellar entrance. They eventually lined the bodies along the grass, beside each other. Most of them looked like they had died from smoke inhalation. Only a few had visible burns on their bodies.

Jesse shouted from the cellar as the final three bodies were removed. "Someone is alive in here! I feel some movement!"

Georgina felt a cold chill spread across her arms, and she rushed to help. Xavier and Samuel lifted the young woman together and brought her limp body to the ladder as Georgina walked with them.

Georgina lightly spread her fingers on the young woman's face, clearing the hair from her eyes. "Sarah," Georgina uttered in amazement. "You're alive, my dear." She grasped the woman's hand, and Sarah squeezed back weakly. "She's alive!" Georgina shouted to the rescuers. "Jeremiah! Sarah's alive!"

A whoop sounded from the back part of the house. Jeremiah shouted, "Get that woman out of there! She has a ferry to catch!"

Georgina laughed happily. "I don't know if she's able to do that yet, but she's definitely strong, alive, and very lucky."

Sarah gazed at Georgina and whispered in a cracked voice. "My husband, where's my husband?"

"I'm so sorry, Sarah," Georgina answered gravely. "You are the only one alive."

Sarah swallowed. "I will be on that ferry. My husband would've wanted me to." She coughed and added, "I might need a glass of water."

Georgina nodded. "We will definitely get you some water."

♎

Fifteen corpses lined the grass on the rain-soaked field. Alongside the trapped runaway slaves, four white slave hunters lay amongst them, stone cold dead. Only the one captured slave hunter was still alive.

Samuel turned, struck the burly man on the side of the head, and poked his rifle in the man's back. "Tell us where Bartholomew is!" Samuel shouted at the man.

The large man spit a loose tooth out and shook his head. "I never met anybody named Bartholomew! I'm telling the truth!" he begged.

Samuel struck him again.

Jesse crouched angrily in front of the captive. "Do you see that row of dead bodies over there?" he sneered, pointing. "That's eleven innocent people you got killed, and along with them, four of your white comrades are negotiating with the devil right now." Jesse stood straight and glared at the burly man. "Did you want to go join them?" Jesse pulled a pistol from his pocket and aimed it at the prisoner.

"Please!" the burly man begged. "I will tell you everything I know. I was part of a group of slave owners who wanted to recover their slaves. That's all. Billy Eastman recruited us and gave us weapons and ammunition. There was never a mention of anyone named Bartholomew. Only Billy and another man named Thomas, or something!" The burly man stuttered and inhaled sharply.

Jesse's eyes narrowed. "My brother put you up to this? I don't believe you." He aimed the gun at the man's head.

Georgina shouted as she lay by Jeremiah and Sarah's side. "Jesse! It must be true!" She stood, remembering the string of events. "They tried to kidnap me! One of the men had said it was Billy! Our brother!" Georgina ran over to the interrogation by the shed. She glared at the burly man who had almost kidnapped her and slapped him viciously. "You should go to hell with the rest of them!" Georgina leveled her own rifle at the man, seething with anger.

The burly man spit out blood. "Please! Stop this. I was misled! Billy didn't tell me everything. I am telling you the truth!" The burly man searched his memory for a small token of something, anything to save his own life. "Don't shoot! I remembered something!" he shouted, briefly stumbling over his own words. "Thomas, the other guy that Billy was with!" He looked up at Jesse, his face sweating with fever. "He was at the house when we all sat down for the meeting. Thomas mentioned something about Bartholomew travelling on his way back today or tomorrow. I can't remember the details, but he definitely said that Bartholomew was returning."

"From where?" Jesse shouted, a dread filling his heart.

The man spat out blood and tried to remember. "Buffalo, I think he said. Yes, it was Buffalo."

Jesse felt his legs go weak and rubbery. He tried to keep the dread from his face but failed miserably. He turned to look back at the expansive Eastman estate. "I have to go," he mumbled at the forest.

Georgina stared at Jesse and sensed the urgency and graveness in his voice. "Zee?" she asked.

"Yes," Jesse whispered.

"Take Sarah with you," Georgina urged, unfolding a ticket for the ferry from her pocket. "The ferry is in Buffalo. Sarah has to be well enough to travel. We must get her out of here or the authorities will kill her."

Jesse stared coldly across the field with a heavy feeling of terror filling his heart. "I will take her," he said stonily, grabbing the ticket. "Tell her to be ready in thirty minutes. I will get the horses."

PART III

THE EVIL WITHIN

Chapter 20

Jesse adjusted his wide-brimmed hat and pulled on his old pair of leather boots. His longish hair grew slightly outside of the hat now, framing his handsomely rugged and lined face. He scowled in the mirror. "I will hunt you down and kill you, Bartholomew," he whispered into the reflection. "If you touch my wife, I'll make you beg for your death." Jesse looked down at his hands, shaking with anger. He exhaled to try to calm his temper.

Xavier and Samuel offered to join him, but he would have none of it. This was between Bartholomew and Jesse Eastman now. Jesse realized that now. It was never a takeover. It was a threat to take away everything Jesse had built over his lifetime. And now, Zee.

"You won't be terrorizing my family any longer," Jesse sneered, as he stared stonily out the window. He jabbed his finger into the air, angrily. "I will hunt you and kill you, Bartholomew."

Jesse turned on his foot and stomped down the stairwell, swinging on the banister at the bottom. He jumped onto the floor and took several large strides to the back entrance. Jesse ran across the manicured lawns to the stable, his breath coming out in angry, testosterone-fueled huffs. He worked swiftly, saddling two horses, his own and another mare. Once the two horses were ready, he led them both out onto the horse path and whistled loudly towards the house.

Sarah exited out of the back sunroom near the library. Her long legs cleared the distance easily as she struggled with her smoke-filled lungs to reach the stable. Several seconds later, she reached the stable, coughing and wheezing.

"Are you sure that you're healthy enough to travel?"

"I have no choice," Sarah replied, coughing up a bit of phlegm.

He handed her a large cloak with a hood. "Here, put this on. The sheriff's men will be here soon to deal with the fire and the bodies. I don't want them to see you." He handed the reins of the mare to her. "This is Lady," he said. "She'll be your ride until we make it to the Buffalo ferry. We will stop to rest overnight as little as possible. I must reach my wife and find Bartholomew."

Sarah nodded nervously and mounted the horse. "Whatever you say, Mr. Eastman," she whispered, her voice scratchy. "I am very grateful to you for your assistance. Did you receive all the ticket agent instructions needed from Pastor Brown?"

"Yes, Jeremiah gave me a map," Jesse replied, patting the folded map hidden in his pocket.

"Good," Sarah said simply, awaiting his next reply.

Jesse's face changed as a chilling evilness clouded over his eyes. He mounted his horse slowly, then looked her straight in the eye. "I will be killing a man on the way. His name is Bartholomew. I expect you to say nothing and see nothing."

"Is Bartholomew the man responsible for my husband's death?" Sarah asked, a shadow of suppressed grief crossing over her face.

"Yes," Jesse answered, knowing that Billy would one day be held to answer for his involvement in this, too.

"Then I can help you kill that man," Sarah answered coldly.

Jesse chuckled gravely. "No, Bartholomew is mine to kill. Trust me." The smile fell from his face as he snapped the reins on his horse. "Let's go."

CHAPTER 21

Barton stepped down from his horse and tied it to a tree deep within the forest. He would walk the rest of the way on foot. He didn't want to raise any alarms with Zee. Last time he was here, she had wanted to kill him! He shook his head and chuckled. It could only mean one thing, he thought. And it was so clear to him now. As clear as the light of day!

That type of anger could only mean one thing, and Barton knew it all so well. His late wife had possessed that same anger when she had caught him having a rendezvous with one of his female servants. Lorena had swung at him, thrown objects at him, and cried with angry tears running down her face. He remembered the day like it was yesterday. He had to cover her mouth so the entire neighborhood wouldn't hear her screaming at him. She was out of control.

It was because she had loved him so terribly much, and he had broken her heart.

He stopped on the path briefly and blinked.

Yes, he had hurt her feelings. He hadn't meant to, of course. It was only his hormones that had raged out of control when Lorena had refused him sex.

Barton continued walking towards the cabin.

It wasn't his fault, of course. Lorena shouldn't have refused his advances. Then he wouldn't have lost control of his hormones.

The ground crunched underneath his feet as a sudden crack of thunder filled the skies. Several raindrops fell through the forest onto his shoulders, as if the devil was consoling him for his misdeeds.

Nothing was ever his fault, of course. Everything that happened was a chain of reactions following what others had done or said. That was just how life worked around him. It always had!

Did he tell Zee the truth about his wife?

No, he hadn't.

He stopped and stared at the dark cabin in the distance.

He could never tell her the truth. Zee would not understand.

But he knew something about Zee.

Similar to his wife, Lorena, Zee was angry. She had wanted to kill him! She almost did! He shook his head in astonishment.

There could be no other reason for her madness.

Zee Collard was almost certainly in love with him.

Barton Mato had to be a man. He would get his new wife and take her home with him. There was no other solution. He could not leave back to Philadelphia without Zee. She was his salvation! He had turned a new leaf in his life when he met Zee Collard. Gone were the days of living an evil existence. He would be the fallen angel that had risen to become good and pure again. Barton would prove to his dead wife's memory that he was capable of goodness. He was capable of being a wonderful husband.

Today would be the first day in his new life with Zee.

Ω

The rain fell lightly but steadily on the horse path to Buffalo. They had been travelling for three days now but they were finally gaining some ground. Sarah was behind him, and Jesse was in the lead. They entered the forest as quietly as possible and noticed that there was no activity on the well-travelled Buffalo path this morning.

Maybe it was the rain, Jesse thought. It certainly makes people choose a different day for travelling. It felt eerily quiet on such a normally busy path, and his senses were on high alert.

For most of the trip, he had been observing strange activity in the bushes. He didn't want to frighten Sarah, so he kept it to himself. Jesse needed time to analyze the slight movements in the bushes. His military senses always came back to him, and his mind slowly began determining what the movement was from. He was certain now.

It wasn't animal behavior. It was human.

As they rounded another corner on the road, a rustle sounded in the bushes. Jesse turned and squinted through the greenery, trying to make out what it was. As they passed, he noticed a lone horse tied to a tree in the distance. Jesse palmed the pistol on his belt and raised a hand behind him at Sarah.

"I think there's someone tracking us," he whispered, pointing at the lone horse.

"What do we do?" Sarah whispered, looking around suspiciously.

"We let him follow us," Jesse stated, his hand ready on his pistol. "There's a creek up ahead for the horses to rest. We'll stop there and see what happens."

Ω

Zee barely slept last night. The thunder had awakened her early in the morning. The rainstorm fell hard on the roof of the hunting cabin. She had tried to go back to sleep, but it didn't work. She lay in bed listening to the rain drumming on the roof, a dread filling her heart. Maybe it was the wrong decision to come back out here without Jesse. Her sons could have easily come back and retrieved all the meat, but she feared for their safety, too. It was a long journey.

"Why did I come back without Jesse?" she asked the darkness of her room.

The answer wasn't clear to her, but she knew deep inside that the country was where her heart was. She felt at home in the country, and her stubborn spirit of solving her own problems always got the best of her. That was the simplest answer.

Zee shifted in the bed, curling towards where her husband usually slept, on the left side of the bed. She ran her hands along the pillow and prayed that Jesse could somehow be here. Zee shivered from anxiety and realized why she was feeling so dreadful.

Barton had filled her with fear.

Zee was not angry with Barton anymore. She was simply afraid of his disturbed mind now. Zee clearly understood that the man was not well. Everything he had said and done was not normal. She had felt the motherly instincts to protect her home and family from this crazy man. Zee knew with 100 percent clarity that if he hadn't left, she would have shot and killed him.

She sat up in bed.

Zee had never killed a man before. A sliver of fear tingled up her spine, raising the hairs on the back of her neck. How did she get into this predicament? Zee wasn't sure. She was just being herself, she thought.

She hugged her knees and jumped as another crack of thunder rumbled over the top of the cabin. "Well, there's no going back to sleep," she whispered to herself. Zee climbed from bed, dressed quickly, and pulled on her boots, checking to make sure the hidden knife was still in her boot. She wanted to go home immediately. They were set to load all the pack horses this morning, but with the rain, she wasn't sure when they'd be leaving. The weather had already delayed their plans by several days.

She sighed and wished that she could just miraculously be back home. The meat was packed up tightly in the cellar, and their bags were waiting at the front door. Scott and James had drunk too much alcohol sitting around the fire pit last night. Zee had angrily sent them off to bed at 3 am when it started raining. They wouldn't be awakening too soon, she knew.

Zee fiddled with her hands, wondering if she should just awaken them and leave right away. An urgency to see Jesse gripped her. What if there was another attack on the Eastman Empire? What if Jesse wasn't safe?

Zee shivered with the thought of losing her beloved husband.

"No," she muttered, lecturing herself. "Jesse is a strong man. He's been through so much. He is fine. Stop worrying, Mrs. Eastman." She smiled at the title. She loved being his wife. Zee was proud to have such a strong, handsome man as her husband.

A small click sounded on the far side of her bedroom.

It was so out of place in the quiet darkness of her bedroom that it stood out clearly. It was a quiet noise, though, one that she wouldn't have heard if she had been asleep.

She turned slowly towards the sound. Zee couldn't see much through the dark rainstorm. The clouds were black and angry, only allowing a brief burst of sunlight, then quickly masking everything with a dark gloom.

Zee's eyes caught a movement outside the dark, rain-soaked window. Had she been seeing things? Was there something out there?

She moved very slowly and crouched on the other side of the bed, forgetting the pistol under the pillow. It's probably just an animal outside, she thought.

Her mind quickly jumped to several conclusions. One that she didn't like at all.

What if it was Barton?

He had left saying that he would never hurt her. But could she believe him?

Her mind churned through the possible answers.

No, she could never trust a crazy man. Barton was truly out of his mind. Nothing she had said had gotten through to him. He was in love with her, and that was that. In his mind, it was final. She could tell in his eyes, when she had the gun aimed at him, that he was insane. There was a wildness in his pupils, almost like how animals look before they are killed.

Something about Barton was very wrong. Zee knew this now.

She heard another click and jumped, slipping down onto the floor.

Someone was opening the bedroom window.

♎

Jesse trotted towards the creek, then jumped off his horse, handing the reins to Sarah. "Let the horses drink, and stay with them."

Jesse crouched and stepped stealthily into the bushes. He felt an urgency like none other to reach the cabin immediately. He had a sudden fear that he was too late. Scott and James had talked about a man from Buffalo who had helped out at the cabin. His name was Barton. At the time, it meant nothing to him. He trusted Zee completely and knew that she would have told him if there was danger.

Jesse had let the small bit of information go and trusted his wife's decisions. He knew that she loved him fully and completely, but all the troubles they were having in their marriage lately could have steered things the wrong way.

A tendril of anger seeped into his blood as he lifted his rifle and aimed at the bushes, looking for any slight movement. He had trouble focusing his mind on the task. Every single fiber in his being wanted to go galloping at full speed to the cabin.

Barton was short for Bartholomew.

It had never occurred to him earlier.

When he heard the words that Bartholomew was in Buffalo, everything clicked into place. Like a puzzle which he had been pondering over for some time, his mind had quickly summed up all the conclusions.

He hoped that he was wrong. Jesse was not a religious man, but his mind began praying silently to awaken Zee and alert her to the danger. His heart pounded in anticipation, and he feared for his wife's well-being. Nothing was more important to him right now.

He heard a twig snap in the distance.

Jesse had to focus and eliminate the threat immediately before him. He thought hard about the best plan, urging his mind to concentrate. He narrowed his eyes down the rifle, following the sounds.

Finally, he lowered the rifle and swung it down. He pulled the pistol from his belt and crouched through the forest silently, closing the distance. He needed to find out who was following them.

Another ten yards closer. He could hear the man breathing. Jesse had circled around him and was now behind the man. He was wearing a dirty hat and hunting clothes. Jesse leaped at the man suddenly, jumping like a tiger, crashing through the bushes.

The man panicked and tried running away, but Jesse grabbed his ankle, tripping him. The man fell flat on his face while Jesse dragged him backwards.

"Who are you?" Jesse yelled, yanking the man's ankle high in the air. "Why are you following us?"

The man screamed. "Please! You'll break my foot!"

"Answer me!"

"I am of no concern to you!" the man yelled hysterically. "I was only paid to follow you."

Jesse stopped and tied a rope around the man's ankle. "Stand up!" He yelled. "Who paid you?"

"A rich man," the man stammered out. "I think he said his name was Barton or something like that."

"Put your gun slowly down on the ground," Jesse instructed, his pistol aimed at the man's head. "Do as I tell you."

The man slowly removed a flintlock pistol.

"Put it on the ground slowly."

The man cautiously placed it on the ground. "Are you Jesse Eastman?" the man asked.

"Yes," Jesse replied. "Why?"

"I was right then," he stated disappointedly.

"What do you mean?

"Barton told me to follow a man with your description from the Eastman estate."

"You've been following us from the estate this whole time?"

"Not directly from the estate, but close enough."

"What were you instructed to do?" Jesse asked, picking up the flintlock pistol and placing it into his bag.

"I was supposed to gallop ahead and alert Bartholomew if I saw you."

Jesse narrowed his eyes at the man. "Why didn't you?"

"Because you had a woman with you," the man replied. "Bartholomew clearly stated that you would most likely be travelling alone or with several other men."

"Sarah put you off then," Jesse answered, chuckling.

"Yes, you might say that."

"Well, well," Jesse murmured thoughtfully and gestured for the man to stand up. "Are there other sentries?"

"Not that I know of," the man replied, standing hastily. "Look, Mr. Eastman. I meant no trouble. I am just a man of destitute trying to earn a few dollars."

"He paid you that much?"

"Yes, Barton is a rich man." The man stood fully and nodded, waiting for instructions.

"Did he tell you to kill me?" Jesse asked.

"No," the man answered. "He was very clear that I was to warn him only. The pistol is mine. I have to live in this forest and kill my own meat. I would greatly appreciate it back, Mr. Eastman."

Jesse rubbed his trimmed beard thoughtfully, then slowly tipped his hat. "I will put your pistol in your horse's bag. That's your horse tied up over there, right?" Jesse pointed into the woods.

"Yes, that's Charlie."

Jesse motioned the man to start walking. "I'll be tying you to this tree over here. I'll secure the ropes well, so it'll take you some time to get freed. By then, I will already be at the cabin ending Bartholomew's life."

The man's eyes widened. "Revenge?"

"No," Jesse answered. "Just ridding the world of filth."

Jesse approached a tree near the creek as Sarah looked up. He knelt down and started binding the man firmly to the tree.

Sarah's eyes widened.

Jesse looked up as he continued wrapping the long rope around the tree. "Don't worry, Sarah," he calmly reassured her. "He'll be able to free himself. It'll just take a while." Jesse turned his attention back to the man and spoke quietly. "I will feed your horse and bring it closer to the creek so it can drink."

Jesse tied the final knot, then trudged towards the horse. He untied the horse and brought Charlie to the creek, speaking softly to the animal. Once the horse was well watered, Jesse tied it to a nearby tree.

Jesse straightened, returned to his own horse, and spoke quietly to Sarah. "We have to go now. We need to get to the cabin as soon as we can."

Jesse mounted his horse and waved at Sarah to follow him. Once he was certain she was ready, Jesse snapped the reins, prompting his gelding into a full speed gallop throughout the forest.

CHAPTER 22

Zee heard the familiar squeak of wood on wood as the window creaked open. Her spine tingled in fear. The bedroom window slipped up gently and stealthily, with a large shadow of a man working it gradually wide open. Her heart quickened and hammered in her chest. She had no doubt in her mind that it was Barton.

A large dark figure dressed all in black started climbing slowly through the window. She could hear heavy breathing as the masked man wriggled through the opening. She immediately grasped her pocket and realized that she had left the gun under the pillow. She inhaled sharply and weighed the odds of giving up her hidden position in order to get the pistol.

The man abruptly got through the opening and stood in the dark. He was a very big man, Zee thought. She crouched down farther against the bed, wondering if she should slide underneath the bed and hide. Then she thought of her two sons sleeping off a night of drinking. Zee couldn't risk their lives by being a coward. She was hidden quite well in the stormy dark morning light. No sources of light penetrated the bedroom. Zee was certain that the man could not see her.

The figure took three strides towards the bed and the crumpled blankets.

She pointed her hands in her shirt as if holding a pistol against the fabric. "Stop right there, or I shoot," she growled in the meanest voice she could muster.

The figure stopped and raised his hands. "Zee? Is that you? Don't shoot. It's me."

"What are you doing here, Barton?" she growled angrily, standing abruptly on the far side of the bed.

"I'm here to take you back home to Philadelphia," he replied, pausing with his next words. "The woods are a dangerous place for a woman alone."

"I'm with my sons," she replied instantly.

"No, you're coming with me, alone."

"I'm not going anywhere with you, Barton," she declared, glancing instinctively at the pillow where the pistol was hidden. "I'm going back to my husband today."

"No," Barton replied, his voice cracking painfully. "Jesse doesn't deserve a woman like you. You are my wife now." He narrowed his eyes at the gun in her hand. His brow furrowed in suspicion, then, deciding to take a risk, he leapt towards the pillow she had been glancing at.

Zee jumped at the pillow at the same time, grasping his hand as hard as she could. He got there first. His fingers wrapped around the hidden pistol, and she struggled to pry them off. Screaming in frustration, she bit his arm, sinking her teeth in as far as she could.

Barton cursed and grabbed her hair, shaking her teeth off his arm. He secured the gun, inspecting it appraisingly. "Is this what you were looking for?" He chuckled, lifting her by the hair.

She opened her mouth to yell for her sons.

Her scream was muffled by Barton's large hand slapped across her mouth. "Shh, my dear," he cooed. "You don't want to endanger your sons now, do you?" She relaxed instantly in his grip. Barton allowed her to sit on the bed for a moment. "That's a good girl. Now, you will be listening to me, Mrs. Zelda Mato."

Zee's eyes widened. "What?" she mumbled against his hand.

"Yes, that's right," he assured her. "We will get married right away. Don't you worry. We will be happy together. You'll see." He glanced down at her with a glint in his eye. "I know you love me, Zee. You can admit it."

Zee felt all the energy drain from her body as the realization hit her like a ton of bricks. Barton was Bartholomew Mato! He was Jesse's most feared enemy! Anger flashed in her mind, then sorrow and regret. Jesse had told her that nobody had ever seen Bartholomew in person. The man had always let everyone else do his dirty work.

Zee had never thought Barton was the same man. Not once! She hadn't even considered it or questioned who he was. He had fooled her! He had fooled everybody; even her sons didn't suspect anything. She whimpered against the hand on her mouth, wondering what her next move would look like.

"That's right, Zee," he chuckled. "You're under my command now." He smoothed a hand along her long hair. "I like this obedient side of you, my darling."

Zee looked up at him pleadingly and instantly decided to play along. She let out a feminine whimper against his hand. Her mind churned with a desperate plan to kill him before her sons walked in. She sat obediently on the bed, trying to give him her best powerless, vulnerable look.

Barton smiled, flashing his white teeth. "That's much better. Now, if you can remain quiet, I will remove my hand,

and we can continue having an adult conversation. If you shout, I may have to kill your sons. You know that, Zee. You'd give me no choice." He kissed her gently on the cheek and stared closely into her eyes, trying to gauge her reaction. "Don't make me do that, Zee. I love you and don't want to hurt your sons."

She nodded and mumbled underneath his hand. "I'll do as you say."

He slowly removed his hand and stood ready for action. When she sat still and lowered her head in submission, he smiled. "Well, well," he chuckled. "You will make a wonderful wife, Zee. You just need to know your place."

Zee looked down at her boots demurely, waiting for her chance.

"Now," he continued. "As I was saying, you will be coming with me to Philadelphia. We will get married immediately, and then it will be your choice where you want to live. I am a wealthy man and can provide you with a perfect lifestyle anywhere in the world." He straightened and leaned back on his hips, spreading his arms wide around the room. "If you want to live in the woods in France, we can buy a boat and cross the Atlantic. It's your choice, my lady."

Zee couldn't believe how crazy Barton actually was. "France sounds lovely," she murmured in a low, sexy voice. She continued looking down at her boot, waiting for him to relax a bit more so she could have a fighting chance. She nodded and flashed her different colored eyes at him for a brief instant. "When will we go?"

Barton exhaled in relief. "You are quite a remarkable woman, Zee. I knew you'd eventually see things my way." He paused, stuffing the pistol in his pocket. "See, God has made us to be with each other. You are the perfect woman for a man like me. I could not just let you go back to your ungrateful husband. That would be such a waste."

Zee tilted her head to the side and smiled demurely. "I suppose you have been right all along, Barton," she replied. "I have been so stubborn about this, and I apologize."

Barton's face beamed into a bright smile of pure joy. "I am so glad. We will be so happy together!"

Zee took advantage of the moment of joy and reached down to her boot. "Let me change my boots, and I will pack a bag, then we will go. Scott and James can return home by themselves. I will leave them a note saying I have left with you."

Barton laughed cheerfully. "That would be perfect!"

Her fingers slipped inside her right boot and grasped the handle of the hidden knife. Her heart drummed in her chest as she seized the moment. "Yes," she murmured, with a hint of sarcasm edged into her voice. "We will be happy."

Barton glanced around the room and noticed her luggage bag sitting by the closet. "I will get your luggage bag, my dear."

Zee pounced at him like a rabid cat, the knife flashing in her hand.

Barton's back was partially turned. He had little time to react to the assault. Zee violently stabbed the knife into his side.

She ran at him with all her body weight and pushed the knife in deep, trying to slice his internal organs. Zee twisted the knife and then pulled it out, stabbing him again in the side with a sharp, precise movement. Barton let out a gasp as the knife hit an organ. Zee pulled the knife out as a gush of blood flowed out. She jumped at him again, this time stabbing towards his neck. The knife slipped and ended up spearing him in the large muscle between his shoulder and neck. His muscles were surprisingly thick, and the knife didn't go in very far. She pushed with all her might but felt the knife yield to his thick muscles.

She tried pushing it in again, but to no avail. Zee yanked the knife back out and attempted to stab him in the throat when he turned around.

Barton's eyes flashed in surprise, then immediately turned to anger. He turned quickly, grabbing his bleeding side and flew his heavy arm across her face, slapping her with a backhanded blow that landed her on the bed. "You stabbed me!" he shouted. "Now, why would you do that?"

Zee's head swam with unconsciousness as she mumbled incoherently on the bed. She tried gripping the knife in her hand, but could feel her grip loosening, and then she felt Barton's strong hand pull the knife from her grip.

"You're a bad girl," Barton admonished, throwing the knife across the room. He instinctively grasped at his side and felt the blood oozing over his fingertips. He tried pushing on the wound to stop the flow of blood. Barton felt a wave of dizziness assault his mind, then felt a sudden urge to urinate. She had most likely slashed his kidney. He felt a trickle of warm blood coursing down from his wounded shoulder. Tears came to his eyes as sadness filled his heart. "You tried to kill me," he mumbled. He shook his head sadly as a sudden rage took over his body.

Zee opened her eyes briefly and watched him reach towards her flaccid body. She urged her body to respond. Her head swam with vertigo. The room appeared to be spinning, but she reacted anyway. Her life depended on it. Zee kicked upwards with all her might, both legs connecting with his abdomen. A sudden whoosh of breath exhaled from his lungs as his body flew backwards, crashing against the wall.

Barton slumped near the closet, flitting in and out of consciousness.

Zee watched briefly, trying to decide her next movement. She should try to flee and get the hunting rifle! Zee moved suddenly and felt a wave of nausea attack her senses. He had hit her hard. She couldn't allow him to strike her again.

Barton shook his head, momentarily stunned. He gazed at her with a scowl forming on his brow. "Why are you doing this to me?" he muttered angrily. "Don't you know that it gets a lot more difficult for me to be gentle with you now?"

CHAPTER 23

J esse and Sarah trotted slowly through the branches when they saw the cabin appear in the distance. The woods were very thick and forested in this area. Jesse could understand why it was so plentiful for hunting.

The horses trotted tiredly to the hitch post at the front entrance. Jesse disembarked as Sarah did the same.

"We will stop for another night and get some food," Jesse whispered to the horse as he tied him to the post, nodding at Sarah to do the same. Jesse peered into the water trough and noticed that the trough was almost dry.

A sudden noise within the cabin caught his attention immediately. It sounded like someone had crashed into something. The walls groaned under the weight of the impact of something or someone quite large. He looked around the cabin to see if one of the horses had fallen and found the horses secured in the stable.

"Stay here," Jesse mouthed to Sarah, holding his hand up in a stop signal.

He heard a sudden grunt within the house and all his senses fired at once. He could smell the dew on the grass, feel the stormy wind in his hair, and hear the muffled noises coming from the north side of the cabin.

Jesse crouched along the east side until he came to the corner, poking his head cautiously around the corner. When he determined that it was clear, he ran along the north side toward the noises. A man was shouting something angrily. Jesse's anger bubbled over, and he strained to keep control of his senses as he approached the open window of the cabin. He looked around the side of the house, trying to familiarize himself with the layout again, and realized with a sudden jolt of urgency that this was where the master bedroom was located. Zee's bedroom. He slid against the exterior log cabin until he was directly beside the open window. He heard the man's voice again, and it was like hearing the devil himself. The madness seeping from the guttural male voice was palpable.

Zee was in danger. He could feel it in his heart and every fiber of his being. He didn't need to visually see what was going on. Jesse knew.

He quickly loaded the rifle and inhaled deeply as the wind blew angrily at the trees, almost bending them over with the force.

Jesse pulled the rifle to his shoulder and jumped into action, swinging into the open window frame, aiming into the sudden, violent scene.

A man stood against the far wall, holding his side. Jesse had never seen the man before in his life. His instincts told him that it was Bartholomew, but he still didn't know. He pulled the rifle up and then noticed Zee scrambling up from the bed. She frogged over the bed and raced towards the door as the crazed man stumbled towards her.

Jesse was disturbed and alarmed, trying to determine the best course of action. Zee was slightly in his line of fire. He couldn't risk it.

Then Zee saw him. Her eyes locked onto Jesse's eyes. There was a moment of surprise and relief on her face. Then her expression straightened. With a momentary nod that told him to kill, she dropped down onto the floor to clear the shooting path for Jesse.

She yelled intentionally. "Bartholomew! Don't touch me again!"

Barton peered at Zee's sudden fall onto the floor. A moment of confusion crossed his face before his eyes settled on the open window.

Jesse stared at him through the rifle's sights. "It's the end, Bartholomew."

Bartholomew narrowed his eyes and ran across the room towards Zee. "I won't let him take you!"

Jesse pulled the trigger, and a loud crack filled the air. In a millisecond, the bullet shot through the air.

Barton's head whipped sideways as the bullet tore into his brain, sending his body flying backwards onto the bed. His body bounced once and then lay on the bed, twitching.

Jesse lowered the rifle and cautiously entered through the window, all the while watching the body of Bartholomew Mato. Jesse pulled out his pistol as he entered the bedroom and walked towards the jerking body.

Zee straightened, and her heart filled with relief. "Oh my Lord, Jesse."

Jesse nodded cautiously at her as he approached Bartholomew, focusing. His actions told her to stay down until the threat was completely eliminated. Jesse took two more strides and stopped at the edge of the bed.

Bartholomew's face was splattered with dark red blood. The legs and arms jerked as Jesse got closer to the body. Jesse involuntarily aimed the pistol at the dying man.

"Is he dead?" Zee whispered.

"I think so," Jesse replied. "He won't stop twitching. This is not something for you to see, sweetheart. Go to the front room."

"No," Zee said stubbornly. "I'm staying right here by your side, honey. Barton can go to hell and I'll make sure he gets there."

At that moment, the bedroom door swung open. Scott and James both ran inside, armed with hunting rifles.

"Mom! Are you okay?" Scott shouted.

"Dad?" James said questioningly. "When did you get here?"

"Who is that on the bed?" Scott asked.

Zee looked at her sons. "That's Barton."

"Barton?" Scott yelled.

Zee nodded her head at the dead body. "Yes, it's Bartholomew Mato."

Jesse picked up one of Barton's arms, and it flopped back onto the bed as the body finally accepted death. The jerking stopped, and the corpse of Bartholomew Mato went cold still.

Zee hugged Jesse warmly. "Oh my Lord, Jesse! Thank you for coming here and stopping him." She broke down hysterically in an uncontrolled series of fight and flight releases. "He tried to kidnap me," she muttered. The anxiety ebbed and flowed out of her body as Jesse turned around and hugged her tightly.

"I'm here, my love," Jesse replied, smoothing her hair as she quivered in his arms. "You don't have to worry anymore. Everything's okay. I'm here, honey."

CHAPTER 24

The sheriff removed the body quickly while Jesse and Zee explained what happened. He took notes, then nodded towards Jesse. "It looks like clear self-defense," he said, nodding at Zee. "You say his name was Barton Mato?"

"Yes," Jesse answered. "He's been threatening our family for quite a while."

"We've had several bounties for Bartholomew Mato. Never had a clear picture of the man, though." Nodding, the sheriff instructed his deputies to load the body onto the wagon.

Jesse coughed politely as Barton's body slumped onto the horse drawn wagon. "My wife and I have a ferry to catch in Buffalo to see family," he interrupted. "If there aren't any more questions, then we'll be leaving tomorrow. The ferry won't wait for us."

"That's fine with me," the sheriff responded. "If there is anything else we need, I'll contact you in Philadelphia." He nodded and waved them goodbye.

Scott and James stayed to help clean up the gruesome mess, then packed up their horses and left as well. The Eastman twins would arrive back to the estate on their own.

Jesse, Sarah, and Zee stayed overnight for a much needed rest then awoke early the next morning. They mounted their horses and set off into the thickness of the woods.

Jesse explained more of what happened back in Philadelphia to Zee. He told her all about Sarah and the fire that had engulfed Georgina's house. "Sarah is a very lucky girl. We owe it to her. I promised to get her to Upper Canada."

Zee held the reins of her horse loosely as she mused over the details. A thought came to her. "Jesse," she said questioningly. "Why don't we take Sarah straight to the Collard farm? I would love to see my sisters again. They could always use extra farm labor. That is, if Sarah is willing."

"Mrs. Eastman," Sarah immediately answered. "An immediate job in Upper Canada is like heaven, compared to what I've been through. I would be most grateful for anything you could arrange."

Jesse chuckled. "So, it is a yes, I suppose." He trotted along the path, his mind churning with gratitude and unanswered questions. "We will see the relatives at the Collard farm then." Jesse smiled back at Zee. "One day, you'll have to tell me what Bartholomew was doing in our bedroom."

"I will tell you the whole story, my sweet," Zee answered. "He was a very disturbed man." Zee continued to explain all the details as they trotted into Buffalo, right from the first time she had met Barton during the shootout in the supply store. "I never once accepted any of his advances. I almost shot him myself a couple of days ago. Scott almost shot him, too." Zee exhaled. "My only regret is not telling you sooner. I thought that I could deal with it myself. We had no idea that he was Bartholomew."

Jesse nodded, content with her version of events. "You've been through a lot," he muttered appraisingly.

"Yes," Zee replied. "Yes, I have."

"You stabbed him," Jesse stated, grinning.

Zee chuckled proudly, thinking back to the string of events. "Yes, I did, with the knife I always keep in my boot."

"I know that knife," Jesse responded, smiling. "He probably would have died soon enough from the stabbing alone. It might have taken him another hour or so. The amount of blood he was losing was a lot."

"Maybe," Zee replied. "But you still saved me, my love."

"I'm proud of you, Zee," Jesse stated. "You handled it as well as you could." The horses' hooves clapped onto the stone-covered entrance into Buffalo. The noise of a distant market teaming with life filled the air. "But you should've told me," Jesse said, glancing sideways at Zee. "I would have killed him a lot sooner."

"I wish I had told you, Jesse," Zee replied, exhaling. "You don't know how many times I chastised myself for not saying anything. I thought I could deal with it myself. I really did." She paused briefly. "You know, I prayed for you to come."

Jesse turned his head to the side, his eyes barely peeking underneath his wide-brimmed hat. "I must have heard you," he replied, chuckling. "I'm so sorry it took me as long as it did. Once we interrogated that thug after the fire, then I knew. I'm glad we didn't kill that bastard, or else we wouldn't have known Bartholomew was in Buffalo."

"How did you know Barton was the same person?"

"Scott and James had spoken of this Barton fellow. I put two and two together. Once I knew something was terribly wrong, I left right away."

Zee smiled as a warm, comforting feeling of protection seemed to blanket her. "Thank you for acting when you did, my love." Zee blinked and fluttered her eyelashes as an immediate flush of love coursed through her veins. "You were my hero today." She smiled.

"I will always be your hero, honey."

Sarah rode quietly behind them, absorbing the conversation and trying not to be intrusive. "The ferry is on the other side of town," she said. "Will we reach the boat in time?"

Jesse replied quickly. "Yes, we will get there with a few minutes to spare. I will buy two extra tickets for myself and Zee. We will cross with you."

"That's mighty kind of you, Mr. Eastman," Sarah replied.

"If anybody asks any questions, we will just say that you're our servant." Jesse smiled and turned his eyes towards his wife lovingly. Everything will be alright, his eyes said.

♎

"Tickets!" the ferry agent shouted as they all stood in a long line up leading to the wooden dock. Most of the people crossing were blacks. Zee and Jesse were only two of a handful of white people. Jesse waited patiently and progressed in the lineup with Sarah behind them. A gusty wind broke branches off a nearby tree, scattering the broken limbs across the grassy area leading up to the dock.

Jesse protectively hugged Zee. "Come here, darling. I don't want you getting hurt." He looked over her shoulder at Sarah. "Stay behind us. These winds are awful."

The blustery weather howled around them as if to emphasize his words. A gust rattled the arm rail ropes on the dock. Then a branch suddenly blew towards them and got caught on the rope behind them. They all jumped instinctively. Luckily, the branch was tangled securely against the rope, but the wind continued its relentless force, buffeting the stick repeatedly against the post. Jesse tightened his grip on Zee and gently urged her forward.

"Tickets!"

Jesse handed the agent three tickets for himself, Zee, and Sarah.

"A party of three?"

"Yes, sir," Jesse announced. "We're going to visit my wife's family in Niagara."

"The black woman is with you?"

"Yes," Jesse nodded.

"Upper Canada is a free haven for slaves," the agent said, shouting against the wind. "Just so you know! If you're bringing your slave here, she may run free."

Jesse grinned. "She's a paid servant. Don't you worry about that."

The ticket agent looked Sarah and the couple up and down. "Go on," he shouted, waving them to step onto the ship. "Welcome aboard. Next!"

The trio stepped onto the ship and settled tiredly into the main cabin as crowds of black people seated themselves. Some were dirty, with mud clearly on their clothes; others were well dressed for the occasion. Jesse was surprised at the number of people they were ushering onto the boat in the descending evening darkness.

It wasn't until 9 pm that the whistle blew and the ship started moving slowly through the waters towards Canada.

Jesse estimated close to fifty people were aboard, mostly all of them blacks. Everyone was quiet, and Jesse could sense a cloud of hope in the air.

He turned his head towards Sarah and saw her eyes beaming in the twilight. He nodded and whispered to her. "Everything will be alright soon."

Sarah's eyes moistened. Her shoulders heaved slightly as she inhaled the freshwater air wafting over the boat. "I know."

Zee laid a hand on Sarah's shoulder. "I know it's been a long journey. We'll be docking at Fort Erie, then we will make our way to the Collard farm from there. It'll be okay."

Sarah's lips smiled in a tearful grin as the events of the past week unraveled in her mind. "I made it," she whispered tearfully.

"Yes, you did," Zee agreed.

"I will be free?" Sarah whispered, her voice cracking with years of unspeakable horrors.

Jesse cranked his head around Zee's hair and laid a free hand on Sarah's shoulder. "You will be free," he stated confidently. "Your new life starts here."

$$\Omega$$

Zee and Jesse walked towards the big white house in the distance. A chill of old forgotten memories awakened in both their hearts. Zee smiled at Jesse. "This is where we first met."

Jesse grasped her hand lovingly and kissed her palm. "Yes, it is, my dear," he replied. "I remember it like it was yesterday. You were bossing around my team of American soldiers while trying to remove a bullet from that young boy." Jesse's eyes glossed over as he remembered the events as if they had happened yesterday. "You saved that boy."

Zee grinned. "Yes, I saved Tommy's life that day."

"You saved me, too," Jesse added.

Zee laughed wholeheartedly. "You didn't need saving." She leaned over and kissed him on the cheek. "You just needed a woman like me to set you straight."

Jesse chuckled and squeezed her hand. "I remember when you opened the front door. I was not expecting a beautiful-eyed country girl to be on the other side of that door."

Zee squeezed his hand back. "And I wasn't expecting a handsome American sergeant to seize my home and turn it into a military hospital."

"Well, I'm sure glad it was your house we picked, my dear," Jesse murmured lovingly. "My heart started feeling joy that first day we met."

"Mine too," Zee replied as they ascended the stone steps leading onto the porch. Sarah followed behind them shyly. "Come, Sarah, you'll love meeting my family."

At that moment, as if on cue, the front door swung open. A middle-aged woman with dark blonde hair ran out. Jesse was always struck by the uncanny resemblance of the sisters. "Zee!" Charlotte hollered, hugging Zee fiercely. "Is it really you? We haven't seen you for years!"

"We've been busy, but it's no excuse," Zee laughed, hugging her sister back. "It's so good to see you! Oh my Lord, Charlotte, it's so good to come home."

Charlotte pulled Zee to arm's length and looked into her eyes. "Does that mean you're both coming back for good?"

Jesse smiled and kissed Charlotte on both cheeks as several young teens ran out onto the porch. Jesse winked at Zee, then turned his attention back to Charlotte. "Yes, it does! We are moving back to Lake Huron next summer!" Jesse announced.

The surprise announcement lit up Zee's eyes. "My darling! Do you really mean it?"

"Yes!" Jesse replied happily. "I was waiting for the right moment to tell you." He lifted his arms in the air, gesturing at the Canadian countryside. "This looks like one of those moments."

Zee squealed and hugged Jesse, almost toppling him over. "You just wanted to see me yelp in excitement!"

Jesse chuckled. "Maybe!"

"Well, that's wonderful news!" Charlotte replied. "It will be a delight to have my sister living closer to us again."

Zee kissed Jesse on the cheek harshly, then felt a small tug on her arm. She turned and noticed her youngest niece behind her. Zee bent down and hugged her niece fiercely. "Julia! You have grown so much!"

"I'm nine years old now!" Julia beamed proudly.

The other teens squealed with delight. "Is it true? You're coming back to live in Canada?" Alice, the oldest, asked.

Zee beamed. "Yes! Next summer!" She hugged Alice and the other two. "Clara! Joey! Oh my Lord, you've all grown so much! I missed so much in the past two years!"

Charlotte gestured towards Sarah, who was standing silently behind Jesse.

Jesse caught the unasked question. "Charlotte, we've brought you a dear friend to help with the farm animals," Jesse said, gently tugging on Sarah's arm. "Her name is Sarah."

Charlotte warmly extended her hand to Sarah. "Sarah? Do you have a last name?"

"No, Ma'am," Sarah answered uncomfortably.

"No last name?"

Jesse pulled Charlotte to the side and quickly explained everything in a hushed tone. When he was finished, he added, "Some slaves weren't given last names, Charlotte. Be easy on the woman, she's been through a lot. She lost her husband in the fire."

Charlotte embraced Sarah warmly and grasped her arm. "Come with me, Sarah," she said, motioning to the front door. "We have been looking for a new farm aid for a long while now. Zee and I will show you how to take care of the cows, horses, and goats." Jesse followed Charlotte into the house as Zee and the others stayed on the porch.

Jesse looked around the old farmhouse and found not much had changed. The kitchen was in the same spot, the hallway and front room were still the same, just with different pictures and furniture. A young man struggled with a squirming baby on the sofa.

"We'll give you a new last name," Charlotte muttered happily to Sarah.

Sarah smiled. "We can do that?"

"Yes! Of course!" Jesse joined in. "What a wonderful idea."

Sarah's eyes lit up. "Can I pick my last name?"

"You sure can!" Charlotte announced. "What will it be?"

"Freeman," Sarah replied with tears in her eyes. "I'm free now." She looked at everyone in the room as Zee and the others came inside. "This is my home now?" she asked.

"Yes," Charlotte confirmed. "We have a guest cottage for the farmhands. You will live in your own quarters, but you will eat with us every night and help run the daily tasks of the Collard farm."

Sarah hugged Charlotte with tears freely running down her cheeks.

The young man on the sofa stood with the baby in his arms. "Zee? Is that you?"

Zee turned her head. "Jacob? My baby brother?" she cried, rushing over to the sofa, stopping as her brain registered the infant squirming in his arms. "Who is this little bundle of energy?"

At that moment, the baby boy almost squirmed right out of his arms and screamed in protest. Jacob struggled and finally let the boy go to the floor. The baby immediately grabbed the end table and stood unsteadily, his legs wavering with his face set in a determined grin. "This is my son, Jack. He was born last year. He's 11 months old now."

"Oh my Lord, Jacob!" Zee shouted. "Nobody told me you had another son!"

"He was a surprise to us all," Jacob responded, jokingly.

Zee bent down to the toddler's height and looked into his determined eyes. "Hi there, Jack," she murmured. "I'm your Auntie Zee." She offered her hand to help him balance as he stood. His legs wavered, and his tiny hand clenched her finger in an iron grip. His right leg took a hesitant step. The look of sheer determination on his face was priceless. "You're learning to walk, aren't you? Look at you. You'll be a strong boy one day with that steely resolve."

"He just started walking a month ago," Jacob added proudly. "Jack's a stubborn one. I don't understand how my sisters have raised all these kids. Jack is a difficult child!"

Zee smiled. "He's a Collard then, through and through."

The room erupted in joyous laughter.

Charlotte shouted over the noise. "It's getting late, you all need to eat something and get to bed. We have lots of leftovers from dinner. We'll celebrate with a good, wholesome farm breakfast in the morning."

Jesse bent down to where Zee was, helping the young toddler walk. "That's right, my love," he whispered in her ear. "Let's have something to eat and then get some sleep. It's been a very long journey getting here." He kissed her on the head and knelt down beside her. "I'm so glad we did it together."

CHAPTER 25

At the end of the week, they had to say their goodbyes and return back to the USA. They boarded the ferry and spent a night at the Buffalo cabin. They had done a good job cleaning previously, but they were still forced to throw out the blood-soaked bed. Jesse and Zee retired to sleep in the spare bedroom. It was a pleasant change. The smaller bed forced them to cuddle all night.

When the sun broke over the horizon, they awoke and set out on the road to get back to the estate. It was a long journey, but they had travelled it many times in the past.

They kissed and smiled as they saddled their horses.

They would be home soon.

♎

"The week went by so fast," Zee mumbled, holding onto the reins, as they meandered through the thick Pennsylvania forest. "It's so hard to believe everything we've been through in the past two weeks. I met my new nephew, Jack, for the first time, we delivered a freed slave to Canada, and saw all my relatives again. Betty, Hanna, and Elise came to see us, too! Oh, and not to mention having to deal with Georgina's house on fire or the crazed lunatic Bartholomew!" She chuckled wearily. "I'm exhausted."

Jesse grinned. "We'll be home soon, my dear. I'm tired too." Jesse glanced sideways at her. "We'll be sleeping together at the estate from now on. I don't care what anybody thinks. I don't want to sleep alone anymore."

Zee's face lit up with an exhausted smile. "That would be lovely." A thought crossed her mind, and her lips curved into a mischievous smile. "But you'll be having sex with me every night then!" she said, feigning shock. Zee chuckled and mused to herself. "I don't know if I can handle it."

Jesse laughed loudly. "I'll be catching up on stolen time, my darling." He pulled back on the reins as his gelding cleared the forest. The Eastman estate loomed on the horizon with the full moon rising behind it. "Don't worry. I'm awfully tired as well, hon. We will probably sleep for a week before we can start feeling more like ourselves. It's been a long journey."

"Yes, it has been a long journey," Zee agreed. "But I'm so glad we made the journey together."

Jesse winked at her, recognizing the hint about the journey their marriage had taken. His heart filled with love and admiration for his wife. She had faced temptation and stood her ground against Bartholomew. Zee was a strong, faithful woman, and he felt grateful to have her as his wife. She was the only light in his difficult days, and he would never forget it again. "I love you, hon," he blurted out suddenly.

Zee tilted her head at the sudden declaration of love. She felt the same relief that they somehow had both saved their marriage from near collapse. With his wide-brimmed hat and leather boots on, she couldn't even dream of a better man. Jesse

Eastman was her favorite man in the world. "I love you too, my dear husband."

Ω

Zee looked out of their bedroom window and could faintly see the charred remains of Georgina's house. It had only been three weeks, but so much had changed. Jesse lay in bed still, sleeping soundly. She could hear the rhythm of his breathing, and she loved the sound of it in her room. He had chosen her bedroom, instead of his, because it was where they had always made love in the past. Jesse had moved in only a few items, but promised to move the rest by the end of the month. There was an old wood dresser full of his clothing and a standup closet in her bedroom now. She couldn't be happier.

Zee felt a warm joy spread through her chest. She mused about how Jesse had changed things so quickly. It continued to confound her what the tipping point had been. It was probably a mixture of the Bartholomew fiasco and visiting the old Collard farmhouse, where they had first met. The memories were so unique and strong between them, that it created this tangible bond, like a strong rope connecting them together for eternity. But nothing in life was forever. She knew this all too well. When she had seen Jacob and his son, her heart remembered her deceased brother Sam. When she helped Jack stand, she remembered cleaning Sam and Jacob's wounds when they were small boys. Her heart still grappled with the pain of loss. One day, she might lose Jesse, too.

The thought smacked into her mind abruptly and gripped her heart. She laid her hand on his chest and made sure he was still breathing. This small movement awakened him. She whispered, "I'm sorry, honey. I didn't mean to wake you."

Jesse rolled over and smiled. "I want to be woken up by you every day for the rest of my life, dear." He reached out and hugged her. "Don't ever apologize for touching me. I love it."

"You've changed so much in the last few weeks, my darling," she blurted out. "I feel so blessed to have you back in my arms." Zee sniffled as a sudden emotion tugged at her heart. Tears welled up in her eyes, and she struggled to contain her sudden burst of unbridled emotion.

"Sweetheart," Jesse mumbled, laying a gentle hand on her shoulder. "I didn't change at all. I just finally stopped pretending to be an Eastman. The man you met during the War of 1812 was always still here." He bent closer to her and kissed her softly on the lips. "I've never stopped loving you."

She chuckled. "And I thought all along that it was me who was searching for my old self."

"I think we both were."

Zee returned his gentle kiss and ran her fingers over his stubbly beard. The scent of sex was still fresh on the sheets, and her inner thighs were still wonderfully sore. True to his word, they took breaks for a day or two, but then he continued loving her inside and out, gently at times and sometimes more feverishly. Every ounce of her body and skin absorbed his loving like the desert absorbs the rain. She groaned and curled her head into his neck.

Jesse wrapped his strong arms around her waist, pulling her back into bed. "Come rest with me, just so I can hold you until the full sun rises." He pulled her hips back into bed and pulled the blanket over them both. Her butt snuggled into his groin as his arms encircled her waist and settled between her breasts, cupping them lovingly.

Zee let out a sigh of contentment as Jesse started kissing her gently on the back of her neck. She murmured and wondered about how things would work out within the next year. "When will we be moving back to our Lake Huron cabin?" she asked softly.

"Early next summer, my sweetheart," he replied, mumbling into her hair. "We still have to rebuild Georgina's house and support her with the new baby on the way. The fire was very hard on both of them. We will need to work diligently to rebuild as quickly as possible. Throughout the restoration, I will make sure that everyone is trained thoroughly with operating the estate so they can do it on their own."

"Do you really think they can do it without you?"

"Yes, of course," Jesse replied. "Janey and Xavier are self-starters. I don't doubt their ability at all. As for Scott and James, they are completely different. They have both said they want to come live with us at Lake Huron."

"Yes, I talked to them yesterday," Zee added. "They'd rather live in the woods." She chuckled.

Jesse nuzzled his nose into her hair and inhaled the sweet scent of his wife. "If we have to build an addition onto the main cabin to make more room, we will do it. It will work out, honey, don't worry."

"What about Johnny?" she asked. "Does he want to stay here at the estate?"

"Surprisingly, yes," Jesse answered, pulling her closer. "He has always shown a keen interest in running the Eastman empire. You know that, dear. But I also think Johnny has a girl in Philadelphia, too."

"He does?" Zee asked, clearly surprised.

"That's what Janey said."

"Janey?" Zee exclaimed incredulously. "How does she know?"

Jesse chuckled. "I have no idea, my dear. Siblings talk, I suppose." He smoothed her hair gently and murmured in her ear. "You smell so good."

Her heart melted, and she relaxed back into his arms. "So do you, my love." She kissed his arm. "Xavier, Janey, and Johnny will be able to take care of the estate, then?"

"Yes, eventually," Jesse responded. "I have no doubt about that. Janey has already talked about moving her family into the estate after we leave."

"She said that?" Zee asked in amazement.

"Yes," Jesse replied, kissing her hair. "Our children are getting lives of their own. They're making their own decisions for their futures. As parents, we need to let them do that."

"I suppose you're right," Zee added, thoughtfully. "But what about Scott and James?"

"I don't know about those two," Jesse chuckled. "They will probably be hunting all the time in the wilds of Lake Huron's forests. It'll all work out somehow, I suppose. We will probably need our sons as we get older, anyway." Jesse pulled her closer and hugged her tighter. "My plan is to grow old with you at our cabin in the woods."

An intense spread of love coursed through Zee's entire body at his words. The warm tingles started from her heart and swept through every limb, right down to her toes. She kissed his arm and closed her eyes, snuggling into his embrace. "That's what I've always dreamt of," she mumbled.

CHAPTER 26

The gravel crunched under his horse's hooves, and it seemed like it was the only thing that Billy Eastman could hear. That awful rhythmic crunching as his horse headed into the Northwest wilderness. It was an unforgiving land, but they had made it this far already. They would keep going until they reached the other coastline. He had heard rumors that there was a beautiful coastline out west, and Billy was determined to find it.

His horse's hooves weren't the only sound. Another two horses followed him, a pack horse and a gelding with a woman on it. She had a rounded belly that was growing larger every day. Her name was Laura. She was the black-haired beauty that Bartholomew had invited to the small house in Philadelphia.

After Bartholomew had left, she returned to the house to announce that she was pregnant with Bartholomew's child.

Thomas gave her money and told her to go away, but she begged him to let her stay in the small house. Billy had watched the drama unfold as Thomas shouted at her to leave. The house had been sold. There would be nowhere to stay, he had told her angrily.

When they had all found out about Bartholomew's death, Thomas mysteriously disappeared.

Billy took the pleading woman and put her on a horse, telling her to leave. But she wouldn't. Laura just continued following him everywhere like a lost dog.

Billy had packed up his two horses and the cash he had kept from Thomas's initial payment. He had never spent a dime of it. His lie was never discovered. Billy chuckled. "I was always smarter than them," he whispered to himself as he patted his bag full of cash.

It took several weeks to get deep into the western wilderness from Philadelphia, but it was worth it. He had no other choice. Jesse had put a bounty on his head to be brought back alive. Billy was charged with arson for the fire at Georgina's and the murders of all the people who had died. It wasn't his fault they had died. Billy hadn't known all the slaves were trapped in the cellar.

He was forced to disappear or face a life in prison. Jesse didn't want him dead. He wanted him locked away for life.

Billy Eastman would never choose that life. He'd rather die. If the authorities ever caught him, which was unlikely, he'd shoot his way out until they killed him on site. He would not die in a prison cell.

Billy had shaved all his hair off and grown a long grey beard. It had changed his appearance so much that he didn't even recognize himself. There was little chance anybody looking at a wanted poster would see any resemblance at all to the old Billy Eastman. He would just have to come to terms with his new dismal life.

He glanced behind him and grimaced. Laura was still behind him, following him blindly to the ends of the earth. The woman was clueless. She had nowhere to go. Sticking to an outlaw's path was not the best decision for a pregnant lady, Billy mused.

"Are you going to come to your senses someday and just leave me be?" Billy shouted behind him.

She shook her head sadly. "I have no choice, Billy," she whined. "We are too far into the wilderness now. I would die on my own."

The horse's hooves clopped on the gravel again. No more words, just that lonely rhythmic sound.

It was an Indian trail they were travelling on. They had to stay out of sight so the natives didn't see them, but Billy knew they most likely already had. So far, the natives weren't violent and left them alone. He had heard that many of the Northern natives had died travelling west after the Indian Removal Act in 1830.

Billy was glad that someone was here before him. At least, they had made the path.

The wilderness rang loudly in his ears as the conversation lulled. Billy wondered where this road was going to lead.

She spoke again. "I cook for you. You don't really want to be rid of me."

"I could sell you," Billy joked.

"Na, you won't do that," she drawled. "I have Bartholomew's child in my belly. One day, that child could inherit all of Bartholomew Mato's assets." Laura smiled wickedly. She was a good girl at heart, but somehow Bartholomew had seeped evil into her soul. He had been a mean, selfish, handsome man. She had only known him for a weekend, and he had gotten her pregnant without a care in the world. "Barton died without a son or a daughter, I heard. So, my baby would get it all. That's why Thomas wanted to get rid of me." Laura scoffed and laughed. "Well, I'm going to have this baby and you, Billy, are going to help me."

Billy chuckled and opened his mouth to say something rude, but stopped. She might have a point, he thought. He could raise the child and seek compensation. Even better, he could demand half the money. "Now listen to you," he replied sarcastically. "Bartholomew was the devil you made the deal with, woman. But at least you have some sort of plan now." He clucked his tongue in thought. "I might be interested in ensuring that you give birth to a healthy Mato baby."

"Good," Laura replied, ending the conversation.

Billy sighed as the caravan continued into the woods, through ravines and mountainous plateaus. He'd never seen such raw wilderness in his life before. It was beautiful and dangerous at the same time. A fear settled in his stomach. He wondered if he was going to die out here. The ravens would be picking at his flesh in the hot, humid autumn of 1833. Billy and Laura hadn't eaten anything other than deer meat and berries. He didn't know if it was enough to survive. Once, he had shot a mountain lion, too. That meat tasted strange, but it was a welcome change.

Something scurrying in the bushes caught his eye. A stray dog whined in the distance. Billy shouted at the annoying animal. "Go away, you little vermin! Get!"

The stray dog jumped back but continued following them cautiously.

"I'll kill you!' he shouted at the dog, waving his rifle.

"Don't kill him," Laura interrupted. "We might be able to make friends with him. He might be useful for security if we start feeding him."

Billy slumped into his saddle. Now he had three horses, an argumentative woman, a future child, and a dog! He laughed at the thought. "We can try," he conceded wearily. "When we make camp tonight, we'll see if the dog comes to us." Billy shook his head at the ludicrousness of his situation. "I still can't believe how I got stuck with all of you," he chuckled wildly. "I suppose it's better than prison." His chuckle turned into a full-throated laugh. Maybe it was the stress of his situation, or something else entirely, but he could not stop laughing.

Billy heard his laughter echo into the empty mountainous valley. It reverberated back to him eerily. He stopped laughing abruptly and gazed thoughtfully out at the western wilderness before him.

Maybe he would find gold someday, he mused.

THE END

Continue following

THE EASTMAN SAGA series

for more books

FINAL NOTE TO READER

The Wild West, as we know it today, didn't start until 1865. This book covers the time periods before the West was opened up. It was only a raw wilderness before the 1830 Indian Removal Act. Thousands of native people were forced from their homes in Southeast America and told to go west. Although the entire period of the forced native migration took place from 1830 all the way to 1841, some Northern tribes ceded and started on the journey earlier. The time period of this novel is limited to 1833; readers are cautioned that there may or may not have been fully formed paths by this time. The Trail of Tears was a long-forgotten piece of history, and I felt compelled to include it in this book, regardless of the possible time conflict.

Most of the North American West was very different in 1833 than how it is today. No roads, just trees, forests, animals, and wilderness. Many Native Americans died on their way west on the Trail of Tears. Various trails were left behind by the 100,000 natives that were forced to relocate, including the

Northern Route, Hildebrand Route, Bell Route, Water Route, and many others.

The California Gold Rush brought many more people out west, but an earlier Georgina Gold Rush also occurred in 1829. This area in Georgia was Cherokee land, although gold miners trespassed anyway, consumed by greed and the quest for gold. Land speculators began to demand that the US Congress do something about controlling this rich land of gold. The American government stepped in and passed the Indian Act on May 28, 1830. The act gave the president powers to negotiate with the natives for their removal to lands west of the Mississippi and provide compensation to native landowners.

Many of the Southeast tribes were heavily invested in agriculture. The lands they were being forced to leave were valuable farm land, cleared, homes built, and ready to move into. Some of the native homeowners preemptively sold their land for good profits and journeyed west on their own. The Northern tribes were fairly mobile and left quickly. Other tribes, like the Cherokee, decided to stay and fight. Some were forced out by the US military.

Travelling on these newly formed trails was a perilous undertaking. Approximately 15,000 natives died from malnutrition, exposure, disease, and exhaustion. The ones that made it were the original pioneers of the West. I stumbled upon this research halfway through writing 1833 Brothers & Sisters and tried to include as much as possible without deviating from the heart of the story. Maybe, one day, I will write an entire spinoff novel about the Trail of Tears and give it the attention it deserves.

Many other notable things happened in the 1830s that have almost been lost in popularly known history. My job as a historical fiction writer is to bring these ghosts to life.

All the characters in this book are fictional. This is one of my few books that contains no historical figures, only the events.

I originally chose to write about the Underground Railroad because of the connection it had with the Niagara Region of Canada, where I live. It was yet another historical mass exodus that has shaped Southern Ontario into what it is today.

The Underground Railroad was a series of concerned and empathetic Americans who aided slaves to get to Canada. Each house was called a station. There were station masters and ticket agents. Rarely were actual trains ever used. It was a coded secret way of advertising in newspapers and through word of mouth to enslaved individuals who wished to escape to Upper Canada.

In the 1793 Act to Limit Slavery, there was a provision that allowed any slave who reached Canada to become a free person. It was the ticket to a life free of slavery for many blacks. In the beginning, only a small number of slaves made it to Canada without help. Word spread after the War of 1812 that freedom for black slaves did indeed exist in Canada. US military officers who made it back to America talked about the freed "Black men in red coats" serving in the British Canadian troops. During the War of 1812, this regiment was called The Colored Corps. It was an odd thing for Americans to see at the time, so they talked about it freely when they returned.

After the Fugitive Slave Act in September of 1850, a dramatic increase of black people escaped America. This nefarious act enabled more slave catchers to pursue black fugitives, even within the freed Northern states of the USA. The Act stated that enslaved fugitives, once caught, could be returned to their slave owners in the South. It led to an exodus of black Americans to Upper Canada. The Act was repealed, but not until June 1864.

The Underground Railroad was created in the early 1800s by a collection of abolitionists, based mainly in Philadelphia. These abolitionists consisted of freed black slaves, enslaved fugitives, Baptists, Quakers, Methodists, Indigenous sympathizers, farmers, white Americans, and Canadians. They started using the term Underground Railroad in the 1830s as a way to build an informal, covert network. Many of these people were average Americans and Canadians who were simply dedicated to human rights and equality.

The routes out of the Southern plantation states started from Mississippi, Arkansas, Tennessee, Georgia, and many other southern states. These lines led through many safe houses along the way through the interior of the USA and the eastern coastline, up towards the Northern states of Pennsylvania, New York, Indiana, Ohio, Illinois, as well as many others. Some of the routes crossed the Great Lakes into Canada, some crossed the Niagara River, and some lines crossed over land borders.

Many terms were used in the covert networks, such as conductors who guided fugitives to points along the journey. Passengers, cargo, and freight were also some of the languages used. Stations are what they called the safe houses where fugitives could rest and be fed. The houses were often identified by lit candles in the windows or carefully placed lanterns in the front yard. To this day, in a Canadian town that sits across from Buffalo called Fort Erie, you can go for a neighborhood walk and see many homes with lit decorative candles in their windows. The Underground Railroad tradition continues on, with future generations not even realizing why they have candles in their windows.

Ticket agents organized safe trips and arranged travel to the candle-lit safe houses, mapping out the extensive journey to freedom. The station masters were the people who owned the safe houses, feeding the slaves, clothing them, and providing a safe place for them to rest. Average Americans donated money to the network, helping to provide the necessities. These people were called stockholders.

The journey itself was very dangerous, sometimes on foot, in wagons, carriages, on horseback, and sometimes by train. The passengers also travelled by boat, travelling mostly at night and resting during the day.

The main terminus was in Upper Canada. Some Canadians opened their homes to the fugitives, providing shelter and a means to integrate into Canadian society. Many former black slaves settled in Upper Canada, in today's province of Ontario. Many Canadian cities have a long ancestry of freed slaves, including Windsor, Niagara Falls, and Hamilton. The fugitives were hard workers and brought many skills to Canada, including cultivating land, cooking, operating blacksmith shops, liveries, and even founding the first taxi company in Toronto.

In total, the Underground Railroad brought up to 40,000 black fugitives to British North America, now known as Canada. It was their ticket to freedom.

The network existed until the end of American slavery in 1865.

Throughout history, migration, spearheaded by acts of government, both nefarious and freeing, forced many Indigenous and black Americans to create a life elsewhere. Through this mass exodus north and west, it created roads, passages, human bonds, and travel routes, some of which continue to exist in today's modern society.

Human spirit and kindness eventually wins. In the process, we all benefit.

I'd like to thank my family for their support and my many editors, historians, readers, and supporters for following along on my journey of spreading the truth of history, not just what we are taught in school.

History matters. God bless you all.

LEAVE A REVIEW

Check out the author's website for behind the scenes blog posts and interviews at:

jaboulet.ca

J. A. Boulet is the passionate author of many historical fiction novels. Raised in a Hungarian refugee family, J. A. was born in Canada and grew up with strong moral convictions, which she has stood behind all her life. Ms. Boulet began writing poetry at a very young age and progressed to short stories and novels easily. She quickly became a history geek and became fascinated with ancestry and the rough path of immigration. Her university studies ranged from photojournalism to accounting. After decades of working in accounting, J. A. published her first book in 2020 and has since published one to two books annually.

She lives in the Niagara region of Canada with her two sons, a crested gecko, a large Doberdor dog, and a small orchard of fruit trees.

Follow her on Twitter, Instagram, Amazon, and YouTube.

All links are available on her website at: jaboulet.ca